RECEPTION

D0839023

KENZIE JENNINGS

9-759-7234850-3450345809

www.deathsheadpress.com

Cover art by Lynne Hansen

For Lucy

(We know it would never have gone down like this. I love you, little sis.)

FOREWORD

I met Kenzie Jennings while waiting in line to hear Bruce Campbell speak. It was at the Spooky Empire convention in Orlando; this was their smaller scale summer event, which had no author guests, and I was just there as a regular ol' horror fan. Kenzie had contacted me beforehand to ask if she could get a book signed, so I messaged her to let her know where I was. She showed up, stayed long enough for an inscription and a quick picture, thanked me, and then left so that she would not be taking up any more of my valuable time.

Her thought process was: *Gosh, it sure was nice of him to devote a couple minutes of his Spooky Empire experience to greeting a fan.* My thought process was: *OMG! Somebody brought one of my books to the convention and I'm not even a guest! OMG! OMG! OMG! Best con ever!*

That led to occasional social gatherings with Kenzie, her boyfriend, my wife, and I. Much sushi was consumed and many movies were watched, including an Edgar Wright theatrical triple feature of *Shaun of the Dead, Hot Fuzz,* and *The World's End*, which I'm just sharing here to make you jealous. We had deep-fried Mars bars (delicious) and jellyfish (less so). She went to my belly flop of a launch party for my second young adult novel. I spoke to her school's creative writing club.

Then she finished her first novel: *Jayne Juxtaposed.* A superhero novel written as "chick lit." I offered to read it.

This kind of thing can be a bit nerve-wracking. When you have sushi with somebody on a regular basis, and there's much discussion of writing during these meals, it makes things much less awkward if you actually like their work. I'm not saying that my thought process was: *Oh, God, please, please, please, please, please, PLEASE let this book not suck!!!* But I really hoped it was good.

It was, in fact, damned good.

She got a contract with a small publisher. She'd sold her first novel! How exciting! How thrilling! And because this business can be filled with disappointment...the book never came out.

But Kenzie was already working on her second book, a horror novel called *Reception* that might sound familiar if you looked at the cover of the book you're reading now. I know the horror market way better than I know the chick-lit superhero market, so I was excited to be a fountain of advice when it was complete.

She sent me the manuscript when it was done. I loved it.

I told Kenzie that she needed to go to a horror writers' conference. Aside from writing a great book, attending a writers' conference is one of the most valuable things you can do for your career. Hell, sometimes it's *more* valuable than writing a great book! Anyway, that conference turned out to be KillerCon in Austin, Texas. "This won't directly lead to a book deal," I told her, "but you'll make contacts that will build a foundation that will eventually lead to a book deal."

KillerCon directly led to a book deal.

And, ooooh, you're in for a nasty treat, kiddies! Cannibals at a wedding reception? C'mon! How can you not want to read that? (Actually, I'm sure many people elect not to read such a thing, but they aren't reading this foreword, either.)

Reception is grisly, weird, and a lot of fun, and here you are, lucky enough to be there at the start of the career of an exciting new voice in the horror genre! Keep your arms, legs, and head inside the ride at all times, so they don't get eaten, and prepare yourself for the bloody delight that is *Reception*.

--Jeff Strand

ABOUT THAT LITTLE DILEMMA...

I wish I could remember the little things that seem necessary.

Little things like quickly changing a flat tire, cooking perfectly fluffy scrambled eggs, replacing an old door lock, and getting tacky bloodstains out of formal wear.

I wish I could just remember.

Blotting with water is just making it worse. The stains keep spreading.

(Was it salt? Hydrogen peroxide? Dish soap?)

My whole face feels gummy with it. The clots have gelled over, growing itchy. It's streaked all over my arms, the bandage, my hands, the front of my dress; it's everywhere. The soap masks the metallic stench of it, that and the underlying sour tang of vomit, but only just. The label on the soap bottle reads "Havenhill Tea Rose," but it smells like discount store floral musk tangy with copper and pheromones.

I scrub until my hands are raw and burning. Bloody crust under my fingernails, rimming my cuticles. The makeshift bandage around my forearm had grown so saturated with blood and dirt, it's useless. My arm still burns. I want to scratch it wide open, scratch it away.

These sorts of little things, noticeable.

My sister Shay softly cries from her space on the floor.

These sorts of little things, unimportant right now.

Shay is slumped against the wall in a fluffy heap of crinoline, satin and gore-spattered beaded brocade. Her ballerina bun that she'd spent a good couple of hours and plenty of money getting into a perfectly rounded knot is partially undone with its bobby pins dangling limply. Matted, stringy clumps of hair are glued to one side of her grimy face. She snorts back a burble of snot. Tears run down her cheeks, twin rivers in a ruddy landscape. Her breath comes in

7

sporadic, tight hitches, kind of like she's hiccupping but she's forgotten how to.

"I spent so much on this dress. I mean, I know it was on sale, so it's not like it's a big deal or anything," she says in-between breathy hiccups, "but it is kind of a big deal when you've paid several bills already, and it's this dress you want. You know?"

"Did it come with spot removal instructions?" My lame attempt at humor doesn't register. It's Shay. She never gets it. Then again, levity isn't exactly the order of the day, not with everything happening right now, not with what's out there.

So it's understandable.

"I just wanted—" Shay's train of thought is interrupted by a stray burp, which then forms into a warbling sob, something she's probably practiced for future meltdowns. This just isn't the time for it.

While I let her finish her thought, oh those thoughts that have been unraveling wildly over the past few hours, I dampen a hand towel under the faucet and then use it to blot at my hands, my dress. Then I toss it just before I get to ripping up one of the resort's thin towels, creating raggedy strips from it.

Sniffling, Shay watches me work. I briefly stop unwinding the bloody tablecloth bandage I'd hurriedly crafted and had wrapped around my damaged forearm, and I glance down at her, offering her a sad smile.

She grimly returns the smile, pats down her ruined gown, and plucks her sticky strands from her cheeks, grimacing as she does. "I wanted to get married, Ans. That's all," she says softly. "Just wanted to be a bride, a wife, all of it. I mean, I know it's so overdone, with all the planning out all the details, the expectations and timing. Everything always has to be perfect and orderly. There's just no room for things out of place. And no time for plan B's or second chances. But, Ans, I wanted to do it right. To do it *right*."

"For Mom and Dad," I add, nodding. I know how it is. I wince at the sight of my shredded arm beneath the last layer of tablecloth-bandage. Just the mere thought of picking it from the raw wound, prising it from nerves and meat, makes me gag. Still, have to do what I have to do, and I start peeling it away from the wound slowly, carefully, and it's excruciating.

"For *Mom* and *Dad*," she says with a sigh. "You know it. I'm the one who can't disappoint them, right?"

8

My skin prickles, itching. The ache behind my eyes thrums. I'll allow myself to believe I'm not angry, I'm not. But I don't like it, even if it is true—the implication that I'm the daughter who can and will routinely disappoint them. This isn't my fault. This isn't my fault. This *isn't* my fault.

"For what it's worth, I don't think it's all that important anymore, considering," I say. Our terrible reminder. *That*. I suck in my breath as I gently tug the last bit of bandage away and examine the damage. I keep having to remind myself that it wasn't—it *isn't* as bad as I'd pictured when it happened, but it looks pretty awful close up in all of its meaty, oozing glory. I run the tap, and hold my arm under the cool water, gritting my teeth at the burn of it, all those exposed layers and nerves...and those germs. Those germs. I'd poured alcohol onto it earlier, not too long after all of it went down. Even still, it wouldn't have done much good on the wound, as it's not a run-of-the-mill scrape of flesh here. There's no antiseptic anywhere from what I've seen, not like I had the time or ability to scour the place for a halfway decent first aid kit. Still, I think there's probably one in someone's car. While we're not exactly able to use a car to get out of here at this moment, at least I can hope my arm won't get so infected I'd have to amputate.

Jesus H. *Amputate*. That's an awful possibility. I sneak a glance at my sister while I rinse my wound.

Shay's body sags, and her eyes have watered over. Her hands are fluttery, fidgety in her lap. She doesn't know what to do with them.

I shut off the faucet, wrap my arm in fresh towel strips, and then settle down right beside Shay on the chilly tile floor, picking at the bloody crust from my eyelashes and strands of hair as I do. I flick the crumbs from my thumb and then wipe the stickier bits on my dress. So much for that waste of money, too.

"You reek," she says, wrinkling her nose at me.

"Well, thanks. You don't exactly smell like violets and pink hearts yourself."

"Pink hearts have a scent? How did I not know this?"

"It's Bath and Body Works' new fragrance. You should try the body cream. So good for the skin."

"I would, but I'm allergic to shea."

"Since when?"

"Since I was old enough to shop for body butter only to find out this little factoid."

9

"Pity. Your skin could use that extra glow like all the real brides have."

"Fuck off. I was a beautiful bride."

"Yeah, you were. Shame it didn't last long."

"You're one to talk."

"I can be done talking, if requested."

"Does it hurt?" she suddenly asks, breaking the empty banter and staring at my arm. "Because we're not gonna be able to go to a hospital anytime soon."

"Queen Obvious states the obvious."

"Just wondering. That's all. Hate to think it'll get infected."

"It probably will unless we can get to Mom's car. I think the first aid kit in there has something to clean it with."

"Hey, just a thought. I might have some Neosporin in my suitcase," she says after a minute.

I chuckle at the thought of it. "It's funny how your suitcase is probably only about... what, twenty feet away from us, but there's no way in hell either of us will gamble and scramble to get it."

She laughs, clamps a hand over her mouth. Not like it matters. They'll hear us anyway. They're everywhere. The thunk-thunk-thunking out there may have momentarily stopped, but like everything happening here, we tended to trust "momentarily" more than anything else.

"Gamble and scramble," she says. "You made a rhyme. A-plus, gold star, extra recess time for you, Pretty McTitty."

"Awww. Thanks, Regina Vagina. I love getting gold stars."

"Anytime, anywhere."

We hold hands and laugh until it forms into tears. Our heads press, and we cry softly together. Shay's grip on my hand tightens. I squeeze back. Then I hug her to me, and she weeps against my neck. My head hurts so badly behind my eyes, the searing pressure alone may cause them to burst or catch fire. And wouldn't that be something? As they are now, it's painful enough to bring the hot tears.

"We took vows, Ansley," Shay says. "We took *vows*."

"I know you did."

"Are they meaningless now? What am I supposed to do?"

"I've no idea."

"What are we supposed to do?"

I can't answer her.

Hell, it's just how it is right now.

10

It'll be better once we figure out what's next. It has to be. God, my head hurts.

Shay looks at me, her expression somber, her eyes red and lined with worry, mascara still holding surprisingly strong, just gelling a little in the corners of her eyes. "So how are we gonna get out of here?"

Good. Fucking. Question.

Suddenly, there's a hard rap on the bathroom door, one that rattles it against the frame of the chair braced against it. It makes us both jump.

They made it in.

I squeeze Shay closer to me, both of us jolted by the noise. Shay's trembling. I am, too. Nausea burns the back of my throat. My heart rate isn't helping matters either. It's hyper, out of control.

A masculine voice comes from the bedroom, right at the bathroom door. It's so low and sultry, it's practically purring in its heat. "Little woman, you can't stay in there forever." Another hard knock, a shimmy of the door, then a loud smack against it, rattling the chair as well. "Shay, stop being a bitch. Open the goddamn door. You hit me so hard with that thing, I think you cracked some of my teeth here. "

"Please," she murmurs against my shoulder. "Make him stop. He needs to stop."

Nathan thumps his hand against the door, and the chair braced against it under the handle rocks. "Shaaaay? Oh, Shaaaay? Shay Ellen! Baby, open up!"

"Fuck off!" Like I'd let him get the last word in.

Then all goes quiet beyond the door. Shay straightens, her hand gripping mine tightly. When I look at her, she has her eyes squeezed shut, her other hand over her mouth, as if that'll make a difference. We keep our hands bound, fingers locked. Our breathing is synchronous, coming in sharp and steady. Inhaling, exhaling, inhaling.

The silence though, that stillness beyond the door, it's unnerving.

It's just like them to play.

ONE

My memories come in linked fragments out of sequence, like anyone else's I guess.

They're in bright Technicolor scenes, like they'd been painted in, and while the color schemes are somewhat correct—the sky is blue, purple, black, or a purple mixed with black, like a bruise; the sun is a dusky yellow; the dead grass is a sandy brown— I often wonder if the brightness, the starkness of the colors, is another withdrawal side effect.

My assigned counselor at the center, Leon, among other things, gave me a giant checklist several pages long on my first day there. He gave one to my mother, too, during the center's weekly visitors' day. Mom had since excused every single behavioral tick and "invisible" condition on my part, claiming "it's probably on the list because (fill in the blank with what I'm experiencing or displaying to her) is a symptom of (fill in the blank with the withdrawal effect), and her counselor has instructed that we must…we *must* be patient and help with whatever she may need." I mean, I could've probably twitched through a robbery followed by a mad killing spree, and my mother would've still brought that up. I think she kind of enjoyed it in a way. It got the conversation going, and she liked the attention for a change.

In hindsight, my "condition" only served to open up the slightest possibility of Munchausen by proxy. Still, she loved me. I wish I could've let her hear and see that from me more often, just little acts of kindness, a hug or two more often, consistent visits to see her and Dad.

My dad though, he didn't accept much. That's just how he was.

I remember that last day at the center. Faces, familiar habits, splashes of color, the tense body language. Leon and my mom chatting on the steps to the front entrance. She'd just signed me out, but not before the on-duty receptionist and the one nurse I couldn't stand gave

12

her the rundown, all the legalese, the firm warnings "out of professional courtesy" that this weekend away wasn't a good idea.

I never once thought it was, either, but Mom was firm with them and the head of the center, Paul or Paulo, I forget his name. He wasn't particularly memorable anyway, not if you were on the outside looking in as I often was. He only came out of the office area of the center if there was a problem involving billing and insurance or if one of his "clients" (the center's term for "patient") was being released midway through court-mandated treatment, like I was. Leon once told me the guy had been one of the best therapists in the state, and he was also pivotal in getting anti-opioid legislation on the ballots with an expansion on mental health facilities and substance abuse therapy. That said, you'd never know it by his obvious apathy at what was happening in his own center.

I was ready to go. Just rip off the Band-Aid. Get it done with. My sister wanted me there by her side, and I still couldn't entirely process it. Me, the family embarrassment. I kept thinking about her and our last outing when I was being fitted for the dress. She'd grown all soft and moony ever since she met Nathan. I didn't mind it up until she'd stopped treating me as a sister and started treating me with flashes of doubt and with what I suspect was a touch of scorn.

My stomach kept performing cartwheels and flips as I popped the trunk of the SUV and set my suitcase inside. The agreement was that I'd have enough clothes for just two nights, but the idea of sharing that amount of time with people I didn't care for kept me from packing in excess as I usually did before a trip. Shay though. I had to remind myself it was all for Shay and no one else, not even Mom and Dad.

Especially not Mom and Dad.

It was promising to be a hot, sticky weekend. The downtown air was a heady stew thick with exhaust fumes, cooking grease, and damp soil. Sweat trickled down my back, and my bra itched. I'd need my second, wasteful shower of the day by the time we reached Hill Country. Mom wasn't in the mood to be hurried along. If there was new information she could wrangle out of Leon, anything involving the state of her eldest and most troublesome, she'd have us leave when *she* was damned good and ready.

Poor Leon. He just stood there sagging on the top step, the weight of Mom's barrage of questions and concerns keeping him from conscientiously answering. Every time he tried to interject, she was quick to come up with something else, some other line of inquiry about my treatment. She hadn't liked him much when she first met him during check-in, and she certainly didn't care much for him right in that moment. Her disapproving gaze honed in on his wild hair and his usual uniform consisting of Atari logo tee, faded jeans, and sneakers. At least he hadn't been wearing that hideous jacket of his that time around, the one with the patched elbows. That was about as "professional" as Leon was willing to get.

I caught a snippet of what he finally was able to say to Mom, only because he'd raised his voice, and that itself was startling. Gone was the cool, easy façade he'd perfected. This version was a Leon I'd never seen or heard before.

"Mrs. Boone, she'll need as much support from you as she receives here. She needs empathy on your end. Walk in her shoes. Try to understand her. The handbook I gave you earlier details her tapering plan, but that's just part of it. Both her body and mind have gone through significant trauma because of the damage to her central nervous system."

Mom seemed as if she was about to say something else, but she stopped herself. It looked as if she was thinking over his words carefully before she shook his hand and then pulled him in towards her. Or maybe it was the other way around. I just remember how close they were, head-to-head, conspiring, sharing secrets about me, the family shame, the walking embarrassment. They glanced over at me, smiling broadly, but their gaze read much more than that. I caught the glint in Mom's eyes, that apprehension and doubt.

Yeah, it was already off to a rocky start.

#

Leon's strange, distant stare and his last words to me before we left him standing there on the steps played on repeat, an extended loop. Around and around, like a recording that's dissolving into white noise.

Remember what I said the other day.

(I do. It's important to remember those sorts of things.)

When you're feeling like everything is sucking all the air from you, you find something solid. Look at it. Hold it. Use its solidity. It will remind you what is here. What is now. It will bring you back to where you need to be.

You will be released from the lie that's keeping you bound.

14

It feels as though every day is a lie "keeping me bound." I can't discern quiet from noise and noise from quiet. And everyone is keeping things from me. I try to not let it affect me, but it's difficult whenever I walk into a room, and everyone's there, and then suddenly the silence is shouting at me to take notice of what *isn't* being said.

"Feet off the dashboard please." Mom said, startling me out of my thoughts. She wrinkled her nose in my direction, clucking her disapproval, and then squinted out at the millipede of traffic ahead of us slowly inching its way out of the city limits.

"Did you forget to bring your specs?"

"Spectacles, Ansley. Don't abbreviate," she answered as she shoved at my bare feet with a free hand. "And, no, I did not. They're back at the hotel, so you're going to have to let me know when we're closer to the turnoff." She reached awkwardly around and wriggled a hand into her bag. She then pulled out a thermos and handed it to me. "Hydrate. You need to drink plenty of water. Leon said it will ease some of your symptoms."

I made a face at her. Even still, she had a point. I just loathed the reminders again and again. The water felt good going down, frosting over the burning in my chest.

I slid my feet closer towards the steering wheel, grinning at Mom as I did, egging her on. She hated it so much. Anything to relieve the tension, the thrumming heatwave that was roiling in my head, the constant swishing of my heartbeat in my ears. The headaches and tinnitus had grown worse over the past few weeks. Leon told me to expect that along with plenty of other withdrawal symptoms. Lovely symptoms like nausea (check), rapid heart palpitations out of nowhere (check), high blood pressure (check and medicated), air hunger (check and try-not-to-call-for-an-ambulance-again-dumbass), tremors (check), and so on…and my real hell was only just getting started.

Frankly, at first, Leon didn't look as if he'd taken to Mom, and the feeling appeared mutual. Again, it was her evident embarrassment, the pressing questions, the idea of anyone in her family needing such therapy. It was Dad's prodding behind Mom's initial doubts. No matter how much Leon tried to convince them both it had been the right thing for me to choose rehabilitation over prison time, Dad didn't shy away from sharing his disapproval. He'd always scoffed at anything involving psychiatric care and rehabilitation.

Leon's one of those people you can't help but like when you first meet him. He greets everyone with a broad smile and a hug, and he

15

never forgets a name, ever. With my folks though, and even when it was just Mom there, he took two steps back and kept it there. His smile, half-cocked, up until those last words on the steps.

I wish I'd heard what he and Mom had said about me.

At the very least, he was considerate enough to give Mom a copy of the *Ashton Manual* with the tapering schedule as he'd promised her, even though she could've easily downloaded the thing online like regular people do in the modern age. Mom despises the Internet though. She hates it so much that it's practically prohibited when everyone's gathered for the holidays at home. Cell phones are often a no-no, too, unless anyone there is working and needs to keep in contact with colleagues. Only good old fashioned, uncomfortable chitchat permitted. Shay and I often spent our holiday gatherings ducking into the bathroom, feigning stomachaches, to text friends and lovers or search for something online. Anything to keep us relatively sane in a household on motherly lockdown.

And, perfect timing, my phone then buzzed in my bag, vibrating a reminder that I was never really lonely against my knee.

Mom loudly cleared her throat in my direction as I fumbled around in my bag for the thing. "Ansley, really now. Can it wait?"

I grasped my cell from its tangled confines in the bag. Glanced at it, muttering a halfhearted apology at Mom. It was Leon, on schedule. He'd promised he'd be texting periodically while I was away. A part of the therapy that I liked, a part that was probably mandatory for me. At any rate, none of us at the center would ever have to deal with our suffering alone. The support was always there.

REMINDER: When you get there, make sure you take breaks, little sister. Practice your breathing. Eat when you're hungry. Drink water on the hour. Don't give in to what isn't there. And don't let anyone have you do anything you're not ready to do.

"How much longer?" I asked Mom as I sent back a quick reply. *Done, done and DONE. Mom's hating this right now.*

Having met your mom, I can pretty much guarantee she'll make sure you'll do exactly as we agreed. She seems to like taking care of business.

Mom sucked in her breath, exhaled a long whoosh of air. Her exasperated sigh, full of dramatics. "Not too much longer now." She reached over and shook my bag strap. "Answer quickly and put it back in your purse. There won't be time for any of that this weekend. I know he's requiring a check-in with you, but you'll have to keep that thing in

16

your room during the ceremony and reception at least. It signals one as anti-social."

I ground my teeth together as I sent Leon a final message.

You have no idea. Don't know if I'm gonna make it this long.

"You're going to be fine, Ansley. It will be fine," said Mom, answering for Leon as well, almost as if she'd known. "Well, your father's none too happy about any of this, what you're going through, but he'll eventually understand. It could've been worse. He knows that. We just have to wait. He can read that Alton Manual and get a better idea of what you're going through. You know he likes to research."

"*Ashton* Manual. Ashton, not Alton. She was an expert. Google her."

"I don't play Google. You know that perfectly well."

"You don't 'play' Google, Mom. It's a search engine. Kind of like a virtual card catalogue but better because it's so much faster with no annoying call numbers to jot down. You should try it. Get yourself out of the late 20th century like the rest of us decades ago."

"Don't have time for it. I'll leave that sort of thing to your father, if and when he wishes to walk that avenue."

Dad. Yeah. About that guy. He'd always been a presence there in the darkest spaces of my thoughts. He was convinced that what I was going through was my own undoing, and he reminded me of it, not through his words but through his actions. Maybe "actions" isn't the right word though. More like "inaction" through passive-aggression. I mean, he'd leave the room whenever mention of the court dates, and then the medication issue, popped up. Get away to the gun range to practice, practice, practice or to the bookstore where he could sit for hours, poring over as many libertarian biographies or manifestos as they had on hand (his mantra was that anything terrible that ever happened was always the end result of one's choices). If he couldn't get away, he'd change the subject to something politically charged so he could vent until he was purple and clenched.

To Dad, my problem, the withdrawals, was, of course, due to my own poor choices in how I handled my crippling anxiety, the panic attacks, the blackouts, the flare-ups. The irony of the matter is that he and Mom and their dour temperaments have most certainly been one cause of my problems. It didn't take crappy, drug-reliant therapy to make me see that. I knew that; I've *known* that all along.

Shay was lucky, but she's always been lucky. Luck and shine just *suited* her. She was a princess at home and in school, holding court

17

whenever and wherever she felt up to it. She's had Dad wrapped around her baby finger for thirty-four years now. Mom, on the other hand, refused to kowtow to Shay's princess act. Well, unless Shay brought up something she knew they both had in common. Quite often, it was clothes shopping and cream tea at one of the many downtown tearooms that have suddenly popped up everywhere, having grown nostalgically trendy over the past decade. Once the shopping-and-scones excursion was over though, the two of them would head off in opposite directions, Shay back to her glamorous life as an upscale department store chain buyer and Mom back to her life of whatever her interest-du-jour is (one day it may be book clubs, another day it may be tapestry circles, I never know anymore). They'd avoid getting in touch with each other until another purse or jewelry sale popped up nearby, preferably in-between where the two of them could meet without complaint.

"Speaking of Dad, is he and what's-his-name still getting on, acting out their libertarian gun-fetishes?" I knew what Shay's to-be-father-in-law's name was, but the headache was getting worse, causing my mind and memory to go all mushy, and I wasn't in reach of my suitcase where I'd stupidly stashed an extra large bottle of Ibuprofen (last minute addition courtesy of a last minute emergency trip to the drugstore much to Mom's dismay).

"Your father has agreed to behave for Shay's sake, even if that means I have to tolerate him with that man for a few more days."

"Man, I'm *starving*. I'm never this hungry," I muttered, forcing the subject to die a sudden death. "There'd better be enough vending machines there to ease the evening munchies."

"The kitchen might still be serving dinner by the time we get there," said Mom, "but if not, I've some granola bars in my purse."

"Granola bars? Are they burger or hot dog flavored?"

"Don't be silly, Ansley. They're just granola bars. I often bring some whenever your father and I have to fly somewhere. Airline companies have been cutting costs down, and it's ridiculous. There's never any food, even cross-country. It's all pretzels and peanut butter crackers," she said. "Anyway, if the kitchen is closed and if you're really that hungry, I'm sure Rex has enough clout to get the kitchen staff to stay late, if need be. He can be irritatingly persuasive, that man."

I fidgeted with my cell in my lap, scrolling through all the old texts, the searing reminders of the breakup that started all of this, the cautious lies, the halfassed apologies, the name of the very pregnant other woman I hadn't even seen coming around the bend, the craziness that refused to settle. I chose my words carefully as I scanned those angry words, all of those angry words. "Yeah, he's kind of a tool, that man."

Mom snatched my phone from my lap and shoved it into my bag, sniffing as she did when she was supremely annoyed. "I'm sure Rex has all the best intentions for his family and for Shay, even if his own sense of respectability and civility shows otherwise."

"See? You can't stand him either, Mom. Turns Dad into a buddy-buddy, macho jackass."

"Don't talk about your father that way."

"Sorry, but I needn't remind you that you can't stand Rex either."

She sniffed again, wriggling her nostrils at the rugged landscape ahead of us. We were on a winding country road that wove us deeper into the crusty dips and valleys of Hill Country. "I don't care for him, no. I don't care for any of them," she said. "However, if he's what makes your father agreeable during social events, so be it. Still, I don't know how his own child can stand his absolutely boorish behavior. And his wife…Delia…"

I could sense she wanted to say more, but Delia, the matriarch of the Card family…She was a hard one to put into words, the *right* words. She seemed all satin and grace. She'd greet you with a sparkle, a laugh, a chitter-chat, a soft squeeze of the arm, but her eyes whispered something else to you, something secretive and knowing, like nothing could ever get by her.

And the way she treated Shay. You'd think they'd been the best of mother-daughter-girly-friends for years. I knew that was even worse for Mom.

"Doesn't hold a candle, Mom," I said softly. "She's not you. You know that, right?"

Mom sniffled and waggled a hand in my direction, as if she was fanning the air of the implication alone. Then she wiped her lower lash lines with a careful, delicate swipe of a finger. She tended to get teary when she was infuriated and jealous about something significant. "Delia has been wonderful to Shay. Just wonderful. And I want Shay to be happy. She's never been as happy as she is when she's with friends."

"Hey now," I said, squeezing her free hand. "I'm here, Mom. I'm your friend, you know."

"You're never around much though, are you? We hardly know what's happening with you anymore, Ansley. When your father got the call that you'd had that breakdown at your work, that you'd been arrested, and all of this, what you're going through now—"

Jesus H. Christ, *that*. It was always going to be about *that*. That itchy scar etched on my workplace, on my social life, on my family's reputation and so on forever and ever. It had been broiling there, bubbling in the wings as the thought of *him* with *her*, their happy family, their cozy-cuddly life together threatened to scald me from the inside out. All it had taken was one more reminder, and it was so stupid. Just a simple, little ping on my phone signaling a text message saying, *You need to leave me alone*. It was the proverbial last straw for me then and there. Of course, it just had to have been at the call center of all places. Right when I was in the middle of dealing with another long-winded customer complaint, of all times.

Apparently, my outburst frightened the hell out of everyone there, including the boss' kids who'd come in with him after my boss had picked them up from school. I wouldn't know though. I'd forgotten most of what happened. It was almost like it all had been erased from my memory altogether, a protective barrier shielding me from the truth about my behavior and everything I did in that moment.

Lots of things were like that though, those missing fragments.

The police report indicated I'd hurled my desk phone at my boss, striking him hard above the eye. There wasn't any permanent damage, thank God, but the written reminder and court documents and legal fees will always be there, my permanent scar. He pressed charges, of course. I was in county for a couple of days before Dad reluctantly posted bail. In the end, courtesy of a sympathetic judge and a thorough (read: *expensive*) lawyer, I was sentenced to a month's stay in a rehabilitation center of "our" choosing coupled with mandated therapy and a year's worth of community service. That said, it was much better than the alternative.

Still, it's yet another scar, another reminder, I was unfit to work, to interact normally, have a life and such.

I was unfit to exist around normal people.

I waved at Mom, signaling her to stop before my heart burned a hot hole deep within me. By that point, my head hurt so much my eyes were watering.

"I know," I said. "I'm sorry I haven't...I didn't mean to keep things from you. I don't mean to do that. It's just you're so difficult to talk to about—Well, like when Simon broke up with me, it wasn't just a passing issue, Mom. It wasn't just some little thing that could've been shrugged off like you always say we should do. He just stopped speaking to me, and the next time I hear anything about him, he's married with a little girl on the way. That's not normal. That's not right. And I couldn't take it. Between that and the prescriptions and the anxiety over every little thing I did, it all made me sick. I mean it, *physically* ill. And getting off the stuff is even worse."

"You could have called then, Ansley. You *should* have called. We could've helped somehow. We didn't know anything."

"I know, Mom. I'm sorry. You're right. I should have. I keep saying that though. I feel like I can't apologize enough for it. You know how it is."

It wasn't that I didn't *want* to call or visit my parents often. It's just that…Well, I didn't want to call or visit my parents often. There's only so much of the tension between us that I can feasibly take.

And, meanwhile, I was cutting my last benzodiazapine prescription down, moving my way into low dose Diazepam, as per strict, hellish instructions. Aprazolam, Lorazepam, Clonazepam, you name it, I'd been overprescribed it *and* its other mellow kin. I wanted a break from the whole anal-retentive tapering schedule. Just some relief. I didn't care about the physical toll it was having on me. My sister's wedding was the real test of self-endurance as to what I could possibly take while tapering off the hell I'd been on to numb myself to everything and then some.

At least Shay hadn't asked me to be maid of honor. Thank God for small favors, I suppose.

The road suddenly shifted beneath us, and the little car jumped and growled its displeasure at us. Mom had turned us off the smoothness of the main drag onto a rocky side road that, according to the rustic wooden sign we'd passed, led to the Montague Ranch Resort. The road itself was lined with desert broom and spiky palmettos, leading us down a winding, bumpy trail.

"So how far are we from civilization? Are we going to be relying on outhouses and campfire coffee or what?" I said. Not like I particularly minded being away from people and noise. I just didn't care to be corralled in with people and noise.

A darkened guardpost with no guard on duty greeted our arrival. The closed iron gates ahead of us kept us from going any further. Mom urged the car to a shuddering halt and set it in Park. Then she rolled down her window and stretched out her arm to hit the call button on the post beside the car. There was a crackle-pop of static and then silence on the other end.

She poked at the call button again. "Hello? Are you just going to breathe into the speaker or are you planning on answering at all?" she snapped.

There was another crackle in response. Then a man's voice, deep and chuckling, came on with a "Sorry about that, darlin'. You here for the Boone-Card wedding?"

"Nooooo, we're here for the whole ranch-hand experience, lassoing, campfire farting, cattle-branding, and all," I said.

Mom shushed me, giving me the old settle-down look only real mothers could ever possibly perfect. Then she turned back to the call speaker and said, "Yes, I'm the mother of the bride. I was just picking up my oldest. Would you kindly open the gates?"

Another chuckle, and I didn't like the raspy-deep sound of it. "Well, hay-loooo! Sure thing, lambchop. Lemme just get the keys to the truck here. Just a min' and I'll let you ladies in."

We sat there in the quiet, listening to the droning buzz of the cicadas, waiting, just waiting.

"Lambchop? For real?"

Mom gritted her teeth, glancing at me in the rosy light of the sunset. "That was certainly Rex. That man."

"What a card, that Card."

Mom's scowl twisted into a half smile. I can't even remember the last time I saw her smile like that. It was the smile that signaled she appreciated the humor even when things happening weren't particularly amusing all in all.

In the distance, headlight halos winked at us just past the gates as the pickup truck dipped and eased its way down towards the entrance.

"Why don't they have an actual guard to, you know, guard the place, and stay there…in the *guard*house?" I pressed. Not that I required an answer or anything, but it was a valid question, I thought.

Mom kept steadily watching the truck as it pulled up and then made a U-turn around, facing back towards the driveway path. After a moment, she said, sort of absently, "It's the only resort I've ever been where the staff wasn't around much at all. Delia said there's a maid service in the morning but only during the weekdays. Restaurant service is minimal, but their lunch was quite lovely. Crepes and fruit salad. I rather liked it. Good choice for the heat."

A tall, broad-shouldered shadow of a figure slid out from the driver side of the truck and gave us a jaunty wave. Rex Card then stepped out in front of his truck, his facial features blotted by the lights behind him. He let out a whoop of a laugh, one hand on his hip, the other playfully wagging a finger at us like we were children who'd done something naughty.

"You gals gettin' here well past the dinner bell," he said with a chortle. "It's not po-lite to keep your family waitin', especially when there's some divine grub to be had."

Mom leaned out the window and said, "Obliged, Rex, if you'd be so kind as to let us in. My youngest is probably worried by now."

Rex unlocked the gates and swung them wide open, motioning us in. Mom pulled up the car next to him. He dropped into an easy crouch near her window. It was the first time I'd seen him since the engagement party well over a year before. He was a good-looking man in his early 60s with curly salt-and-pepper hair, a perfectly trimmed mustache and a broad smile bearing too many teeth to count. His eyes though, like Delia's, they showed something lacking, something inexplicable. They were alive, yet their light had long since gone cold.

He winked at me. "Lookit you there, Missy Prissy. Been awhile. You feelin' any better? They get you good n'healthy?"

I glared at the back of Mom's head. That wasn't what I'd wanted anyone to share. I know she could feel the heat of my stare against her neck, but she kept her focus on Rex who didn't avert his gaze from me until she spoke.

"She's well. Thanks, Rex. We'll meet you back up at the courtyard." With that, she rolled up her window and eased the car past Rex who waved us in, his smile forming into a blank line as he did.

"What exactly did you tell them?"

She pretended like I hadn't said anything and kept her eye on the trail as she drove on.

"Mom. Answer me."

She blew out a long exhale, as if she'd been holding her breath, trying to keep it all in. "Shay had already mentioned something to Nathan about it. Just that you had been ill and needed some time in a facility but that it was nothing serious. Nothing for anyone to worry themselves over." Mom glanced at me, her face crinkled. "And she's right, isn't she now. Nothing to worry about. The alternative would've been much worse, but they don't have to know that."

Nothing. Right. Shay and I would certainly have some words. But first, all I wanted was to knock back some Ibuprofen and take a long soak in the shower to get the stink of the long drive off me.

Then swallow a pill crumb.

It was going to be like that this weekend. Sheer hell.

I just wasn't aware *how* awful a weekend in hell could be.

TWO

I don't know exactly how long I'd been sitting there on the edge of my bed. I was fresh out of a lukewarm drizzle from underneath the showerhead, attempting to check my email on my cell with shaky-twitchy hands, but it must have been awhile since the violet streaks of light had long since disappeared from between the cracks in the heavy wooden door to my suite. Stray streams of water from my wet hair cut shivery trails down my back, so I ruffled it a bit more in a towel and then turbaned it over my head. The towels weren't heavy and soft as they ought to be at a hotel. Instead, they were thin and rough and didn't do much to get one dry. There was a hairdryer that had been placed in a velveteen bag that dangled from a hook on the bathroom wall, but I didn't feel like plugging the thing into the only socket available and maneuvering my way around the tiny bathroom in order to get my tangled hair dry. So I let my hair dribble water, forming little puddles on the cold concrete floor of my suite.

"Suite" probably wasn't the right word to describe the room. The resort itself was designed to look like something out of a western, a little pueblo village with cobblestone paths leading to tight alleys, courtyards, doorways, and rock gardens, one of which was part of the natural landscaping surrounding an algae-choked swimming pool. Some of the paths led to wooden doors to what seemed like would be cozy casitas, like the one I was staying in. The inside of them was another matter altogether.

If any place were to make one feel imprisoned, it would be within the guest rooms. Mine didn't have any windows at all, making it feel like the interior of a cave. The main light to the room was out, its lightbulb having fizzled and died when I attempted to turn it on, so I had to rely on the dusky light of the little table lamp on the scuffed nightstand. I'd needed to charge my cell, but most of the free sockets were nothing more than a spaghetti-jumble of exposed wiring. I'd tried to plug in my cell in a socket in the bathroom beforehand, but there was

25

no place to set my phone. There was no bathroom sink countertop at all. Instead, the sink was little more than a deep marble bowl with a wide drain and a swan-necked tap, a completely impractical attempt to appear modern and stylish. The cord couldn't reach the toilet tank, so I couldn't set the phone on that either.

Evidently, that didn't matter anyway. There was no signal out in the middle of an obvious nowhere. After a third, fourth, and then an angry fifth attempt to move about the room, trying to pick up something…anything…to grant me a bar or two, I plopped myself back down on the edge of my bed and scrolled through the much older messages from Simon, ones that had grown scarce and sporadic, brusque and short, once the days, then weeks, then months, had passed. I hadn't trashed any of them. That record of a dying relationship had grown into a frantic obsession for me, one that Leon had tried to ease out of me through my therapy sessions but couldn't.

Simon's last message to me was simple and telling.

You need to leave me alone.

It was the finality of those words that broke me in pieces. That was the day I went ballistic at work. The fact that I'd not been able to get an updose on my benzo prescription only made it worse.

I felt something tickling my thigh in light, airy touches just below the cuff of my shorts. A spider had gotten confused, apparently mistaking my leg for a part of the dusky, drab surroundings. Normally, I would've screeched and leapt away from the bed, frantically shaking myself free of the rest of his invisible friends that might have landed on me as well. Instead though, I used the edge of my cell to gently ease him off me and onto the damp, pebbly-rough floor.

The room's cranky AC unit clicked on and rumbled. It had been perfectly placed beside the bed as well, so that would be a plus when I finally managed to sleep. The in-house rotary phone suddenly came to life as well, ringing and rattling on the glass-topped dinette table against the wall. When I went over and answered it, all I could hear was a crackle of static, and a broken, barely recognizable feminine voice said, "Ans…Here?" and then the line went dead.

I hung up the receiver and then picked it up again and put it to my ear. Again, no signal. Just a hollow, low-pitched whine. It sounded like it was picking up the sound of the wind from a far-off place. I tried dialing "O" as that usually worked at hotels, often signaling the front desk to pick up. Still, nothing.

"Hello?" I said into the receiver. "Anybody there?"

26

The wind on the other end of the line whistled softly at me. There was something else there though, something almost out of reach, but one of my many withdrawal symptoms, as it turned out, was a bit advantageous. When there was sound, whole sound, perceptible sound, it was often sharp in my ear, causing the pain to streak down my neck and tighten and twist nerve endings further.

I swear to Christ, in that moment, I heard a voice on the other end of the line muttering something I couldn't understand, not even a bit, and right then, I wasn't in any sort of mood to take it.

"Hey, who is this?" I said. "Speak clearly because I can't understand anything you're trying to say—"

A voice then came on. Masculine and raspy. A rattle-cough.

I slammed down the receiver before whoever it was on the other end could answer, and I briskly rubbed my arms that had gone goosepimply all over. I'd had my fair share of crazy, never mind when it came from me and was evident all over my emails and text messages to Simon. The detox unit of the rehab center held all-day, all-night screamers, criers, and babblers from all over the state, all in various stages of withdrawals, many who had stupidly tried to quit cold turkey. The babblers had been the worst because their words either came out in random bursts of mumbo-jumbo, or they kept repeating the same mantra over and over again. One of them had everyone on the rec floor completely bonkers with his constant, roaring complaints about being hungry and the lack of a 24-hour snack bar. It was much more problematic for those of us who sometimes got wavery-nauseous at even the slightest thought of eating anything at all.

When he finally got his wish as soon as the unit had a working vending machine installed, he tried to hit everyone up for money. The foolish among us would offer him a couple of dollars, only to later discover that instead of eating the junk food he'd buy, he'd merely hoard it in his room. I don't know just how much the attendants discovered there, but I do know he'd hidden some of the food in between his mattress and box spring. They'd pulled out a number of flattened bags of mushy Doritos and Cheetos. The bottom of the mattress and top of the box springs were stained in bright orange globs of Cheeto dust. He'd screamed for the attendants to put the mattress back and "leave (his) food alone, Goddamnittohellandfuck!"

So crazytalk in general, *that* I could handle. It was the hiss of the sound itself that had been creepy and so... *final.* The voice hadn't sounded familiar, so I couldn't place a face to it whatsoever. I tried dialing again, if anything, to attempt to get a dial tone out, but there was nothing on the other end but dead air. I couldn't figure it out – If someone was able to pick up somewhere around the resort, the phones couldn't be completely fried, could they? How did that work exactly (or not since that was the case)?

There was a soft rapping on the door, which gave me a jolt, causing me to nearly slip on the floor when I turned around.

"Ans, it's me. Open the door, dumbass!"

I could barely hear her through the heavy door, but it didn't matter. All it took was 'dumbass' and I was grinning like a nitwit, instantly feeling the anxiety melt away. I unlatched the door and opened it wide.

It was my little sister Shay, a sight. Her auburn hair had been recently cut into angled edges that skimmed down, just touching below her shoulders. Her wide brown eyes gleamed mischief as ever, which was comforting. I'd missed that. That said though, she was also deep in "impress-me" mode. Instead of her usual tee-and-tight-shorts combo, she was casual chic in a white men's dress shirt (probably Nathan's because she was like that), chunky bracelets, rolled jeans and Keds. Like a Banana Republic ad. Shay was the only reason why I'd agreed to go through with the wedding. If it had been any other relative or friend, I would've turned the touching offer down without question. Shay though…Shay was my lifeline to something feasibly normal and whole, decent and real.

Plus, she was holding out a soda and a paper bag of something that smelled so wonderful, all fried and greasy, and hell if I wasn't famished. It was often like that while dealing with withdrawals, the appetite suddenly showed up when I'd no idea I'd been hungry for so long. Other times, the mere sight of food made me want to spend the next few days hunched over the toilet bowl.

As hungry as I was though, I didn't know if I really wanted it. My heart was still dancing after the call.

Shay's smile twisted into a quizzical frown. "It's bratwurst, your favorite. I had Nathan and Charlie pick it up in town just for you since you and Mom couldn't make it to the rehearsal dinner," she said, shoving the bag and drink at me. "Let me help. 'It's great to see you, Shay. Thank you for being *so* thoughtful. You're an awesome little sister. I don't know what I'd do without you.'"

"Did you call me earlier?"

"Yeah, but the line went all funny," she said. "I was coming down anyway. I just wanted to say 'hi', see if you were all right. Mom said you were hungry."

I opened up the bag, my appetite winning over. The spicy, oily-rich aroma alone caused my stomach to burble a reminder that it was high time I ate something. Then I beckoned Shay inside, but not before I gave her a swift peck on the cheek and a grumbling, "Thanks, butterbutt."

"Sure thing, titty-tata." Shay sauntered in and made herself right at home, plopping down on the bed. She grasped one of the bedposts, making a face at it. "It's ostentatious, right? Too fancy? I don't like the furniture. It screams luxe comfort but feels like something out of The Princess and the Pea...or like Nana's house. She was always into style over comfort. Sort of. Kind of. Okay, she wasn't stylish at all, but she tried, right?"

"Don't forget, she was the one who kept all the 'parlor' furniture covered in plastic sheets," I said as I made myself as comfy as I could in the overstuffed armchair in the corner. Then I promptly dug right into the bag of fries and bratwurst. Everything was as I'd imagined, all greasy good, food I'd totally regret later because that's just how it was for me.

"Why did she call that room a 'parlor,' like she was expecting gentlemen callers over for cards and brandy...?"

"She liked the idea of gentlemen callers," I said around a mouthful of fries.

"Until they actually came over," reminded Shay. "Then she did everything she could to keep them *out* of the parlor and at the kitchen table, having them drink that nasty Turkish coffee she made so they'd sober up and leave her alone to her romance novels and endless games of Solitaire."

"Nana would've hated this place. Too dark and dreary. She liked happy colors, floral wallpaper, Hummel figurines carefully placed everywhere," I said. I took a long swig of my drink, something cherry-flavored and calorie-dense wonderful.

Shay wrinkled her nose as she peered all around the room. "Friend of Nathan's family runs it. Most of them are out for the weekend, except for some of the kitchen staff, their cousins, who are amazing cooks. They had these steak kabobs for dinner tonight, and the meat just melted in your mouth. I don't think I've ever had steak that tender."

The curiosities never ended. "I thought you were going vegetarian now."

Shay's face went all dreamy soft, her eyes glazed over. "Nathan said I needed to up my iron and B12 intake, and eating red meat was the best way to go."

"Aww, girl, I'm so glad you gotta a guy who eat-shames and mansplains such important info for your little girlbrain to take in."

"Don't be like that."

"Seriously though, what's up with that?"

I'd obviously struck a nerve as Shay suddenly transformed from girl-in-love soft to steel and salt. It had been happening off and on since...well, since *Nathan*. I didn't like that version of Shay, that Nathan-influenced, Nathan-can-do-no-wrong version of Shay. Her jaw tightened, her voice chilly. "Nathan cares about me, Shay. Maybe if you had someone in your life who cared as much, you wouldn't be such a bitter bitch about every little thing that makes other people happy."

"I'm not bitter," I said as I crumpled up the empty bag and then tossed it into the wastebasket. Then I removed the makeshift towel turban from my head, unraveled it, and used it to pat down my damp locks. "Bitch, yes, sometimes. I'll own that. But 'bitter,' no. 'Bitter' should be reserved for little girls who long for tiaras and kingdoms but instead wind up with good old-fashioned chauvinists who control their every move. "Bitter' is the moment when those girls wake up and realize, too late, that everyone else isn't in the same boat after all because everyone else had enough sense not to take it."

Shay slid up on her feet and then loomed over me, trying her best to appear as if she had some semblance of control, but I knew – I always knew – lately, she was often ready for a fight to break out between us. My condition. Always my fault. "At least Nathan didn't run off with someone else and start a family with her," she said.

"Ouch. You're actually gonna bring out the big guns while I'm out of detox? That's just mean."

"Did you like the brat? You kinda wolfed it down like you hadn't tasted anything so good in quite awhile there."

"Don't fucking change the subject, Shay. You brought up Simon, so say whatever it is you wanna say."

Shay cleared her throat, one hand steady on the door handle, readying her to leave, the other clenching and unclenching as she did when she was trying not to explode. "I just think you should take a good, hard look at yourself and deal with your own issues before you pass judgment on anyone else."

"Noted. Duly."

Her voice softened, if just a little. "I wanted you to be a part of this. I know you don't believe me, but it's true."

"I guess I have you to thank for getting me out for a couple of days."

"Ans. Come on."

I let that simmer for a moment, both of us silent. Then I said, "Admit it. You just wanted to see me in a bridesmaid's dress."

"Okay, I wanted to see you in a bridesmaid's dress."

"How much does Dad owe you?"

"What?"

"How much did you bet him that I'd agree to wear it? You know he doesn't think I have it in me. He thinks I live and sleep in shorts and jeans, and it pisses him off. We're supposed to be ladies after all."

Shay couldn't keep a straight face, and she muffled back a giggle just before she said, "Fifty."

"You bet fifty bucks?"

"Fifty cents."

"Fuck the hell right off."

She let out a gasp. "Language, Ansley! So unbecoming."

"Go suck a lollicock."

Shay grinned at that and opened the door. Then she turned back to me once more, her face crinkled in thought before she softly said, "It was Nathan's idea by the way."

"Idea for what?"

"For the bratwurst," she said. "He remembered it was your favorite. He knew just where to go in town to get you one."

"What'd he do, have them inject it with laxative?"

"Ansley, seriously."

"You should know by now I take any Nathan niceness with a side order of suspicion."

"Whatever. I'll thank him for you since those little meaningless things like manners often elude you."

With that, she left. I knew it would take a couple of hours before she cooled down, cleared herself of my annoying habits. Those habits. I'd always been great at getting under one's skin. Deflective trait probably. I swirled the crushed ice in my soda cup around and

31

around, the tumbling sound of it momentarily blocking the voice that had stilled my heart earlier and had since returned, poking through my thoughts.

My stomach suddenly went sour. The taste in my mouth, acrid-greasy and cloying. I tossed back some of the dregs of crushed ice left in the cup, crunched them between my teeth, hoping they'd soothe away the acid-churning happening inside of me and the timpani orchestra pounding over and over again in my skull. I'd taken enough ibuprofen to destroy the remainder of my innards earlier, once I'd been able to tear into my luggage. Still, it hadn't done much in ridding me of my headache. Instead of ice needles and jagged blades stabbing away there, it had merely lessened to an actual throbby ache.

Then my body went warbly, and the room spun and dipped as soon as I stood up. My knees popped. My eyes watered. I felt shaky and weak. You know that feeling you get when you're about to throw up, when you know something horrible is about to happen to your body, and the very thought of food makes you feel chilly...? I suddenly felt it up and down all over, the thundering palpitations knocking the air from me. I barely made it to the toilet before all the soda, bratwurst, and fries came pouring out in a hot, gooey torrent, the force of it yanking my jaws wide open.

Apparently, I hadn't been hungry after all.

Even so, my stomach, completely emptied of its contents, loudly disagreed.

No phone signal. No promised WiFi access, even though the welcome brochure that had greeted me on the dinette table upon arrival had indicated otherwise, so I couldn't do any further, obsessive research on withdrawal symptoms. The bizarre conflict between stressful stomach and hunger pains had to have been one I'd not experienced until then.

I felt a cool ribbon of air coming from the bedroom tease along the side of my neck and arms, easing me a little out of my miserable state. I wiped the sour grunge from around my mouth with a piece of toilet paper, crumbled it and tossed it into the toilet bowl with the acrid remains of my menu for the day. My head felt hot and hollow. I needed sounds though. I needed *something* to distract me from the sickness, so after I brushed the rank tang away around my teeth and tongue, I made my way back into the bedroom and turned on the only bit of decent, working technology, the wide flat-screen TV on the wall in front of the bed. Besides the distraction, I just wanted anything to let

32

me know we weren't really out in the middle of bumfuck nowhere, thirty miles from lights, the sounds of traffic, and people – glorious, noisy, chaotic *people*. Couldn't stand to be near them, yet I needed them, *all* of them.

The only channels I could access were local stations, and there wasn't anything worthwhile on aside from one of the many awful singing competition shows that just didn't know how to die a horrible death and some syndicated sitcoms that were funny in the '90s, back when they were relevant and still politically incorrect. I didn't need a laugh track though, so I left it on the local PBS station where some grandmotherly British sleuth was enjoying a spot of tea with the village constable. It was mellow enough to soothe the headache down a bit and noisy enough to fool me into thinking there was some civilization around. I took my nightly benzo bit, washing it down with the last dregs of watery soda.

Then I climbed into bed and buried myself deep underneath the musty comforter, willing myself to sleep while my brain screamed that it was on fire.

#

If it wasn't the sudden, loud CLICK and griping of the AC that woke me up, it was undoubtedly the last image I had of Simon getting a sledgehammer dead center to the face that did it. There was an explosion of blood, brain and gristle, and then I found myself wrapped in a sweaty tangle of sheet and comforter. My hair felt matted and damp. My mouth, full of cotton and sand. The droning whine in the room, as it turned out, wasn't a residual sound from my dream but from the TV reminding me that, at 3:15 in the morning, PBS didn't pull all-nighters.

My stomach cramped something awful, burning and twisting my insides into hard knots. As soon as I sat up in bed, the room bounced, and I could hear the swishing sound of blood rushing in my ears. I turned off the TV with the remote and sat there in the inky darkness, listening for a moment. I thought I heard someone or something tapping on the door to the suite.

There was a scratching sound, barely perceptible, coming from the other side of the door. I clicked on the bedside lamp and slowly slid out of the bed. Underneath my bare feet, the concrete floor was chilly and sticky, undoubtedly from condensation. The state was so

33

humid and miserable this time of year, and there didn't seem to be adequate ventilation in the room whatsoever.

Whatever it was beyond the door gave it a tap-tap-tap, startling me. It sounded like someone was hammering on it with gentle force.

"Hello?" I said softly and whistled. "Who's there?"

The tapping sound stopped. I waited for an answer, a voice, anything. It would've helped had the room had windows. I'd be able to catch a shadow, something out there, even in the dark of the hellish early morning hours. I pressed my ear to the door, listening closely, carefully, trying not to let my imagination and fear run off hand-in-hand with my sanity.

Tap.

Tap.

It sounded like long fingernails clicking against the wood.

I wasn't about to run out there without a weapon, so I stalled a bit, bracing myself against the door just in case whatever or whoever was out there tried to ram the door open. "You gonna say something, have a conversation, light chit-chat out there…or you just planning on scaring the shit out of me for the rest of the night?" I said as I stuck my foot out in the direction of my bag that I'd dropped on the floor beside the bed.

I hooked the bag handle onto my big toe and dragged the bag towards me. Then with one hand still braced against the door, I crouched down and used my free hand to rummage around in my bag for the pepper spray I know damned well I'd brought for the trip. At least, I'd presumed I'd brought it. My hand grasped around something that felt like a pepper spray container, but it revealed itself to be a fancy lipstick case, some retro-cutesy gift from the bridal shower goodie bags awhile ago. I didn't even use lipstick.

I tossed the thing back into the depths of my bag and felt around the bottom near the slick liner. Using my back to brace the door, I snatched up my bag and snaked my hand all around the inside of it. A sharp thump to the door caused me to drop the bag and slide right down to the floor, my rear end hitting it hard. Some of the bag's contents had tumbled out onto the floor. The tube of pepper spray had slid under the bed along with a number of stray coins and some lint-shaggy, butterscotch Life Savers I'd apparently had a family of collecting and growing in my bag. I scooted over to the bed and reached underneath, feeling around for the pepper spray. Once I had it grasped tightly in my hand, I slowly eased myself up, unbolted the door lock, and swung the door wide open.

The air outside was muggy and stank of rotting vegetation. There were no outside lights on in the exterior edge of the resort where my room was located, but there was a fingernail curve of moonlight that was just bright enough for me to discern the lines of hills and valleys and bowing trees dotted here and there in the distance. The soft light of my room helped as well, acting as a dim searchlight, ready to capture anything scuttling around right outside the room.

There was no sign of the door scratcher though, nothing out of the ordinary. My heart still rapidly pounded away, undoubtedly unconvinced there was really nothing out there. Fight or flight instinct urged me to avoid the possibility of the former and take on the offer of the latter, but it wasn't enough for me then. I would've rather faced it head-on, whatever "it" was actually, confronted it, made peace with it, if anything, so that I could go back to that blissful sleep I so desperately needed, so I slipped on my sneakers, snatched up my room key and cell phone, and headed out, but not before locking the door behind me. I still didn't like the thought of whatever it was that was outside getting in and hiding in my room, waiting for me there in the closet or bathroom or a darkened corner. There were lots of places to hide in that gloomy place.

I walked along a pebbly path, using the flashlight app on my cell as a light. There were no visible signs of life, aside from the waving shadows and buzzing gnats frantically zigzagging in the faint light. When I rounded the corner of the building, the warm glow of lamplight came from somewhere ahead of me, so I switched off the app, shoved the cell down in my shorts' pocket, and trudged on, heading straight for the light.

"You lost, little lady?" someone growled right behind me. The hot, acrid stench of meaty breath warmed the back of my neck and curled around me.

And my eyes went runny, my head went heavy all over, my heart rate thundery.

I spun around, stumbling, waving my tube of pepper spray around in front of me. I fell backwards and landed smack dab in a bed of something painfully prickly. Needles pierced my skin, poking hot, jagged points through my shirt, my shorts, all over my hands and all down my legs. I flailed about, trying to heave myself up, but every time I put my hand down to brace myself as I tried to get up, I wound up

35

making it worse by attempting to reach around for actual ground. My body went into panic mode, shaking, my breath coming in ragged hitches. I managed to clench my way through the pain and heave myself up off the bed of cacti. Then I wiped frantically at barbs I couldn't see whatsoever that had stuck through my clothing and into my skin. When I ran a hand into my pocket for my cell just to get my strong light back and check the damage, shine it on whoever was out there with me, my pocket turned out to be empty. The cell had apparently slipped from it into the cacti bed.

"You've gotta be kidding me," I muttered as I patted myself down, if anything, to be absolutely certain it had fallen out. And as my luck would have it, it wasn't there at all.

I wasn't about to try and get the thing when I couldn't easily see it down in the cacti bed, but I couldn't get back to my room in the darkness, not with whoever was out there, teasing me, scaring the hell out of me. I would've certainly used the pepper spray had I had a clear view of my tormentor.

Bile formed in my throat. My body trembled all over. These weren't withdrawal symptoms; this was fight or flight, fight or flight. If I high-tailed it back to my room, I'd not be able to feasibly "high-tail" it because I'd have to feel around, letting the buildings, any physical landmarks guide me somehow in the dark. If I made my way closer to the lighted area of the resort, I'd still risk running into whoever it was out there with me, but at least there'd be some sense of civilization, and I'd be able to see him clearly (face him, make peace with him, STUPID) than if I were heading back in the darkness.

Also, there was the off-chance I could find someone out in the creepy hours of the early morning who could help me get my phone. Off-chance, barely a possibility, but there had to be a few employees around. Mom had mentioned something about staff not being around, apart from some cooks or something, but she was prone to exaggerating details sometimes. Hell, what kind of a resort doesn't have a front desk worker on duty at the very least?

Right when I started for the dimly lighted area of the resort, someone grasped my upper arm. I screamed, cutting the dark, and a voice went "Shhhhh."

I turned right into a tall figure as I once again held out my pepper spray. A flashlight clicked on, its beam right underneath the chin of a man's grinning face.

36

"Soooo…whatcha doing out here at hella clock in the morning?" said the man with a chortle.

And I sprayed him right in his eyes, the fucker.

THREE

The guy howled, dropping his flashlight on the ground. "What the *fuck*?" He pawed at his eyes, balling his hands and rubbing frantically.

I shoved him while he was unsteady, and he fell backwards, landing right on his ass. At least he hadn't tripped into the cacti bed. Small favor for him.

"Goddamn, girl, what is *wrong* with you?" he said with a groan.

I picked up his flashlight and waved its beam in his direction, if anything, to get a closer look at the creep.

He must've been in his 40's or so. It was often hard to tell middle-aged men's ages precisely as they all seemed to dress as if the grunge era had never really left the building. He had dark, ruffled hair and five o'clock shadow attempting to be a weak beard. Solid build. Etched scowl. He looked like he'd both inflicted and taken a few swings in the past couple of decades.

Yeah, he fit right in with the locale.

I dropped to a crouch right beside him, waving his flashlight beam right at his face. "I'm sorry, what's wrong with *me*? Really? No, no. What is wrong with *you*, not me," I said. "Not me. *I* was out looking for the prick who kept scratching at my bedroom door, that same prick who scared the holy fuck out of me a few minutes ago…and the *same* prick who caused me to fall onto a cactus and lose my cell."

He sniffed, wiping his wet, red-rimmed eyes with the back of his hand. "Look, I'm sorry if I scared you, but I swear I wasn't trying to do that to you. That isn't me. I mean, hell, look where it got me. Eyes on fire. Ass broken in half." He scrambled up to his feet, rubbing at his sore backside. "I have chronic insomnia, so I just walk around until I get tired and my thoughts go quiet. Runs in my family. Well, my father's side. Mom and her kin could sleep if there was a Cat. 5 hurricane happening outside."

"So you really weren't the guy who crept up on me and said, 'You lost, little lady'? Because that was something I don't want to relive ever again."

The guy gave me a perplexed grimace, his nose crinkling, eyes all narrowed. "That's pretty creepy."

"It's creepier when someone says it right in your ear, and you can't even see them," I said, gauging his reaction carefully. One thing about being in a rehab center, you can learn a lot about how to lie effectively, and you can pick up on the ones who try it out and fail at it. It's too bad none of us had the patience enough to play poker.

He took a long, hard look at me as well. We might as well have circled each other, like a standoff. We were in the territory for it. He stuck out his hand, motioning for the flashlight.

I held it away from him for a moment, eyeing his hand. Then I looked him in the eye and said, "You try anything funny, anything weird, and I will beat you down. I'm not kidding. I will beat you down."

The guy chuckled and then froze, realizing I wasn't joking. "Oh, I believe you. You're sparking there, girl. What's your name?"

"It's not 'girl.' That's just patronizing."

He held up his hands in defeat. "Wasn't trying to be." He held out a hand, this time for a shake, and managed a somewhat decent friendly grin. "Charlie Dughall. I'm in the wedding happening here this weekend."

The name clicked, but his face didn't register. I tried to remember if he'd been at the engagement party. Couldn't recall. There'd been so many people milling around my parents' house then. Shay liked big parties with lots of company, not my thing. I'd stuck with a couple of fellow introverts in the den, watching their kids play some card game with spells, weapons and characters out of a Tolkien series.

I shook his hand anyway, which was rough with callouses and warm. "I'm Ansley. Unlucky bridesmaid in the wedding party."

His expression suddenly shifted as realization crossed his features. "You're the one who's in rehab."

My face went hot. "And *you* can fuck right off," I said just before I snatched his flashlight from his grasp and tromped past him, shoving him aside, heading back to the cacti to find my phone.

The fact that my family informed complete strangers of my goddamned personal business was infuriating enough, but the guy, whateverthefuck Charlie, tailed me, attempting lame apologies again and again, and that pissed me off even more. I didn't need apologies about the truth of the matter. I didn't need pity either. I just wanted certain things in my life not to take the forefront of every damned bit of information about me.

I didn't even want to know just how *many* people at the wedding knew that about me. I was pretty sure my epic meltdown at my workplace, followed by my arrest, had also been mentioned, a little side tidbit of gossip, cutting and real.

"Hey, I've had problems with alcohol myself. Still do. Among other things I'm not proud of. Hasn't gone away. Hell, everyone has their vices," said Charlie. "But you...*you*, on the other hand, you're doing something at least. The rest of us, just a buncha cowards when you think about it."

"I don't think about it. I live it, and I'm reminded all the damned time," I muttered, willing the guy to leave me alone. "And I never had a vice. I wasn't addicted. Newsflash, buddy: Not everyone who's in rehab is an addict."

"Didn't say that."

"You don't need to *say* anything," I said as I wove the flashlight beam around the prickly plants. "It's what everyone leaps right into. All that conclusion jumping."

"Okay, so why were you there?" he said. He blinked hard and rapidly for a second, squeezed his raw eyes shut, opened them wide again, attempting to clean them out.

I guessed he hadn't been told *everything*, which was a relief. I watched him for a good minute before answering, "I'd been overprescribed medication by some shrinks needing an obvious kickback. Apparently, people aren't supposed to quit them cold turkey, but no one gave me any warning. So I've been like this ever since."

"What'd you need the medication for?"

"Just full of questions, aren't you, Charlie?"

"Well, maybe you didn't need any medication, I don't know. I'm just gettin' to know you s'all."

"I didn't need the medication I was prescribed, no. No one needs that shit." I swiveled the light at Charlie's face. "You know, I could do with some help. I dropped my phone somewhere around here."

40

"Give me back my flashlight, and I'll be glad to assist," he said flatly, wiping at his eyes with the back of a hand.

I wasn't about to oblige. There was just something off about his voice, his overall demeanor, something chilly there skirling underneath the surface warmth. It didn't help that he liked to talk, and I hated it, all that forced, nosy conversation. Folks around this area of the country loved to talk and talk, and there was nothing particularly engaging about whatever it was they'd kept talking about. My father hated it, too, and when forced to converse with another husband and/or business associate, he often managed to twist the conversation around so that it was on subject matter that was best left to showing off rather than talking about. From what I've learned from Mom and, primarily, Shay over this past year, it was how he and Rex (kind of sort of) bonded over guns and mutually agreed-upon paranoid conspiracy theories involving government takeovers. They went sometimes to the local range together whenever they felt overwhelmed by chit-chatty types, not even offering to take another stray introvert along with them. As much as my father stresses needed civility, how important it is to be polite, quite often, when forced into an uncomfortable social situation, he doesn't abide by his own tenets.

I could feel Charlie watching me as I swung the beam this way and that around the prickly growth, searching for the cell phone. "Eyes off my back please," I said over my shoulder. "I don't like people staring."

He eased a bulbous bit of cactus aside for me with his boot. "There ya go," he sniffed. "Right there, kitty cat. Careful now. It scratches, too."

I shined the light right at his face again, blinding him once more. "Really?"

"What? What did I do this time?" he said, squinting against the beam, holding up a hand at it.

"Kitty cat'? Because I'm assertive? You know, you could be a little more original, a little less archaic. I don't think comparing women to cats is trending online these days."

Charlie scowled at me, glaring in the bright light. His eyes were still raw and watery from the pepper spray. His cheeks, shiny-wet. He reached down, shoving the cactus plant aside, and picked up my cell from off the ground. He took my hand in his own and smacked the cell right into my palm.

"Hashtag Here's-Your-Goddamn-Phone," he said. Then he grabbed the flashlight out of my other hand and turned to leave.

The thought of being in the dark, alone again, with whoever else it was out there, kept pounding away at me, strumming my fear in my ears. I tugged Charlie back towards me, grasping his wrist, pulling him in, willing him not to leave. "Wait a minute," I said, pleadingly.

But he snatched his arm away and held a warning finger out for me not to touch him, to back off.

"I'm sorry. I'm so sorry," I said. The desperation in my voice made me inwardly cringe. "Please don't take anything I say personally. I'm sure you've also been warned about my wayward acidity. Overt bitchiness. It's just a coping mechanism. That's all."

Charlie suddenly widened his eyes and rapidly blinked out a stream of tears. He then rubbed at them again with his free hand, aggravating them further, groaning as he did. "Burnin' like a hellfucker," he mumbled.

He pulled at the bottom hem of his tee, yanking it up to his face, his eyes. He blotted at the corner of his eyes while I got a pretty decent view of the taut lines of abdominal muscle laddering down, a thin line of dark hair in the center pointing one in the right direction.

Of all times, of all places.

"I gotta get back and wash this shit out of my eyes. Can't be blind and take care of the groom, stumbling down the aisle like a jackass," he said, dabbing away at the burn.

And my head felt as if there were searing pokers prodding away inside, behind my eyes, through my temples. The pain, it wasn't out of sympathy for him. It was a signal that I needed to get back to my room, drink a gallon of water, and try to get back to sleep.

"Come on," I said, taking him by the arm, willing to risk it a second time. "My room's probably closer, just around there. I owe you a hand at least. You can wash that crap out before you go back."

Charlie hesitated, which was certainly understandable, all things considered. I offered up what I hoped was a genuine smile. It felt real for once.

And it seemed to do the trick because he tightened his mouth in a grim line, gave me an exasperated sigh, and then waved me with his flashlight hand to lead the way, so off we went to my room.

I've always known there are some moments you just simply can't turn around and high tail it back, start fresh and clean, rewind the reel a bit with renewal. When Charlie finally acquiesced and took my offered hand as soon as I opened the door to my room, we could have done that differently.

We *should* have done that differently.

#

I don't know how it happened. Or even why it happened. It just did. One of those quick snapshots in time exists there, permanently sealed now in my memory photo album. They're just brief images, flashes of what once happened or *might* have happened. Some of them appear a lot better, much more colorfully, clearly happier, than they actually were.

Charlie was there, sitting on the foot of the bed, head back, putting the drops in one eye at a time. I had a towel at the ready for him, so that he could blot. He briefly squeezed his eyes shut after each application, temporarily rendering him blind. His hand tightened around mine, and he gently tugged me in towards him, his legs on either side of me. I handed him the towel, thinking that was what he'd actually wanted, but the part of me on fire got the other signal first. Naturally, it was the wrong signal. It always was. I just wanted to make the burning stop, any distraction would do, and one was right there, one strong hand pulling at the back of my head, moving me down into his kiss. His lips were soft and pliant against mine. He tasted of smoky scotch and peppermint. Inhaling the heat of him in was too much, too intense, too raw even for me.

I untangled myself from his hold, pulling away from the kiss. Charlie looked at me quizzically, and I could feel his hand roaming my back, tugging at the hem of my tee shirt, wrapping it, knotting it in his grasp. Neither one of us had anything to say, nothing rational, no excuses or apologies. I just didn't know how to proceed. That sort of impulsiveness was something I'd been long used to, but I didn't care for one night stands with strangers. After Simon, I'd certainly had my share of regretful nights, waking up in bed with this guy and that, all of whom held the same facial expression upon realizing who was really there beside them, one of either confusion or disgust or a combination of the two. Clearly, beer goggles had played a hand in the night before. I never understood it. I'd just never thought of myself as physically appealing. Leon had instructed me again and again not to succumb to such thoughts about myself, and while I'm not quite as bad about it as I had been, every so often, that nagging, sticky sliver of self-hatred edges its way into my psyche.

When a guy like Charlie comes around though, well, it's kind of a turn on. I'd like to think it's the poison in me that does it.

"Sorry. It just seemed right, I don't know. Maybe it's just the idea of a wedding. Expectations. Something there," said Charlie, his gaze tight on mine. While his face clearly marked his apology, his hand played naughty, lightly teasing along the creases of the rear of my shorts. "Kinda cheap turn though, right?" he whispered. "I mean, we already had a bachelor party for the guy. Enough is enough already."

I reached behind me, halting his roaming hand in a firm grip. He flinched and withdrew his hand, held it up to me in another apology. "I've overstepped. Again, I am sorry. This is weird. It's weird, right? It's just that…You're just…You're a beautiful woman. No matter what though, I respect boundaries. I shouldn't have done that. I'm serious, I'm sorry," he said, bracing himself to stand up.

I gently pushed at him, forcing him back down on the bed. I ran a finger around his jawline, memorizing its angles, the feel of his prickly skin. "Fair warning," I said as that finger traced his lips, idling there. "You've already been told I have issues. And I'm not into regrets, so if you're the kind of guy who later pretends like it never happened, you'd best run along now."

Something flashed in his eyes, something dark and unidentifiable, but I caught it and held it, filing it away in storage just in case I'd need it at some point. It was gone though, replaced with need. His hand slid back around me, but I caught it in my grasp and moved it to my front, gently shoving it down past the waistband of my shorts, forcing it underneath, guiding his fingers onward. He was awfully good with those fingers.

He kissed me properly then.

Later, he kissed me where it mattered in the moment, and when his teeth found my clitoris, the lights behind my eyes went hot, and I finally let go.

FOUR

It's not like I'm not used to men leaving. I am. Beer goggles, remember. I just don't particularly care to be reminded that they do. The scent of Charlie's skin was strong, like wet grass and diesel. The smell was what woke me from a drowning sleep, so, of course, I thought he was still there, wrapped up in musty sheets and scratchy, thin blankets with me. Wasn't so lucky, as it were. His smell lingered in my hair, the pillows, the sheets. In the weak light of the bedside lamp, I couldn't even see an indentation there in the bed. There was only his scent left behind as a cold reminder. He was just like the rest, apparently, ready to high-tail it on out of there once he got a clear look at the woman lying next to him.

Not like I wouldn't run into him during the wedding and reception.

Hell if I regretted anything.

Scratch that. Hell if I regret anything, present tense. (Oh, but I do. I really do.)

I always hated sleeping naked in hotel sheets. It sounds a lot sexier than it really is. My skin felt tight and crawly all over. When I managed to roll out of the bed, blood pulsed loudly in my ears at the sudden strain of movement. My back muscles burned, so I stretched, forcing myself to crane my neck forward, my arms stretched out in front of me. The crackle-pop of bones, tendons, ligaments shifting there, an ever-present reality, not of aging necessarily, but out of utter apathy. I'd stopped caring much after Simon. When I bent my arms, grasping at each elbow behind my head, one at a time, everything went red and spotty. Pinpricks of light darted about in front of my eyes. The pain forced me to my knees on the chilly, damp concrete floor. The worst part was that I had to keep myself from reaching for my pills. I was allowed to half it and take a crumb in the morning and a crumb at night, if I needed to. I stupidly decided a single dose at night would be

45

best, as I'd only needed something to sleep since nothing else had ever worked. However, that would inevitably leave the day – from sunrise to sunset – wide open for every goddamned symptom that suddenly popped up out of its own raw oblivion.

At some point, I was to begin a liquid titration, and the mere thought of it made me queasy. The process of it, whittling the tab down even further and further, until I was finally free, gave me no sense of comfort whatsoever, no sense of relief.

Breathe, Leon whispered from somewhere deep within. *Whenever you feel tight inside, just breathe. Four-seven-eight, little sister. Recite that. Remember that. Four. Seven. Eight.*

I breathed in for four seconds, held for seven, released for eight. Breathed in, held, released again. The burning sensation in my temples and up and down my back fizzled down to a low simmer. My eyes were watery, and all I could see was a crimson wash of color. I had to blow my nose as well. It was as if every bodily fluid was stuck inside with a need to be released along with the knots of tension all over my body.

My cell lit up red from its spot on the nightstand, announcing its dying battery life at a meager 20% remaining. When I reached over for it, my head suddenly went fuzzy, spreading a dry numbness down my spine and across my neck and chest. Heart attack. Wasn't that a symptom in women my age? Numbness? Tightness? Shortness of breath?

You're fine, said Leon, reminding me that I'd been through this before. *You're experiencing more symptoms of your withdrawals. Your heart rate will increase due to panic. Focus on the sounds around you. Block out everything else. It's just noise. That's all it is.*

I couldn't breathe. I couldn't take in a breath at all. I was dying. It was happening.

You're not dying. Block it out.

But I couldn't take in any air. I needed to lie down.

Get up, little sister. Don't lie down now.

If I lay down, I could just stay there, die in bed. Slowly decompose, a wilted corpse. Cute.

Get the fuck up.

Someone pounded hard on the door, jolting me from my panic. Cold, clammy air surged in, forcing me to move. I was up on my feet, moving, moving.

Now answer the door. It's wedding day.

46

"We're eating, Ansley." My dad, on the other side of the door. I could hear the hesitant note there in his voice. He never did know what or how to say much to me. Even when I was young, he just said it as it was. Little emotion. All business. He wasn't like that with Shay, his golden source of fatherly pride. I suppose it ought to have bothered me more than it actually did.

"It's eight fifteen. You need to join us for breakfast before the kitchen closes at nine," he said.

And I'd almost forgotten how much he always hated it when I slept in.

Just like that, though, I could breathe. I never would've thought it would be my father responsible for breaking me out of my tight, choking panic. I quickly slid on my shorts that I'd apparently shed on the floor beside the bed along with my sleep tee. As for the underwear, I had no idea where it could be. Commando would have to do.

Another rapping and I went over to the door and leaned my head against it, my breathing coming in long, steady gasps. I could hear my heart ease down.

"Ansley? Are you there?"

I lightly touched the door, feeling its chilly graininess under the pads of my fingers. Solidity, Leon. Right there.

"We've gracious hosts, Ansley. They'd like to see you at some point." The chilly disappointment was evident in my father's tone. "I suggest you get yourself together. Right now."

It was enough for me right then, right there. I slid the deadbolt aside and pulled open the door, instantly saturating everything in a sheen of blinding, white hot light. I shielded my eyes with a shaky hand, squinting at him.

I'd not seen him since the engagement party, and it surprised me that even though it had only been a year, he'd grown much greyer, much more haggard, less his dapper, gentlemanly self. It was me, I was sure of it. I'd done that to him. My issues. My sorry state. His linen suit was rumpled, his dress shoes dull from an evident lack of a routine shine job. Even his beard, usually so neatly trimmed, was thatchy and uneven. He seemed smaller, too, like he'd shrunk some in the wash, creased and crinkled.

He also smelled of stale cigars. It wasn't like him.

He would never have lost sight of himself like that. Shay had learned to keep herself trim and together by paying close attention to

47

him, following in his shadow. I wondered what she thought of him now and what she must've really thought of me for doing that to him.

It was *me*, wasn't it?

Or was it the strain of letting his sparkling youngest go, watching her set off on a new path with a beau in tow?

Or was there something I'd not been told? That could easily be a possibility. Lately, I'd often been left out of the proverbial loop due to my change in residency, so to speak, never mind the fact that my father had paid quite a bit of money for me to stay there, quite a bit of money for *all* of it.

"Hi, Dad." Routine civility. Not like I had a choice in the matter. He paid for a lot of things, including the cushy wedding digs, exposed wiring and all.

He gave me a long once over, his lips tightening in disapproval, and I realized how I must've looked to him, schlubby tee, no bra, cutoffs, face puffy, hair everywhere. I realized, and as it normally went, I didn't care.

"Get yourself together," he said. "This isn't a vacation. It's important that you're present for your sister during her wedding day."

"The wedding's not until seven. And it's not like she asked me to be maid of honor. I just have to get my hair done, put on a fancy dress, and then spend the evening being delightful, looking like I give a shit about everything, right?"

He froze, unable to speak. I didn't get pleasure out of being blunt with the guy, but once in awhile, it put things in perspective for him, the realization that his daughter – that "other" one – had formed a life outside of his understanding and had…well, she'd been through some hell. Whether or not it had been "self-inflicted," as he'd often reminded me, was entirely open to interpretation.

Personally, I believe we don't choose whom we fall in love with and get antsy over. I don't see how anything like that could be considered "self-inflicted."

"I'm sorry." I couldn't leave it like that with him. We'd never bond, but at least, I could be kind, I suppose. "You know I'm cranky when I get up in the morning. There was this ongoing joke at the center that my best days were ones when I wasn't on early shift duty in the cafeteria because they'd have us up at six—"

"I don't want to hear it," he said. "And you're not to talk about it while you're here. Do you understand?"

"*I'm* not—Are you kidding me? You're kidding, right? Shay's apparently been telling *everybody* about it. I'd be surprised if she hadn't said anything about it to the staff here, too. Aren't they Nathan's friends as well?"

Dad held up a hand, shaking his head at me. "I said I don't want to hear it. Now straighten yourself up, put on some nicer clothes, and be so kind as to make an appearance before breakfast is cleared away. You can manage that, can't you?"

And with that, he disappeared back into the white sunlight, huffing away to tend to groomsmen, reluctantly hang out with fellow father-in-law, or whatever it was fathers do during a wedding day. I immediately felt right at home because once more, Shay was in the clear, and I would get the prodigal daughter treatment as I had for a good while since.

I kept my hand up, shielding my eyes from the light as I took a look around at where we'd landed, where the wedding would actually be held. It hadn't been particularly helpful to come at night. Not much of a view then. Not necessarily much of a view of civilization in the daylight either. There were several connected casitas leading down the cobblestone drive towards a little chapel and a wide fountain lined with colorful tiles, a fountain that was, surprisingly, active and burbling. I couldn't see past it as the drive curved down the hill. In the distance, ruddy brown hills sloped up and down in sporadic peaks, edging the dusty landscape. Bits of green sprinkled along the crests, reminding us that the drought was seemingly slowly ending but that it would still take quite a bit of time to come close to undoing the damage. The air was hot, promising a sweltering afternoon and evening, not exactly an ideal time for a wedding in the countryside.

To Shay though, it didn't matter. The sooner she could get hitched, the better. I never understood what the rush to anything so drastic was all about. I suppose it would make sense if a baby was on the way or if time was just slipping away quickly for the couple, but Shay was young and making a good living for herself. She'd mentioned wanting to have a family, babies and such, but only recently since she and Nathan had gotten serious.

I had to remind myself that Shay was as conventional as everyone else, unable to think and then act differently, away from the herd. Small-town sensibilities and expectations, they tended to stick.

It wasn't like I'd not thought of what it would be like to marry Simon. Not only that, but there had to have been that sort of

49

conventionality in me for me to have been so angry, so batshit crazy, about his having married another woman.

I often felt as empty as the land around me. I didn't have a place. I didn't have any concrete hopes and dreams anymore. I didn't have aspirations or goals. All I knew was that I'd felt more at home, the happiest, with other troubled misfits, in a rehab facility of all places.

The far-off sound of a plane coming from somewhere in the wide, open landscape snapped me out of my daze, reminding me that my immediate goal was to get the wedding shit over and done with so that I could start again, wherever and whatever that was.

#

I managed to swipe a mini muffin and an overripe banana from the leftovers at the breakfast buffet in the dining hall. Dad had been right. The staff was a stickler for time, so they'd already started piling dirty dishes and buffet platters onto carts, readying them to be swept off to the kitchen. I'd not brought much in the way of proper casual attire, according to what I saw of the other guests lingering there in clusters at some of the tables that had been set up specifically for the event. Apparently, morning was for chunky jewelry and bright, crisp summer dresses, linen suits or dress shirts and chinos. It was not for a button-down shirtdress ("Wear something button-down, Tits McGoo, so you won't mess up the 'do," Shay had nagged on the phone days beforehand) accessorized with thrift store leather belt, $5 flip flops, and my beat up bag. My bag was kind of weighing down my already achy shoulder and neck with its extra load of phone charger and old-fashioned address book (I never trusted storing vital info in a phone that was proven quite often to die during the worst possible times). Nevertheless, I was going to find an adequate place to charge my phone, even if I had to do it in someone's car.

A towering, flapping woman in a flowy turquoise dress, her wrists loaded with shiny gold bangles, flitted from table to table, chittering and pointing things out to a sour-faced girl in standard black-trousers-and-white-blouse waitstaff attire, who seemed to be there to note whatever was wrong, according to the swan. Flower arrangements were plucked and fluffed; place cards were laid out, ready to be set in their proper spots once breakfast was finished; chairs were rearranged; the antler-adorned chandeliers were dusted free of cobwebs and on and on.

50

While I was gathering up my meager breakfast, someone sidled up from behind, and I could feel hot breath on my neck. "Hay-lo, Ansley Boone. Been a long time, girl." The voice, darkly husky, laced with something toxic. The musky tang of Old Spice and smoked meat that lingered there. I didn't want to turn around. I didn't want to see him. I didn't want the reminder that *he* was actually going to marry to my little sister.

"Hey, Nate. How's it hangin'?" I said and then popped the mini-muffin into my mouth. Blueberry, tartly sweet, not my favorite, but I was hungry, and it eased the tension happening, pounding there in my head. Low blood sugar, high tension. Answering the guy, well, I didn't care, but for Shay, I'd keep it civil while scarfing down my breakfast.

Nathan's arm went around me, deliberately brushing against my waist as his hand grasped the handle of the pitcher of orange juice. "Pardon me, little lady, while I partake in a beverage," he said with a low chuckle. He slid up beside me, loudly clearing his throat as he pretended to be interested in the act of pouring juice into a plastic cup.

I took a step back. My body was growing uncomfortably hot and itchy. "So," I said, in mid chew, and then swallowing down the last bit of sticky muffin, "Shay says you've relieved her of her vegetarian habit. Good going, you." I snatched up a napkin from the stack and wiped my mouth with it.

Nathan tossed back his drink and then smacked his lips loudly. Then he made a show of tossing his cup into a nearby wastebasket. "She does like her meat tender n' juicy," he said, turning back to me with a wolfish grin. "Who would've thought that angel would just go to town on a choice cut? Like she'd been deprived all her life of a tasty piece of rump."

I wasn't about to play, take the bait, whathaveyou. That was what he did when Shay wasn't around. He was like a frat boy who'd consistently failed to graduate from adulting school. Luckily, I didn't have to hear anymore from him because Delia Card, his mother, came up from behind him, silently, coolly, in a musky, floral cloud of Chanel No. 5. She placed a hand on Nathan's arm, signaling him to straighten. Nathan cleared his throat and faced his mother, kissing her on the cheek, ever the good son.

"Your friends are growing restless, my love," she said, keeping her ice queen gaze locked with his. "You boys should take up

51

the Dughalls' offer of a trip into town. We're in need of more table wine. Your groomsmen's gifts should be ready to pick up as well."

He smiled warmly at her, an act that was disarmingly human of him. "As long as they don't drink without me, we're good. Thank you for letting me know, beautiful," he said and kissed her squarely on the lips.

As if I hadn't gagged enough already since arriving there.

Delia pried him away, laughing up at him in a voice rich with champagne bubbles. "The ladies have hair appointments in a little while, so you and your friends make do in town without us. Now off you get," she said, shoving playfully at him, urging him towards the door.

Nathan smirked once more at us before he headed out of the dining hall. And Delia turned into me, beaming, while I set down my banana on a nearby table, one that had apparently been recently occupied judging from the used cutlery and wadded paper napkins there. Delia then took my hands in her own. Hers were dry and cold. Her bony thumbs rubbed at my palms, the thumbnails gently scratching.

"How are you doing, Ansley?" she asked. "Your sister says you're...*renewed* from your facility stay. It's good, yes? I'm not all that familiar."

I wanted to bolt. Right then. Right there. Fuck the wedding. But the pull of Delia's magnetic gaze, and her surprisingly strong grip, kept me there, locked firmly in place.

You're on display, but you can own this. Educate, Leon whispered.

I offered Delia what I hoped was a nonchalant smile. "Yeah, I'm learning how to make my withdrawal symptoms moderately bearable. I couldn't have come otherwise. When you've been medicated like that, you don't just quit cold turkey. You can't stop without some help."

"You know, there was once a situation with one of Rex's many wayward cousins," she said, almost deep in thought. "Heroin, or something awful like that. He'd been in and out of methadone clinics, rehabilitation facilities, various hospitals... In the end, he took his own life. Jumped from the 15th floor of his brother's workplace. Cruel to come to such desperate finality, affecting everyone he'd ever loved, especially his own children. He had three little ones who never really knew him. I think they're here with their grandmother and mother. You

52

should meet their mother. I'm sure she can provide you with much needed empathy."

I never know how to react to those kinds of examples offered in sympathy, what others consider a "parallel" situation. They rarely ever are. As for meeting up with a widow just to commiserate about something so tragic, never mind something that has nothing to do with my own situation, well. I just nodded at Delia, let out a little murmur. Nothing comprehensible, no words to misconstrue. As I've learned, it's all I can ever do in response.

A fly buzzed around Delia's carefully sculpted and pinned updo, hovering there, aiming for a landing spot. A friend joined him, and Delia made a face, creasing her glossy skin in strange places, creating fresh grooves she'd undoubtedly inject at some point. She released one of my hands to swat the pests away, and all of the blood rushed back into my hand to my fingertips, making it tingle all over in tiny sparks.

She chuckled, a dry rasp of a sound. "This is what happens when one ventures out in the heartland. Carcasses attracting all sorts of pests. Bound to be plenty in this awful place."

I laughed along with her, a polite response I suppose. Maybe a little in agreement. At the very least, we had something in common: We both hated the resort.

Still, Delia's thumbnail from her other hand dug into the center of my palm, burning it. I couldn't think of a kinder way to pull away though, so I gritted my teeth through the pain. She gripped it tightly, but her gaze was honed in on someone behind me. She smiled broadly and gave a little wave with her free hand.

"Sweet girl, look at you there. That hair and dress, so lovely. You and your mother have impeccable taste," she said, beckoning, her voice suddenly caramelized and sticky. "Your sister's been sharing. Such fortitude and courage. You're lucky to have each other through this. Quite a time to celebrate new livelihoods, new beginnings."

Shay came up beside me and put an arm around my shoulders, squeezing me into her. She was radiant in a daisy-patterned sundress I'd not seen before. Then again, it's not like I would've recognized her as my sister anyhow. These people, they'd done what I'd failed to do as her older sister, great role model that I am. As for the Cards, they'd obviously turned her from low end casual, to high-end chic.

She grinned at me, breaking the spell. Back to the girl I knew well, if only for a moment. "Yeah, I mean, I wish we would've known more about what was going on with her, but Ans...She's never been the type of girl to let anyone in that easily."

I felt the blood rush to my cheeks. It's not like I wouldn't have said anything. They all *had* to know some pertinent details, right? Otherwise, I would've spent time in county prison rather than simply overnight in jail. She knew that. Our family had just never been the kind to air out emotional difficulties with one another, not until lately.

The momentary distraction my sister caused allowed for me to twist my hand from Delia's grasp, scratching the palm roughly in the process. When I glanced down at it, I saw that blood had started to well up in a crooked line down my palm. She'd actually broken the skin there. I grabbed for a paper napkin on one of the buffet tables. At least it would give me an excuse to move away from Delia, who was cooing over Shay's dress, having Shay turn this way and that so that she could admire it from all angles.

I blotted at the scratch and then squeezed my palm, watching the blood seep, strawberry splotches forming on the napkin. I don't know what came over me then. I was trembling and feeling hollow. I think it was a strange dose of curiosity, something pulsing and lingering there inside of me, egging me to bring the napkin to my nose and take a whiff. The coppery scent of it, of me, usually sent me gagging to the nearest toilet, but in that moment there, while Delia and Shay chattered about patterns and designers, dresses and fluff, all I wanted to do was inhale into my napkin, smelling myself, what made me, *me*.

Shay caught me smelling my napkin and made a face. Her nose wrinkled, her gaze went flinty. She subtly shook her head at me, mouthing a perfectly rounded "*What the fuck*," all the while she kept up her conversation with Delia. Delia was beckoning for a group of people who were collecting themselves from one of the dining tables, so she didn't notice that Shay was paying only the slightest bit of attention to her. I quickly crumbled the bloodied napkin and tossed it into the trash bin near the utility table, feeling my face and neck go hot. If I could have traveled back to that point in time as an observer rather than a participant, I wonder if I would've been repulsed by my actions because looking back at it now, I couldn't say what exactly had come over me, why the hell, *what* the hell possessed me to do that. I'd like to blame the withdrawal symptoms, but I don't think—I don't think *madness*—is anywhere on the list.

It was bonkers of me.

Even still, my headache had returned, pounding away; my heart was doing an unwelcome dance routine in my chest, and I felt my stomach twist and wring itself. So, naturally, in the moment, then and there, I chalked my actions up to side effects.

Lucky for me, I'd disposed of my guilt in time as Nathan, Charlie, and a couple of bearded guys and their bored-looking dates had come over from the table to join Delia and Shay. Charlie had his hand roaming the back of an absolutely stunning woman with lustrous dark hair and eyes like liquid ebony. He laughed as he enjoyed a joke with Delia and Nathan. His date caught my eye, held my gaping stare, capturing it, trapping it alive. Her eyes still on me, she said something in Charlie's ear, her hand with its crimson fingernails and flash of a sparkling diamond cluster, cupping against his cheek, muffling her words to him alone.

And right then right there, Jesus fuck, I wanted to hide under the table, dive into the trashcan and bury myself, camouflage myself behind the nearest potted fern, be anywhere but there in that moment. My body was growing sluggishly heavy, and my feet felt as if I'd attached them to weights at first, like I couldn't move at all. I gritted my teeth and managed to swivel on my heel and made to leave, but Delia called out.

"Ansley, have you met Nathan's friends? Come over here, dear heart, and we'll have introductions all around."

I halted there, barely having reached the exit to the lobby, and turned around. I had a quick once over with a shy smile, nodding at each of them, working to memorize faces, avoiding Shay and Charlie, not to mention Charlie's gorgeous date and her intense scrutiny. (*Was that an actual engagement ring she was wearing?*) Nathan gave me a subtle smile. The others, they looked as if they'd rather suck paint than socialize with me. It was obviously Shay's world now; everyone looked like they'd be comfortable in a Ralph Lauren ad. Just wasn't my scene.

"I—I'm sorry. I just have to make a quick phone call. Work-related stuff. There's a signal in the lobby, right?" I said with a nervous chuckle, hoping it didn't come off as too unsettled. My stomach had just about reached my esophagus and was burning, stuck there.

Stupid me, I couldn't avoid the pull of Charlie's gaze. He shook his head at me, a barely perceptible movement, and his lips thinned shut.

Shay, apparently, had seen the entire silent conversation he and I were having in that brief moment. Her eyes went round. She

55

sucked in her breath, and Charlie's beautiful date suddenly heard that. She looked at Shay, and then at me, back at her, then at me once more, trying to make out what was happening there, right there, in that moment.

Nathan was quick to answer, breaking our little drama. "Wait, I thought you were out of work. Weren't you laid off?" he said with a smirk. "Didn't you injure your boss or something?"

I flashed Shay a scathing look. Hell if I was going to be the guilty one during the entirety of the wedding. Her expression softened. She chewed her lower lip, something she does when she's caught and unable to sweet talk her way out of it. Delia looked at me with an ever so slight trace of pity in her eyes. I couldn't take it anymore, so instead of trying to come up with a witty comeback of an excuse, I turned and left, hurrying out into the lobby, hoping I'd not run into another person I really didn't want to explain my behavior to.

I'd almost reached the main exit doors from the lobby that was busy with guests checking in and asking questions and a couple of confused-looking desk clerks in resort uniforms, the first hotel desk staff I'd seen since arriving at the place. I made my way over to the desk and then waited patiently in the line.

For the record, I know this seems like something insignificant, something irrelevant to what was going to happen later. Many of the details in this probably do, but in this, everything matters, even the smallest, mundane detail.

Like what went on at the front desk.

The elderly couple in front of me, the two of them prim and preppy in matching pastels and visors, were talking to a desk clerk, and they all seemed tense, strained. The desk clerk, a red-haired, sun-freckled girl, fresh-faced and overwhelmed, who couldn't have been more than nineteen, kept apologizing. To be honest, I wasn't paying close attention to what they were saying to her, and looking back on it now, I should've moved closer to them. In the moment, I was still flustered about what had happened in the dining hall and was worried that any one of them—Charlie, Shay, Delia, hell, even Charlie's date— was going to come after me with questions I really didn't want to have to answer.

If I had paid more attention to what was going on at the desk rather than worrying about my own insecurities and guilt, I probably would've gotten a sense as to what to do later. Think about it for a minute though. We just never know what to do because most of the time when the shit goes down, we're flat out blindsided by it. Even when there are alarm bells ringing away, we never pay close enough attention to them because civility has us shrug such things off rather than follow our primal instinct to flee or fight.

And sometimes, you just don't really know what *is* actually happening.

I was standing there, keeping an eye on the doorway leading to the dining hall, catching only snippets of their conversation, just words, nothing strung together cohesively. Words like "sorry," "plastic covering," "bedding," "refrigerator," and "clotting," don't usually connect well together, do they?

I heard all of that, and nothing about it registered as anything but...well, weird. Just that. The fact that I can still form a picture of it is enough for me in the moment, but in hindsight, what would I have really done had I honed in on what was actually being said? They could've been talking about an array of different things, from changing bedding to stains on the mattress to chilling food they might have brought to...Oh, fucking hell, who am I kidding, right?

Then again, I might not have heard anything, really.

But, hey, old people. I plan on, *hopefully*, being one of them in the not too distant future, but they're generally batty. And that's exactly what I chalked it up to—they were elderly and cuckoo, and I could've easily excused it as dementia, expressing one's batshittery. Wasn't *I* just a little bit batty, too? Had I heard what I thought I'd heard?

When it was my turn, the couple turned away, and the woman collided right into me. She laughed and squeezed my arm. Then she apologized with a friendly smile and a "Ran right into you, didn't I?" I didn't recognize either of them, but since the only ones who were at the resort were guests of the wedding, I naturally assumed they were from groom's side of the family.

I watched the two of them head off in the direction of the lobby entrance as the woman clasped her husband's hand in her own. They stopped just before they reached the doors to say hello to another older couple who'd just come in, both sweaty and loaded down with travel gear and a bulky, but beautifully wrapped, wedding present.

The desk clerk coughed to get my attention. "May I help you, ma'am?" she asked.

I turned back to her, offering her what I hoped was a breezy smile. "Yeah, what's the best place around here where I can get a signal? There's barely one bar on my phone in here. I thought there was supposed to be Wifi, too."

Before the desk clerk could answer, I felt a squeeze, a bit of firm pressure on my shoulder, signaling me to stop what I was doing. "Talk to you for a minute, Ans?" Shay said softly from behind. I felt myself being propelled around as she led me to a corner of the lobby that poured into a tiny hallway with a dainty cushioned chair and two doors announcing men's and women's facilities.

"I was asking because I was just curious...Why isn't there any reception around here?" I asked Shay just before she roughly pushed me through the swinging door of the ladies' room.

FIVE

I stumbled inside, barely catching myself against the air dryer on the wall. I whirled around, right back into her. "Jesus, Shay. What wrong with you?"

I knew what it was though. She really didn't have to tell me; I'd read it all over her face. I supposed I should've felt some normal amount of guilt at any rate. Maybe it was karma, meant to be my fate from here on out. After all, I've been in love with a married man for a while now. "Taken" men would inevitably have to be my troublesome weakness.

Shay latched onto it quickly, furiously. "Are you fucking joking? What do you think you're doing?" she hissed at me, her face mere inches from mine. She then checked underneath the stalls to see if anyone was there and had heard the commotion coming from the two of us. Quite a pair, we were. Once she saw the coast was clear, she was right in my face.

"I saw the two of you looking at each other like you had some dirty, little secret. He's *engaged*, Ansley. You are not going to do this on my day. *My* day. You are *not*."

Her breath smelled of bananas and coffee tinged with a trace of something else, something dark and salty-crusted. Her teeth had been methodically whitened, probably a professional job courtesy of mama Card. Dad would've never dished out the bread for such a…what he'd probably call…a "frivolous" expense like that, not even for his favorite. He and Mom had been smug about their frugality throughout the whole ordeal, leaving much of the cushy expenses up to the Cards, who were into keeping up with appearances, something my family tended to eschew. Frankly, I wondered how much Mom and Dad had invested all in all for their own daughter's wedding—Dad's pride and joy; Mom's source of constant comparison.

59

"Listen, it wasn't like he made it evident," I said. Seriously. No indication. No apparent guilt. "You know, you might even ask him one-on-one if this is a regular thing with him. I get the feeling he's got a few on the side besides a lousy one-nighter with the likes of little ol' me."

Shay never likes it when I take a dig at myself, so I took a shot and continued with my downplay. Anything to cream character. "Okay. It was wrong, Shay. A stupid moment of weakness. Leon warned me that destructive behavioral patterns often breed other destructive behavioral patterns, if anything, to mask the one that started it."

She clenched her teeth, readying herself for her own retort, something biting about my therapy no doubt. An apologetic silver-haired lady in a sleek orange sheath dress opened the ladies' room door wide to lead in a chain of giggly little girls, no more than five or six years old, curly-haired, prissy ducklings. Shay and I crowded near the sinks, watching the flock of them in silence, smiles on. The silver-haired woman pointed two of the girls into one stall, reminding them to lock the door, and she led the remaining one, probably the youngest of the bunch, into a stall with her.

"Can we talk about this later? When we're not surrounded by wedding guests and their kids?" I whispered, keeping my head close to hers. "You have to get ready, don't you? Isn't that a bride thing? Don't we have hair appointments?" Truthfully, it wasn't something I was looking forward to, being stuck in a hair salon with Shay, her best friend, our mom, and Delia Card, but it was all I had in the moment.

"Yeah, we do," breathed Shay. It came out forcefully, like a big sigh. "You might want to take their spa deal, too," she said, grimacing down at my hands. "Christ, Ans, you've got to stop chewing on your nails like that. Your cuticles look like you've been mauling them."

It was always something. If not the nails, the clothes; if not the clothes, the body; if not the body, the hair, and so on. "It keeps me from swallowing the whole bottle of pills I brought," I joked halfheartedly. "It's either my fingernails or my delicious babies."

"Are you serious? You brought your—I thought you were off them. What the hell, Ans? What kind of a rehab facility lets—"

I interrupted her before she could get me totally wound. "I'm *tapering*. It's fine... So is Charlie's fiancée coming along with us, too, then? Is that why you're freaking out about it?" Anything. Anything to get off topic. I was so goddamned tired of having to explain myself to family who refused to pay attention to me.

"Her name is Nabhitha," Shay snapped. "She happens to be one of the most gracious people I've ever met."

"Nabhitha. Swank name for a swank lady."

Shay pursed her lips into a tight line. She inhaled deeply, let out her breath in a long exhale of air, and said, "I can't—I can't believe you and Charlie...It's like you don't even—" She stopped, chewed on her lower lip.

"Don't even what?" I prodded.

"Never mind."

"Don't even what, Shay?"

"It's not important."

I wasn't about to let that go though. "No, no. You don't get to drop it now," I said. "Say whatever it is you were gonna say."

She hesitated before speaking. She was choosing her words delicately, like I'd break if I heard it. "It's like you don't even care about outcomes," she said softly. "You don't care about what happens to other people. Even more, you don't care about *yourself*, Ans. It's like you've lost all self-respect. You just do whatever suits you at the time, and you don't care if it hurts anyone."

Granted, it may have always seemed that way from the other angle, of that I'm sure, but it was utter bullshit. It wasn't true from my end. It wasn't true at all. Before I could come to my own defense, we heard the toilet flush in one of the occupied stalls. There was a little whisper of encouragement, followed by another flush. The stall doors then unlatched and the little girls and the woman in the orange dress came out, the little ones giving us curious glances, their chaperone apologetic as she herded them to the sinks.

Shay nodded in the direction of the door, signaling for us to go outside. I followed her out into the little hallway outside the lobby facilities. She then turned and looked at me directly.

"Be honest, Ansley. Are you planning on testing Mom and Dad while you're here because the last thing I want to have happen on my wedding day is for there to be tension," she said. "I invited you to be in the wedding because I felt that you were really trying hard. I want no outbursts, no drama, no theatrics, Ans. It's bad enough that we still argue about Nathan. I just can't stomach any of that stuff right now."

"I know. I know," I said. My face was burning. My stomach, flip-flopping.

61

"Mom especially can't take any drama like that, ever since—"

"Since what?"

Shay hesitated before continuing. "She had a minor heart attack. She had a decent recovery, but the cardiologist said her heart won't be as strong as it had been," she said. "It was awhile ago, right around the time Simon split up with you."

And suddenly, everything else seemed utterly inconsequential. "How come no one told me this?"

"Dad said he'd tried to get in touch, but he couldn't reach you, so I tried. He was so upset. I've never seen him hurt like that. I caught him crying once on the patio," she said. "I even emailed you about it, Ans. You used to respond to emails, even the ones Mom used to send out. You remember? The ones with the links to the cats behaving badly videos?"

I managed to smile, all things considered. "And the jumping baby goats."

"Oh my God, those goats!"

We shared a little chuckle, just enough to keep us in the moment. Then we just stood there, unsure of what to say, how to feel, how to continue.

"I'm so sorry, Shay," I said softly. "I wasn't thinking of anyone else. I don't shut people off like that though. I was just—"

"You were just what?"

"I was just broken. I needed to be away from everyone."

"Well, that didn't do Mom any good, did it?"

"Apparently, it didn't." I didn't know what else to say, what else to do, how to respond. "I should talk to them. Maybe when all of this is done…"

She nodded primly. Then after a thoughtful minute, she said, "I can't believe it though, that you— "

And there she went again. Choppy thoughts, implications, accusations, leaving me waiting for a straightforward response. It's what *she* did sometimes. "Yes? That I what?" I said.

Shay tossed me a look. "Seriously, Ansley. Charlie's Nathan's *best man*. I thought you didn't do clichés."

"The best man's a cliché? Yeah, okay, I suppose he is, and yeah, I did him. Done did him good, girl."

"Shut up," she said. "It's not funny. It's so wrong."

"But it felt *so* riiiiiight," I softly sang.

62

Finally, she snickered, and I almost joined in when the woman in the orange dress emerged behind me, shuffling the train of little princesses out of the ladies room. Shay gave the woman a perfectly bridelike, dazzling smile, showing off those pearly whites. Since my back was to the door, I made a face at her, and then played it off by waving at the little girls, who kept giggling amongst themselves.

As soon as they'd left, Shay went dark and somber. I took a step back at her sudden change in temperament.

"We're not still fighting, are we, even after a laugh?" I asked, offering up a hopeful grin.

"Be honest with me," she said, her voice low, "I thought you were off the meds. Isn't that what landed you in rehab to begin with?"

"I went over and over this with you, but the wedding...it's turned off everything around you. Such selective listening," I said, but when Shay put on her I'm-about-to-throw-a-fit grimace, I softened my words. "Look, I know the joke was stupid. You know me. I'm a smartass. But yes, in all seriousness, no jokes. I told you I am still on the meds. I have to taper off *slowly*. Otherwise, I wouldn't be able to be here on your...on your important day."

"I'm sorry," she said. "I was so caught up in all of this, everything here, I guess I must've missed that part."

"Well, yeah, kid, you're getting married. You're allowed to be distracted. It's practically expected of you. It says so in the bride's handbook."

Shay's mouth rounded in an "O" in melodramatic surprise. "There's a *handbook*? How was I not aware of this?" she said with a grin.

"Page 290, chapter twelve, and if memory serves, it states, 'The bride must always be distracted with wedding shit that won't matter once she's married.'"

"No, I don't think so. Bridal handbooks wouldn't use the word 'shit.'"

"You're absolutely right. I'm sure it stated 'fecal matter' though."

"That sounds much more believable, if slightly repetitious."

"I promise I'll behave from here on out," I said with my palm up in reverent oath. "On my honor, Princess Bitchface."

"I'll hold you to it, Lady Dickdouche."

I wrinkled my nose at that one. "Dick douche? Do they really make those?"

Shay feigned a look of absolute seriousness, her brow creased, her mouth in a pursed scowl. "Oh, I should think so, and I bet it's dreadfully painful. According to what I read online, a dribble of vinegar and these skinny pipe cleaners are involved in the process."

"The Internet has answers for *everything*."

We shared a giggle. Our childish fun was short-lived though as Mom found us in the little hallway and beckoned for us to join her in the lobby, giving us both a disapproving look as she did. "What on earth are you two going on about?" she said as we came out from the hall into the bright lobby.

I shrugged and gave Shay a knowing glance, practically daring her to follow my lead. "Personal plumbing matters," I said, barely containing my grin.

Shay burst out laughing, and Mom sighed at the two of us. "Ladies, settle-settle," she said, shaking her head. "Delia has the car running out front. We don't want to be late for our salon appointment." She gave me a quick once-over, scrutinizing my face, my hair, as we made our way out through the lobby doors. "Ansley, I strongly suggest you have them straighten your hair...and have them keep it out of your face. And don't roll your eyes at me. Grown women don't do that in public. It's unbecoming."

"I think she should keep it curly, Mom. It's her natural look, and it works with the whole ensemble we've planned," said Ansley, halting our group just as we reached Delia's gleaming BMW SUV, quite possibly one of the cushiest cars I'd ever seen.

Delia craned her swan's neck out the window from her place behind the wheel, a wide, open smile stretching across her perfectly unlined face. "We can compromise on what to do with Ansley's lovely hair when we get there, my darlings."

"Ansley can make decisions for herself, you know. She's been doing that for the past twenty years. She even pays taxes on occasion," I grumbled, just loudly enough for certain women in my company to hear.

Shay opened the back passenger door on her side and squealed when she saw who was inside. Emma Holiday, Shay's thoroughly girly best friend from college and Emma's pouty six year-old son, Bryceson, were squished together in the second row, at the opposite end, leaving one seat open for Shay, while I was obviously to sit to the little back row that barely consisted of an extra two seats.

64

Emma gave me a little wave, beaming. She was the kind of woman who laughs at everything, even if it's not particularly funny or just entertaining. I think she was a work-from-home/stay-at-home mom sort, but I'm not entirely sure. She smiled at me as I hesitated to get in.

"Bry-bear," she said to her scowling little guy, "Hey, plummy plum, why don't you sit in the back row behind Momma so that Shay's big sister can sit with us. She won't be able to fit back there in that tight spot like you can."

He crossed his arms and pretended not to have heard her, choosing to squint straight ahead and keep up with the pouting. His little feet kicked at Mom's front passenger seat, and before Mom could say anything, Emma placed a firm hand on his knee, pressing him to stop. Kid was going to grow up to be a real gentleman. I guess that was to be expected when his one fatherly role model had up and left Emma when he was just four years old. It's probably the only personal thing I really knew about Emma's family, but the strain on Emma had been evident during the engagement party last year. She'd tried to hide it by laughing at everything as she usually did, but quite often, her laughter was obviously forced and automatic, like it had been drilled in her to keep up the charade. Shay—I'll give it to her—she kept the comfort level high enough so that she was always there with Emma, filling her wine glass or rubbing her back. I was amazed she was able to keep the focus balanced so well that night. I remember her whispering things to Emma, the two of them sharing funny secrets, probably in-jokes from college, and I'd longed for something like that myself, a best friend, someone to share more than just family crap.

I'd always assumed Shay was my best friend, but it took me a good while to figure out that certainly wasn't the case when she proudly proclaimed Emma had the title. Then, naturally, later on, I'd hoped Simon would've filled that spot for me.

Oh, the foolish things we want to believe, the things we wish were true.

It took a purple lollipop from Emma's purse—"Prepped with doctor's office bribes," she said to me with a giggle—for Bryceson to agree to sit in the back. I slid in beside Shay, and we were off.

Twenty minutes into the ride, I, somehow, may have had remnants of purple lollipop stuck in my hair.

Fuck it, I thought, at least we were on our way to the salon.

I didn't hear the argument happening there at the salon between Delia Card and my mother. As tempting as it was to push up the roaring dryer helmet in order to catch up with what exactly was going on, I stayed put, knowing perfectly well that whatever they were going on about wasn't any of my business, and frankly, since I was already an obvious source of contention among my family members, I figured it would be best for me to stay the hell out of it.

Judging by the expression on Shay's face, her mouth tightening in a prim line, Shay wasn't in the mood to intervene either. She kept turning her head this way and that, examining herself in the mirror. Her ballerina bun was perfectly centered and round on the back of her glossy head. Her own hairdresser for the day—undoubtedly at the highest level of the hierarchy, whatever that was—pinned loose strands carefully, also while examining every angle with a meticulous eye.

Shay met my stare in the mirror. She rolled her eyes at me, emphasizing her annoyance. I hadn't really noticed until then how tired she looked without makeup. It's always been tiring with our own mom. I couldn't begin to imagine what it was like having to juggle expectations of both her and another. Delia Card even went one step over the line of appearance obsession.

I just didn't understand why a woman like Delia—even a man like Rex Card—would place such importance on having a wedding at a "resort" that they clearly knew was falling into ruin. Sure, Shay had emphasized that it was a family friend's business, and the Cards had wanted to keep it afloat. Still, since appearances were clearly what it was all about, everyone could've still been supportive of a close family friend and had just the wedding ceremony there for a single evening rather than over an entire weekend.

My hairdresser bent in front of me, blocking my line of sight, barricading me from seeing the back-and-forth happening between my mom and Delia. "You doin' okay there? Not too hot, is it? I can cool her down a little," she said with a wide, toothy grin.

There was coral lipstick on her front teeth, but I got the feeling I'd have to shout that fact of the matter at her, so I just stared at the stain, silently willing her to leave me alone and move out of my line of sight. She lifted the dryer and poked at my hair that had been set in giant curlers. Mom had wanted it straightened, but Delia had insisted curls, and Shay, too far along on the dark side, had agreed with Delia. At the time, I wasn't remotely interested in either argument about my own damned hair. I'd tried to get some compromise underway between both sides, letting them know I could've just as easily gone with the beach waves trend that was slowly inching its mad way across the land of perpetually big hair, big makeup, big tits, big everything. However, Shay came to Delia's defense—pinned curls—and that ended the matter much to Mom's annoyance.

Frankly, from what I'd seen well before everything, Mom was rapidly coming undone. She looked as if the weight of all things bridal had just knocked the last hints of youthful energy, which she once was known for, right out of her. Both she and Shay, actually, looked exhausted.

Delia, on the other hand, despite the fillers and nips and tucks, seemed to grow younger with each new problem or dispute about Shay's day. Was I crazy or did Delia look as if an entire decade had been removed from her complexion, which was glowing with health and vitality, such a stark contrast with my mother and sister's ashy skin.

Vitamin E, biotin, royal jelly, retinoids, hyaluronic acid, stem cells, *something*.

"Gonna let that set for another five, okay? We'll see what we have when it's dried a bit. If it's looking like it won't set well, we can always straighten it like your momma wanted. It'll be pretty either way," said my hairdresser with a wink, and she pushed the dryer shell back down over my head but not before I caught a snippet of the argument between Delia and Mom.

Delia softly said, "Patricia, you know I wouldn't want anything less that the very best for Shay on her day, so you *must* allow me to cover the bridesmaid and Maid of Honor's expenses, too. I recommended this place, and I know it's a bit over the budget you'd set."

As soon as the dryer went back down, the roar of it once again preventing me from hearing a thing, I saw Mom go red-faced and stiff all over. She said something to Delia in response, but judging from Delia's quizzical expression, whatever it was Mom had said, it had been too low for Delia to hear. I suppose I ought to have been able to fill-in-the-blank with whatever it was Mom had said, but Mom's normal, acidic bite-backs had been subdued since we'd pulled up to the resort last night. In fact, she looked hurt when she said whatever it was she'd said to Delia. Her eyes grew watery, and her forehead creased. It was the same look she had on whenever Dad sided with Shay about whatever it was Mom had disagreed with. Not only did her facial expression change, her posture did, too. Most tend to sag and wither when rejected, but Mom's posture tightens. Instead of curling inward, she goes into dancer stance. Her neck tugs with the tension, like a marionette, causing her back to lift and straighten.

Delia took a step back from Mom. Her hands made birdlike movements, fluttering as she tried to soothe Mom, ease her down. But Mom had already taken out her wallet from her giant purse ("One must always be prepared with supplies," she often said to us girls whenever she saw us with our little clutches and chain purses).

She then said, quite loudly and surprisingly clearly, enough that even I could hear her, "This is a wedding, isn't it? They're *my* daughters, Delia, and adhering to some sense of tradition is fundamental to our family and my daughters' upbringing. Understand?"

Shay met my reflection again in the mirror. She offered me a tired smile, and I knew then she'd approved of Mom's decision and her words. As I'd mentioned once before, I'm sure, when it came to shopping—and hair salon expenses do count as "shopping" among the Boone ladies—Mom and Shay were often on each other's side, and there was no way Mom would back down when it came down to it.

Delia, essentially, would have to go fuck herself.

But Mom would never say something so crass now, would she?

68

SIX

Everyone was quiet during the trip to our "ladies' luncheon," something that Mom insisted upon despite Shay and Delia's press to get us all back to the resort.

"They've put out lunch there, Mom. Nate just texted. They've got roast beef for sandwiches, lots of salad choices, that iced tea you liked..." said Shay, giving me a quick side jab, not just a signal to agree with her, but also a reminder that when crammed in together in tight passenger seats, there's still always room to poke one's sibling in the ribs.

Emma oooh'ed at the mention of iced tea. "I don't know how they did it, but I swear it tastes just like Momma's sun tea we used to have in the summer, sitting out there on the porch swing, swatting lovebugs floating around."

"Emma, how is it you manage to make everything sound delightfully romantic?" said Delia, punctuating it with a tinkly chime of a laugh.

Emma chuckled. "Practice. Gotta see the beauty in everything. That's what we're trying to teach Bryceson right now. Hopefully, it sticks. Right, Bry-bear?"

Bryceson answered with a grunt and a sharp kick to the back of my seat. That kid.

"It's a wonderful lesson. Something we'd, regretfully, been too busy to impart upon Nathan," Delia said with a sigh. "One of the many reasons why I find the new motherhood trends so inspired. Such love and commitment shown. Very humbling."

Oh, it was so tempting, the idea of responding to Delia's lamenting about her lack of essential parenting. I held my tongue to the

69

point where I was on the verge of chomping down on its meat. The throbbing headache I'd had only just started to simmer down. I'd come to expect that it would always pop up during the worst possible moments, especially during a family event. Reliable. Predictable. I wasn't wrong. Alas, I'd already downed 800 milligrams of Ibuprofen, and I wasn't about to take more. Over the counter painkillers were even advertised as being just as dangerous when taken in actual pain-killing dosages (Hint: 800 milligrams isn't nearly enough to knock out what I was continuously going through. Instead, it just turned what was a sharp, jabbing pain behind my eyes to a sore thrumming).

My bag suddenly vibrated loudly in my lap. The thing had been partially charged on the bedside table in my room when I stupidly realized then that sockets came in pairs, and my bedside table lamp was working just fine. It's another symptom, I think, that sudden lack of common sense and resourcefulness that was once a part of me. I used to always be able to come up with a quick, simple solution. Now, though, I just give up easily, exhausted at the thought of having to think of something useful right then and there.

Once I found my phone in the depths of my bag, Shay was already in nosy-sister mode, peering at the thing when I unlocked the screen. I used the side of my body to push against her, signaling her to mind her own business, causing her to lean into a giggly Emma.

Shay just pushed back, smirking at the phone in my hand. "Who's Leon, and why is he asking about the wedding?"

"Don't worry about it."

"Who's worried? He's on your phone, and you're obviously on a first-name basis with him," said Shay.

"He's just a friend," I said as I sent him a quick text back, letting him know everything was fine, and then I pushed the cell down deep into my bag.

"Just a friend-friend or a boyfriend friend?" pressed Emma, giggling.

There was an exaggerated sigh from the back seat. "There isn't any boyfriend friends! That's not real! You can't have boyfriend friends!" Bryceson shouted.

Both Shay and Emma burst out laughing. " '*Aren't*,' plummy plum. 'There *aren't* any boyfriend-friends,'" said Emma in-between snorty giggles.

"I know, *Mom*. That's what I'm trying to tell you."

"Bry-bear, you need to be as sweet as the honey you like."

Shay nodded at the phone. "So? Leon?"

"For goodness' sake, Shay. He's her therapist," Mom snapped.

Shay was finally quiet for a moment before she asked, "How appropriate is it for a therapist to text his patients like that, outside of office hours?"

"Mind your own business, Shay," I mumbled, half-hoping she heard me, half-hoping she didn't.

"If you're gonna be rudely texting your therapist about what's happening at my wedding, it becomes my business, Ans."

"No, it doesn't. Patient confidentiality," I said. "Look that up. It's a thing." Right then, my headache had blossomed into something much bigger, its branches seeking every other nerve ending in my head, neck, back, and limbs.

"Patient confidentiality goes out the window when you're texting right in front of me like a rude-ass bitch," said Shay, and then she gasped and cupped a hand over her mouth.

I heard Mom loudly suck in her breath, signaling her exhaustion and expected disapproval.

Shay gave Emma a sheepish look, whispering to her an "I'm sorry."

"Mom, she said *two* bad words! She should get wall time when we get back to the hotel."

Emma waved off Shay's apology, shaking her head. She was trying hard not to laugh. "Bry-bry, adults are grown-up enough to be naughty sometimes," she said. "When you start paying Mommy rent and helping her with the bills, you can say all the bad words you want."

"But what about school, Mom?"

"What about it, plummy plum?"

"If I help pay bills, can you tell Miss Hanley I can say bad words at school, too? We can tell her I'm being reponsible."

"Re-spon-si-ble," corrected Emma. "Responsible. Say it again, Bry."

"Reponsible!"

"Just remember, plucky ducky," said Emma, "bad words are for grownups. You can tell Miss Hanley anything you want once you help Momma with the electric bill at least."

Delia burst out a husky chortle. "If you can pay utilities during summertime, little one, you can pay for anything."

"I can pay anything, aaaaaaaand I won't have wall time anymore!"

71

"What's 'wall time'?" whispered Shay.

"That's when you do something bad, and you face the wall and stay there until Momma says you can play in your room. One time, I was in wall time for *seventeen thousand hours*," Bryceson lamented with an exaggerated sigh.

Shay laughed. "I'm sure it *felt* like it was seventeen thousand hours, Bry-bry."

"It really *was* seventeen thousand hours. It was *that* long. I counted them forever."

"It's the only thing that's seemed to do the trick," whispered Emma, low enough so Bryceson would have to strain to hear her. "My perfect little con artist usually gets away with murder."

"I get away with murder," Bryceson quietly concurred from the back seat.

Shay and Emma exchanged one of those looks reserved for the closest of friends, like something out of *Anne of Green Gables*, like they knew what the other was thinking. They shared soft giggles, and Shay took Emma's hand in her own, lacing their fingers together.

That friendship. I don't know if it was jealousy or withdrawals, but my heart went all fluttery, and a bubble welled up in my throat. I wasn't having it, whatever it was. I'm chalking it up to jealousy as it often ran in muddy rivers through my family. My mom was jealous of my dad's doting upon Shay. My dad was jealous of men with adult children who hadn't even set foot in a rehab facility. Shay was jealous of women who seemed to have it all together. As for me, I was jealous of happiness, closeness, sisterhoods, and lovers. My jealousy often triggered the spasms in my gut and sides, made me flushed, and caused my breath to run ragged, symptoms that were similar to the withdrawal effects. The thought of the one I'd loved with all my soul, Simon with another woman, a wife now, the two of them with a child, made me feel wretched, wasting away, like I was rotting inside.

I felt my hand being lifted from my lap, another wrapped around it, the fingers stroking. Shay was holding mine in her other. I looked at her, and she offered me a brief, tender smile just before turning back to Emma and snuggling against her friend.

"Shay, you need to keep your head up," Mom said, eyeing her youngest in the compact mirror she was holding up. She'd been dabbing at the makeup forming beige grooves in the lines around her

72

mouth. "You'll make a mess of your hair, and I doubt anyone here will be able to properly set it the way you like it."

Shay straightened, cleared her throat. If anything, Mom knew just how to pick on the things that made us ever so slightly insecure.

Mom then turned in her seat and gave me a once-over, her mouth tightening in disapproval. "I brought my Mason Pearson brush. I'll let you use it. It should take care of that nest."

"Mom, *really*," Shay said with a puff of breath. I'll hand it to my sister: she could always match disgust with disgust, mirroring our mother's exact expression whenever something was so obviously impolitely expressed.

"No, none of that 'Mom, really.' That hairdresser did a dreadful job, curling Ansley's hair like that. It should've been straightened as I'd requested."

I couldn't keep silent at that. "Don't you just love it when people talk about you like you're not even there?"

"I think Ansley's hair is gorgeous. A touch of old Hollywood glamour. All she needs is some Revlon red and ta-da," Delia purred. She'd been half-listening, half in that odd daydreamy state she sometimes has. Her gaze was off, directed somewhat at the road in front of her, somewhat at what was ensuing in the passenger seats.

"Ansley's hair is perfectly fine, Mom," said Shay. She had let go of my hand, but she was still gripping Emma's. "You're just upset things didn't go your way for once. Sometimes, it just doesn't though, and during *my* wedding, it certainly won't."

And that's how and when Mom decided to grant Shay the old Boone family silent treatment for pretty much the remainder of the afternoon.

It's such a shame the timing of it couldn't have been worse. There are so many things they could've said or done tactfully, and everything would've been shrugged aside, no big deal, onward with the next problem. And they could've gotten along.

They could've gotten along.

#

Mom had chosen a German bakery and café in town that had huge picture windows holding panoramic views of the ruddy and green spackled hills that surrounded the area. There was a wide patio area where we could've eaten, but the heat was squeezing us into its

73

steaming blanket. By then, everyone was famished, but Shay was anxious about all of us eating "such heavy German stuff" before the wedding festivities. Mom was at that point where she really had no interest in indulging Shay at all.

When it was fresh, the Boone silent treatment was at its worst. It would play out as if Shay was completely invisible to Mom, even when Shay was right there in the moment. Dad was even worse. He'd eat at the dinner table as if he were alone rather than surrounded by chatty women. He could easily tune everything out and made a show of getting up and walking to the other side of the table to reach for seconds of whatever was on the menu for dinner. He'd then bring the serving platter or dish back to his end of the table and plonk it down right in front of him, just out of arms' reach for any of the rest of us eating. Whenever we asked him to pass the food, he just kept right on eating, and Mom would throw down her napkin, get up from her chair, and storm over to Dad's side of the table, pick up the serving dish of whatever it was that had been requested by one of us, and then set it down in front of whomever wanted more of it, shooting Dad a stabbing glare as she did. A right-back-atcha moment that probably entertained anyone from the outside looking in, but to us, it was just another petty display that was, irritatingly, routine.

At the café, Mom took charge, making sure Shay was completely out of the conversation with the dirndl-clad, overly chipper server about the food there. Whenever Shay piped in with a question about a specialty, Mom talked over her question, asking the exact same thing Shay had asked, as if the inquiry had been entirely Mom's own, confusing the server even more.

Had I not been engrossed in watching their little display, perhaps I would've been triggered by Something Not Quite Right, something off about the luncheon just like the brief pieces that were always there, right there in the moment. I realize now, too little too late, that I've been failing to be observant, even halfway reasonably cognizant of my surroundings and the people around me. It's a mistake I won't make again, or so I promise myself now, looking back on everything that's happened. Even so, there's always still a part of me, a nagging doubt, that keeps telling myself, it's just the things I *think* I feel, the things *think* I see, the things I *think* are happening. In all, I can't wholly trust my instincts anymore, so that promise to myself is even up in the air.

Anyway, the crusty mood between Shay and Mom was on the menu du jour for our ladies luncheon whether we'd ordered it or not, served on the side with our overly salted sauerbraten and spaetzle. Emma and I exchanged uncomfortable grimaces every so often, in-between bites, both at the food and at what was ensuing between our hostesses (and my family members). The food was making me feel sluggish and uncomfortably warm. My headache had also returned, pounding behind my eyes and down my neck. Shay and Delia had been wise in ordering a green salad and a slice of oniony flammkuchen, undoubtedly better on the stomach than the heavy meal Emma, Mom, and I had set upon ourselves.

Bryceson, oblivious to the tension, munched noisily on a mini-bratwurst wedged in golden, crisp brochen. Sometimes, kids had all the luck.

Emma burped and said, "I feel all tight like a sausage."

"When embarking upon a new culinary adventure," said Mom, "it's always best to try out the specialties of the house. It would be rude otherwise." I noticed she'd aimed that dig at Delia, but Delia was much more interested in Bryceson's blissful chewing.

"Not if everyone's going to be too bloated to fit in their dresses tonight," Shay grumbled. She chased a last bite of the savory tart left on her plate with her fork, deliberately scraping it around the plate rather than stabbing it outright and eating it. She was testing Mom, and the best way to do that when at a restaurant was to play with your food like a petulant kid instead of eating it as an adult would.

Mom didn't take the bait. Instead, she continued the cold shoulder routine she and Dad had trademarked. Like Delia, her focus honed in on the adorable antics of the actual five year old in our company.

"You enjoying that?" she prodded with a half smile. "It's a lot like a gourmet hot dog. All natural ingredients, all probably not particularly good for you."

Bryceson stopped his chewing long enough to scowl at Mom. "I'm not eating any candy, so it's gonna be good for me. No sugar innit," he said punctuating it with one of those exasperated eye rolls only a surly five year-old could possibly get away with in my mother's, never mind *his* mother's, presence. He then tore into his brat with all the toothy ferocity of a cub, growling as he did.

My mother couldn't contain her smile. She reached over to tousle his hair and then promptly patted it back down, sculpting it back into its careful mess, brushing it out of his eyes. Bryceson made a face at her and then nodded and kicked in time to the loud oompa-oompa beat of the Volksmusik playing over the cafe loudspeakers.

Having casually observed what was tightening at least half of us at the table, Delia found a door wide open, a virtual invitation to take over and ease the tension from us all, even her soon-to-be daughter-in-law who was fast becoming impatient with Mom's treatment.

"Well, I don't know about you, my lovelies, but I've had such a wonderful time with you all," said Delia. "Delightful company, delectable food, and with such lovely creatures all around me. I couldn't be more at home." She was looking at me when she said it, and I'll admit, it made me feel flushed all over. No matter what I thought of her, no matter what I think of her even now, she has always had the uncanny ability to soften the room and everyone in it. She could charm a wing off a butterfly, a stinger off a scorpion, the blood right out of a tick. All of those terrible analogies and then some. Delia was It.

Mom couldn't stand that fact either, naturally.

"And how would you know it's 'delectable'? You've hardly had a bite of your lunch, Delia," Mom said with a soft chortle.

Bryceson was quick on the draw to say with a smirk, "Shay didn't eat her food, either, Missus Boone. If you don't empty your plate, you won't get ice cream floats, and you can't go tubing onna river when you're done with your wedding stuff. Don't you wanna go tubing?"

Emma laughed and pulled Bryceson against her. He squirmed in her arms, trying to break free of her firm embrace. "Bry-bear, do you remember what I said about paying bills?" Emma murmured into his hair, and then she kissed the top of his head.

Bryceson slumped against her. "I can use bad words if I help pay bills. But I didn't say any bad words," said Bryceson as worked to stifle a yawn.

"You can also have all the ice cream floats you want, and before you eat those ice cream floats, you can go tubing as long as you'd like," Emma continued. "Momma's friends don't have to eat their food if they're not hungry, and I don't think they're all that hungry, Bry-bry. Wedding days get everyone all flustered and feeling funny in the tum-tum."

"*I* was hungry, so I ate *everything* on my plate!" Bryceson announced loudly enough so that the rest of the café patrons looked in our direction.

"And did you find it *delicious*, darling?" Delia asked him with a twinkle. It was the first and last time I saw her being playful with a kid. She never struck me as being the jokey type, and I remember wondering how she'd been with Nathan, how it was growing up in *that* family. There was something sticky and potent about her relationship with her son, something there that just didn't sit right.

Now, though, I think I can only imagine how it was. It was undeniably nothing like what I'd thought then.

Bryceson shot Delia a scowl. "No, I didn't. It didn't taste nothing like a hot dog."

"That's a double negative, Bry-bry. Double negatives mean the opposite of what you really want to say. Instead, you say, 'It did not taste like a hot dog,'" corrected Emma as she dipped the corner of her napkin in her glass of water and then dabbed the sides of Bryceson's mouth with it, wiping away the yellow stain before it started paying rent.

"It did NOT taste nothing like a hot dog."

"Not exactly, but that's okay. We can work on that," murmured Emma as she kept trying to keep Bryceson's hands down as they seemed to be everywhere as he was attempting to keep her from cleaning his face. "And you need to stop that right now, sir, because Momma's trying to clean your face."

The server was then back at the table with the check, which she handed promptly to Mom as she was the one who kept wiggling her fingers in the direction of the tab in the waitress' hand.

"You ladies find everything all right?" asked the server, who was eyeing Delia's plate. "Not much of an appetite today?"

Shay beamed up at her. "Oh, no, it was all delicious. I just have to get into a wedding gown this evening, so—"

"Well, my goodness! Congratulations on the happy day," said the server, offering a lopsided version of Shay's smile back at her. No matter how hard others try, they can never quite match it. "Been there, too," she said with a nod. "You know that brioche craze that's been goin' on everywhere? That French bread's kinda sweet-tastin'? I had me a five-for-five brioche French toast platter at the Pancake House right before my nuptials. Comes with eggs, grits, hash browns, bacon, all the fixins. You know what I'm talkin' about? Well, we had t'get some safety pins for my dress, and after that, there ain't nothin' worse than attemptin' to pin a dress that was originally fitted just right, especially around them titties of mine. Always a curse."

I bit my tongue to keep from laughing, and I saw Mom turn a lovely shade of beet. Delia seemed to be paying only the slightest bit of attention, that flat, empty stare of hers honed in on Bryceson and his squirming self. All he wanted to do was get out of there, and I couldn't say I blamed him one bit.

Shay giggled in polite sympathy as was normally expected from a bride out on a ladies' lunch, but I knew perfectly well she was dying to burst out laughing as much as I was. "Oh, it's not that area I'm worried about," she said to the server. "As you can plainly see, I've much more corpulent matter around the waistline, my upper arms, my jelly belly. I owe all this to fine alcohol and movie theater candy."

"Girl, you're 'bout as slender as a Slim Jim. What you frettin' over?"

"Now we don't want to interrupt her while she's working. She has a lot of customers at the moment, and it does her no good to hijack her time while she's on the clock," said Mom, obviously to Shay but without the directness. She was looking directly at me when she said it, signaling me to cut in.

But I didn't care to stop it. I needed a laugh. It's been one of those weekends where everyone seemed lacking in a sense of humor. God knows, it was needed then, and we could do with some now.

The server waved a hand about. "Naw, it's all good. Frida just come in, so she can take up the slack. It's fine. Today's all about bridin' an' weddings, ain't that right?" she said with a grin directed at Shay.

"And a good set of Spanx to flatten everything down, titties, bellies, and all that." I answered, directing it at Shay, specifically, but like Mom, I knew how to play the Boone games, so I kept my attention sharply focused on Mom whose eyes grew wide.

Shay, Emma, and the server seemed to find that uproariously funny. As much as Shay and Emma tried to stifle their laughter, keeping it as ladylike as they possibly could, it didn't work. The two of them shrieked at the exact same time, pointing at each other when they did and then cough-chortling around their own glee.

Bryceson, not one to be left out of anything the grownups found hilarious, chuckled and nodded enthusiastically. "Titties and bellies and all that!" he shouted, his little fist pumping in the air.

Naturally, that only added to the hilarity, causing everyone, apart from Mom and a dazed Delia, to laugh until the tears came, sides were hurting, and eye makeup went all gloppy. Shay dabbed at the corners of her eyes with her napkin as Emma puttered, easing her cackling little guy down so that he could dig around into her bag she'd set on the floor near her feet. Mom looked at me, her lips tightening, forming her disapproval, but what else was new? I knew the game. It was safer to turn to me to blame anyway, even if she was still ignoring Shay. Anyhow, Shay wasn't paying the slightest bit of attention. She was still coming down from her momentary happy high, motioning for Emma to clean around her eyes. Emma got the signal, reaching down into her bag and digging out a compact mirror.

As Shay calmed herself down and Emma got the black gunk out of the corner of her eyes, Mom folded in some cash with the tab and handed it to the giggly server with a clenched grimace as if she was constipated; it was her automatic go-to look of disgust when she didn't know the person she was having to deal with.

The server caught Mom's eye and loudly cleared her throat and straightened her stance. "I'll be back with the change, ma'am," she said, patting a thank-you signal on the check fold.

"No change."

Our server softened. "Well, much appreciated. Hope you ladies have a wonderful afternoon, and many happy returns on your wedding day, sweetheart," she said, aiming that last bit at Shay, who smiled at her. The server nodded curiously at Delia and Shay's barely touched lunch. "You two want a to-go box?"

Shay waved it off. "I'm fine. I don't think I'm going to be able to eat anything else until I get this day over and done with."

"Gotcha, Mrs. Bride. How about you, honey? You still workin' on that, or do you want to take that home with ya?" said the server, her eye on Delia.

But Delia was off in her own world, wherever that was, entranced with Bryceson and his rummaging through his mother's bag. Her eyes had gone dark and glassy, and she swallowed something back rather forcefully, like she'd taken in some air and found it too hard in the throat. Her fingers had curled so tightly around the handles of her purse that her knuckles had gone white and knobby. I don't even think she was even aware that we were watching her.

"Delia," said Mom, "do you want to finish your meal, or should we have it put in a doggie bag for you?"

It was right then when Delia broke out of her strange spell; it was as if she'd woken up and realized where she was and whom she was with. At the time, I chalked it up to the fact she hadn't been particularly interested in eating anything, and a lack of nutrients could make anyone go funny, but really. What kind of person doesn't get the joke and join in on the fun? Well, besides Mom and her ever-obvious Boone cold shoulder.

Delia shook her head at the server, beaming up at her, a ray of grace and light as ever. It did the job, putting the server at ease. "It's fine, really, dear. I'd rather not take it back to the hotel. But you tell your masterful chef that I loved what I tasted, really, every bite of it," said Delia to the server. "I don't know what's wrong with me. I'm usually famished around this time of day. I think it's the awful heat of the summertime here. So oppressive. Saps me of what little energy I have left at my age, and it does nothing worthwhile for the appetite."

The server nodded, understanding, and she gave Delia a friendly tap on the shoulder, a little squeeze, and I swear, I think Delia flinched at being touched. It was so subtle; there was a tiny wince, and her grip went even tighter around her purse handles.   Since I was sitting beside her, and our knees were practically knocking together. One leg was bouncing so subtly, I didn't realize she'd been shaky like that until I placed a cautious hand on top of her own. My attempt to relax her down to earth caused her legs to freeze, her whole body to halt in its tension. I met her gaze, trying to smile in support. Delia stared me down with her diamond-cut eyes, and I went cold and numb all over. My mouth was sandpaper dry, and I felt something sour and foul rising up inside of me.

If I listened closely enough, I could almost imagine I didn't hear everyone buzzing around me, like a noisy hive. If I listened closely, I could hear the song in Delia's gaze.

SEVEN

"Is there a decent ladies' room around here?" I mumbled to the server. I shoved myself up out of my chair and then bent to snatch up my bag.

She pointed me in the direction of the rear of the café. "It's clean, and we like to keep it that way."

As much as I was attempting to squeeze some actual manners for the day, since it was Shay's and all, I didn't have time to offer an apology for suddenly having to bolt to the restroom. No stalls, and, thankfully, no waiting. I locked the door behind me, knelt in front of the toilet, and gagged right into it. Something wanted to come up. It was whatever I'd felt deep down when Delia stared at me. Not only that, while I was used to my heart rate escalating during random intervals throughout the day, that time, it was different. My heart was pounding hard at the gates, but it kept skipping a beat every so often, which forced me to calm down and take deep, steady breaths. I wasn't planning on having heart failure this weekend. Nevertheless, my endocrine system was having none of it, and I threw up everything I'd just eaten. I vomited just enough times to make my head throb and stab me again and again from behind my eyes.

I won't chalk it up to food poisoning. That one's far too easy a scapegoat, and food poisoning effects don't often show up right away like that. I suppose I can readily claim the sudden need to purge on the usual benzo withdrawal suspect, but looking back on it now, right *now*, sometimes there are things one cannot easily explain away.

Like the very idea, the very *thought*, that Delia and her eyes, Delia in my head, had somehow, quite literally, made me sick.

81

I rinsed away the sour taste at the sink and then wiped my mouth with a few paper towels. The place had the soft two-ply stuff that is often set out orderly and straight in a neat container in the middle of the two sinks. They were even absorbent enough to clean up all the water I'd splashed around in the sink when I was gargling and spitting.

There was a light tapping of a knock on the ladies' room door, and I heard Shay's muffled voice say, "Hey, you doing okay in there? We're fixing to leave."

"I'll be out in a minute," I said to the door. "Food here is crazy rich and heavy. Sticking to my guts right now."

"Don't be too long or we'll leave you stranded here with nothing to eat but crazy rich food, yo."

"Wait. 'Yo'? Um, 1991's calling and wants Vanilla Ice back."

"I meant it, turd-ette. We gotta go. We're on at seven, and we're losing the rest of the afternoon here with all the German-ese descendants sitting around, eating their schinkennudeln."

"Hey now, I think that may have been offensive, Shay, but I'm not entirely sure. I don't think 'German-ese' is a real word, and 'schinkennudeln' just sounds like something that would make Mom batshit if she heard anybody say it," I said as I gaped at myself in the mirror over the sink. My hairstyle—in its chestnut-colored, perfectly pinned, wide curls—didn't match the ashy complexion it was attempting to frame.

"It's just ham and cheesy noodles. You know, the kind of food we were never allowed to eat because of Mom's ridiculous aversion to melted cheese. We *so* missed out when we were growing up."

"Yeah, I get that, Shay. Listen, would you tell everyone I'll be right out when I'm done here?"

"Sure, let's see if Mom decides to pay attention to me."

There was a dark purple-blue tinge around both of my eyes, signaling to me that my concealer obviously hadn't done its job well. I just didn't want to turn to pancake makeup as it clogged my pores something awful. Even still though, Shay would demand I cover up the entirety of my face in a mask of Max Factor Pan Stik. A blood vessel had bloomed in one eye, staining part of the sclera in a tiny blotch of red.

It was if I hadn't slept in quite a long time. Truthfully, I hadn't, so I often had stray circles around my eyes with some saggy baggage tossed in along the way. But I looked beyond exhausted there, and I could feel it all over my body, sluggishly rolling through my bones. It was the type of exhaustion where my soul had been stripped from me, leaving me feeling as if everything else was speeding by and whipping around me, and I was the only one there stuck in a puddle of treacle, unable to move without it gripping my feet, my arms, my head, my torso, everything about me. All of that aside though, my heart was still thundering wildly in my chest, and as it was, it seemed the only thing I had in me that could possibly move somehow. I had to tell myself that vomiting normally does that to a person, rending her wobbly and weak.

As for my lovely death mask, I wasn't planning on putting on any decent makeup until closer to the time of the wedding, and luckily enough, no one, except Mom perhaps, would even pay much attention to me. Still, I didn't want to go back out there looking as if I'd actually puked up what had been going acidic in my gut, so I took out my little highlighter stick I always kept with me (heck, it had even promised to "wake up" my face on the packaging it had come in) and swiped it high on my cheekbones, down the line of my nose, and under the brow bone. Then I patted in the stuff as best as I could. At least I'd look tired *and* shiny then. There wasn't anything I could immediately do with the area around my eyes. It would just have to do.

And I'd have to get used to the idea that there was something, quite frankly, *vampiric* about my sister's to-be mother-in-law. Then again, isn't that the joke about mothers-in-law, that they were (kind of sort of) monsters?

One big, hilarious joke.

#

Can I ask you something?

{…} You can ask me anything you want. As long as it doesn't have to do with me having to call 911, looking like I've been complicit in whatever it is you planned. Comprende?

LOL. I don't need a partner in my evildoings. I'm an independent kinda girl, quick to handle herself in sticky situations.

You def. are, little sister. So what is it you wanna ask?

Don't laugh. It's going to sound nuts, & I don't want to come off crazier than I actually am. Is it normal to feel like you're outside of yourself, looking in at what's going on, and you know something's going to happen, like something's coming, something bad, & you don't know how you're going to handle it because you're not actually there?

{…}

Leon, please. I'm serious. I feel all jumpy and paranoid, & I don't know why. I don't know what it is, & I'm scared I'll lose control.

Derealization and paranoia are among the symptoms of withdrawal. Did you consider that?

Yeah, I did, but I wasn't entirely sure.

You also have to consider the fact that you're in a strange place surrounded by strangers (except for your family). It would make anybody anxious. Here's what I think you should do: Try talking to one of your family members about this. It might help alleviate some of your concerns. You could even have an honor system where your family member could keep an eye on you, checking up on you every hour to see how you're doing. Your mom or sister would be great at it.

That will make me even more paranoid, L.

Not if you settle down by deep breathing and tell yourself she's looking AFTER you rather than looking AT you.

The only fam. member I think will go all in on that is Shay, but she's kinda busy getting married and all. Too much on her plate.

Now you're giving me the "but," and you know damn well I don't do the "but," girl.

LMAO! "I don't do the but"! Did you really just text that??

Wasn't meant to be funny but I guess some levity will cool you some. Laughter = best medicine.

Yeah, I needed that. I don't think I'll ever NOT find that funny.

If that solution doesn't suit you, try a little visualization like we practiced. Remember the beach bar with the palm trees and hammocks whenever things grew too stressful during your time here? Use that.

There's a nice courtyard here. I could always duck away and hang out there. It's being strung with lights for the wedding, but I don't think I'll interrupt anything.

There you go. Sometimes it's good to have a wedding at a resort.

If you want to call this place a "resort," yeah. $220 a night for darkness, outdated furnishings, scratchy linens, loose wiring, no signal in the rooms and outlets that don't work isn't exactly resort-like. Have to text you from the only space where there's a weak signal now,

& that's in the lobby. People see me as they're going in and out of the bathroom, & it's just weird.

Call it a resort or whatever else you want, but keep that courtyard place in mind for when things go sour and the walls start closing in.

Thanks, L. I will.

And remember if things get too hot over there, I can be on the road in no time at all.

I know & appreciate that. Here's hoping you won't have to waste any money on gas though.

Not a waste if things get out of control, little sister. You stay frosty. One more thing: Don't panic. Sometimes what you think is happening is much bigger in your head.

Yeah yeah & drink plenty of water, right?

Absofrigginlutely.

EIGHT

I've never been the type of woman who wears dresses, and it often shows, especially when the dress is designed specifically to keep some things tucked in and make other things stick proudly out. It's a common plight of a woman readying herself for the onslaught of middle age. Certain parts are inevitably destined to encounter gravity. Other bits just suddenly appear out of nowhere, all white and wiry or creased and crinkled. I'd only just made the discovery of a skin tag right on an armpit, and we ladies in the center of things were all going sleeveless. I'd begged Shay to let me have a shawl at least for the portion of the reception when dancing was on the agenda (God, I fucking hate dancing), but Shay was having none of it.

As she flitted about from one end of the suite to the other, checking up on this and that, Shay was practically being chased by the woman Delia had hired to do her makeup, one of the resort employees who just happened to appear on the very day of the wedding. I kept my lips zipped, suppressing the natural inclination I had—that everyone in the wedding *should* have had—to ask where they'd all been hiding. The place had been void of almost anyone in an employee uniform last night. Suddenly, the place was alive with uniforms buzzing about. It made me wonder if they only appeared whenever some big, fancy event was about to happen, and then they vanished when things went back to a quieter state. It didn't make much sense to me, and I wasn't the only one who'd thought it was uncomfortably off. Had my sister not been so blinded by wedding festivity planning (ugh) and the idea of marrying (double ugh) Nathan, maybe she would've been a little more savvy and had seen the many negative reviews about the place on Yelp, all of which held the same concern I had, besides the obvious room issues—that there had been no employees around at night, and nighttime was quite often when patrons discovered what was working about their room and what wasn't.

If only *I* had checked Yelp much earlier, if anything for my sister's sanity, and had I known then what I definitely know now, well…

"I don't see anything, Ans. Just slather on some of that airbrush gunk Emma brought. She said it was made to cover anything, and it won't stain your dress," said Shay as I held up my arm for her to examine the hideous growth on my armpit.

I pointed it out to her, wincing as she gripped my arm back, using as leverage. "It's right there," I said. "I don't usually wear sleeveless, so it's not like I would've noticed beforehand. I think it just popped up over the past few days."

"You didn't see it when you shaved? I always catch them when I shave there, among other places I won't get into," said Emma from her cozy spot on the chaise. She was half-keeping an eye on Bryceson, who was adorably suited up and quiet for once as he filled in superheroes in a coloring book, and half-paying attention to whatever Shay was up in arms with in the moment. Emma looked a little *too* comfortable there for a maid of honor. She wore her blissful state well, too well. Weren't maids of honor usually supposed to be just as stressed out as the bride?

I suspected a benzo was the culprit. Xanax was often the go-to for those suffering event panic. My mother used to keep them in Grandma's old credenza, along with the usual hangover "cures" conveniently placed behind the liquor bottles. It was her version of what a bar should contain. The last time I was over there, all of the medicine, all of those "cures," had been hidden away from their usual homes, along with the liquor. Yet Dad had managed to uncover a bottle of single-malt scotch from somewhere in the house, probably his newly established man cave that had once been Shay's room. I know it had been for my own sake, my own "benefit," something my dad had never failed to remind me (as if preventing anyone from easily accessing a bottle of booze in our house would seriously help me in my own recovery). To which I often responded with the same thing over and over again, that I wasn't a goddamned addict.

"Does anyone have a bandage?" I asked. "Anything that will blend in with my pit…?"

Just then, Mom and Delia—all dolled up and ready in rich, dark colors—came sweeping in through the French doors to the courtyard, in mid-chatter about something guest-or-family related, both of them seeming agitated by it. Shay gathered up her train and stormed over to them, her cheeks flushed and eyes shooting blades directly at the two of them.

"Where have you been? We're due in twenty minutes, and Ansley's having a ridiculous crisis that I just cannot deal with right now," she snapped.

"How is it ridiculous when you expect us to look like we give a fuck, Shay," I muttered, just loud enough for her to hear.

And, apparently, loud enough for Bryceson to catch on and cling to it. "Like we give a fuck. Like we give a fuuuuuuuck," he sang as he concentrated on coloring in a cape. I was starting to like that kid.

Instead of chastising the little guy, Emma merely chuckled and brushed back his hair from his eyes. Definitely Xanax.

"Ansley Mary Boone," Mom hissed. "There is no need for that language, especially in front of children."

"Bryceson doesn't care. That kid is a forty year-old man in a five year-old's body," I said as I examined my armpit's deformity in the mirror.

Emma let out an airy chortle. "It's true. I mean, have you heard middle-aged men lately?"

Bryceson whipped around, gaping at his mother. "If *I'm* forty years old, I can pay bills, and then I can say all the bad words I want."

I grinned at him in the mirror. "A lot of the forty year-old men I know would concur, my man. You'll have to pay your taxes too, don't forget."

"I will. I'll pay taxes even though Daddy doesn't like paying taxes. He says that all-the-*time!*"

Shay and I issued Emma a curious glance at that little revelation, and I only just caught the look on Shay's face as well. For a best friend, apparently Emma hadn't revealed much to Shay about her ex having come back into Bryceson's life, never mind her own.

Emma shrugged at Shay, waving off the thought of it. "He's finally up-to-date on his child support, and he wanted to see Bryceson. I figured, whatever. Couldn't hurt. As long as I didn't have to deal with him outside of that."

"Why didn't you tell me? I could've helped," said Shay as Delia and the resort makeup artist, or whatever she was, finally got

Shay to sit down at the vanity that had been set up specifically for such occasions.

"What could you possibly have done, girl? This isn't about anything other than Bry-bear getting to know his Disneyland daddy with his fancy new condo and blonde lay on the side."

"Blonde lay on the side," echoed Bryceson as he scribbled like mad.

Mom sucked in her breath, probably at Emma's candor in front of a kid. I felt like telling her it was the benzo doing the talking for Emma, pointing out the obvious that was right there for all to witness, but I got the feeling she would've have cared little about such matters when a wedding was happening. Mom came over to examine what I was picking at in disgust. Like Shay, she gripped my arm up over my head and squinted at what I knew perfectly well was there.

"What is it? I don't see what you're upset about, Ansley."

"Mom, it's right there. It's a skin tag, and if I have to wear something sleeveless, I'm gonna have to cover that up somehow."

"We need to get you some setting spray," said the makeup girl to Shay, her voice barely above a whisper. "It's just the last thing before your dad comes to get you." She turned to the rest of us and said, "Mom one and Mom two, you need to be out there, sitting in your reserved places."

In an instant, or so it felt, Delia was also there at my side, armed with something that flashed in her hand. She reached up with it and I heard a sharp CLICK of metal on metal, snapping closed, and it felt like something had just sharply bitten me underneath my arm. She snapped her fingers, frantically beckoning for the part-time makeup girl to get something from the opened makeup case that had been set on the vanity. The makeup girl rummaged around in the case before she pulled out a wad of cotton balls, a mini-bottle of antiseptic and a Band-Aid that would certainly do the trick.

"It will bleed just a little bit. Nothing for you to fret over," Delia said as she swiped the cotton and bandage from the makeup girl, who promptly returned to preen over Shay. "But you're a sturdy lady, aren't you, Ansley? You seem to understand beauty and pain, taste and blood. They go well together in the right moment, don't they?" she said softly, just loud enough for me to catch it. I threw a quick glance over her shoulder, trying to catch Shay's eye, Mom's, anyone's. They were rightly wrapped in whatever drama the bride was concocting at the moment.

I didn't like the look of Delia's smile either. Too-perfect teeth hiding behind those designer red lips. She dabbed at the wound she'd created under my arm, softly humming a tune that was vaguely familiar in the spinning fog I was in. Something crisp like autumn days and catchy, something I sort of remembered from back when I was Bryceson's age, maybe a little older. She shook the bottle of antiseptic before she tipped it, wetting another cotton ball. I think it was the thought of having her touch me that had me take the damp bit of cotton from her. Her smile dissolved into a sneer, her face darkening as she watched me soak the fresh wound and the reddening area around it.

"Perhaps you should ask Charlie to lick it for you. He'll clean it up quite nicely, like he did your salty, little pussy," she said so quietly, I'd barely caught it in its entirety.

"I'm sorry, *what*?"

Delia's suddenly twisted into an edge of a baffled smile, one that was awfully authentic. "What's that? Are you quite all right, my lovely? You look a little peaked."

#

You know those moments where everything around you just becomes a hazy wash of colors and light, but you can't discern any perceptible shapes or outlines of the people there? The sounds are just low white noise in the background. If someone touched you on your bare skin right then and there, it would shock you into a comatose state, forcing you into a dark oblivion you'd never be able to return from. That would be it.

And you know this. You've always known this.

It would be the end of you.

In that moment, when the bridal suite became a whirlwind mesh of blinding, deafening pastels and cacophony, I felt Delia's hot breath against my face, and all I wanted to do was run far away from her. My legs were heavy, rooted there. I knew if I tried to lift one and then the other, it would feel like pulling them out of a vat of glue.

My quickening pulse was thunderous in my head. Burning bile rose in my throat. Delia's expression had softened as quickly as it had grown dark beforehand, and somehow, I knew if I even mentioned what she had said, what I'd actually had heard from her, she'd be quick to brush it off and frame it as wedding stress, that I was hearing things, that I'd need plenty of rest after the ceremony, maybe even another month added on at the center. Delia would gaslight me because she was *good* at it. She'd done it before, I was certain of it, and she'd not hesitate to do it again, even to someone she barely knew.

She knew what she was doing, and thanks to my own personal predicament, she knew no one would believe a word out of me.

I didn't know if *I'd* believe me either.

"You're flushed, Ansley. Are you all right? Should we have someone fetch you some ice water?" she said. Her voice dripped with saccharine-soaked concern.

Mom tore herself away from Shay to check on me just as my dad, tuxedoed up and looking completely unsure of what to do, joined us in the bridal suite. The wedding organizer, the woman who'd been fluttering about in the dining hall, was there as well and motioned for all of us to take our places, but Mom shot her a quick warning look, instantly shutting her up. The planner nodded and turned her attention to Shay, Dad, Emma, and Bryceson, who had fallen awkwardly into his role as ring bearer. She gave him the little velveteen pillow and crouched down in front of him to detail his directions.

"Ansley, if you feel like you need to sit or just rest in your room, it's perfectly fine," said Mom as she felt my forehead and cheeks. "You're feverish."

"I'm good, Mom. I am. You need to go out there and—" And the room kept turning itself inside out, making me lose my balance.

Mom was there to grip my arm and straighten me, patting down the front of my dress as she did. Her face was etched with worry. "When was the last time you drank some water?" she murmured.

"Should I go out there and tell everyone we're running a little late?" asked the planner.

Shay whirled around, facing the three of us on the other side of the room, her nostrils flaring, cheeks blooming red. "Do you need some time, Ansley, or is this just one of your moments that we can bypass for now? Seriously," she snapped. "I'm telling you all, I am getting married *tonight*, and that's the end of it. I am so sick of dealing with her bullshit. It's always something. *Always* something," She directed her anger right at me, hitting where it hurts. "Do you need a Valium, Ans, or is that one of the drugs on your naughty list?"

"Shay Ellen, that is quite enough," Mom scolded. "Both of you need to pull yourselves together, become ladylike, or you will be spending the remainder of the evening apologizing in a microphone to the guests and staff here. Do you understand?" She was looking right at me when she said that.

My head was buzzing, going numb. A part of me thought I needed to do something to get Shay's attention, to make a scene, to force the family to get the hell out of Dodge somehow. Nothing about this was right, and Delia, who kept nodding and frowning in perfectly practiced empathy in Mom's direction, had just convinced me well enough that nothing about this was right, nothing about the whole experience felt right, and that Shay was about to marry into a family of creeps.

By then, everyone there was staring at me, as if I could just trigger the correct move to make. Even Delia had on a mask of concern, but her icicle eyes were lit in amusement. It's was as if she liked seeing me squirm, as if she was daring me to say something stupid and call her out on what I'd heard, but I wasn't about to give her the satisfaction no matter what my gut was advising me to do.

And something kept nagging at me, that prickling going up my spine, spreading to my arms, the chill of it traveling to my fingertips. Something wasn't right. Bubbles of bright color popped when I blinked. Then everything went all blurry again.

"Can I have a moment to—?"

But I couldn't finish whatever it was I was trying to say. I remember feeling as if the floor was coming up, just out of reach, and it was Shay who caught me that time. She'd suddenly bolted right for me and hoisted me up by the arms. The room rocked. She put her cold palms against my cheeks, and it helped cool me down, but something was still off, like the air was rippling, and the ringing in my ears blocked out whatever it was Shay was saying, something in the fog over and over again.

The crack in her voice was rising, verging on hysteria. She turned to Mom and the others in the bridal train, shouting at them, frantically motioning them out. Mom seemed about to speak, none too happy about how things were going, but Shay shot her a look that instantly shut her up and had her urge Emma, Bryceson, the assistants, and Delia out the door, away from the tension.

When Shay turned back to me, her eyes were wide and manic, and I could've sworn I saw a blood vessel burst in one of them, creating a red road map of mad squiggles. I wanted her eyes to stop, to keep silent.

I wanted *her* to stop.

None of that felt exactly as it should have in that moment.

#

There are blank spots. I can't remember much of the in-between during key moments. Does anyone though? For me, however, it happens often when there's tension, and my head hurts, and I can't hear much that I probably should. I barely remember fuzzy bits and pieces there in the bridal suite. The whole room was saturated in soft, golden tones coming in through the windows of the bridal suite; the sun was announcing the reclining hour, signaling the early evening.

Shay was saying something to me, her eyes surprisingly clear and bright. I was moving towards her, reaching out to her with the bridal bouquet in my hands. I don't know how they got there, but it seemed that I would've done that anyway. It seemed right. She smiled as she took the bouquet from me, so I presumed everything had settled between us somehow while I wasn't entirely there. I gathered up my bouquet that had been carefully set on the loveseat nearby, patted down my dress here and there, and got into place, readying myself to lead her out the door to the ceremony

By then, my mind had come back into focus. I was there with her, and all I could think about in that moment was whether or not there were alternate exits out of the place in case I really needed to run.

In case each and every one of us needed to run.

NINE

The dining hall was alive with laughter and color. I've since forgotten much of it, how I'd even gotten there, from the bridal suite, to the ceremony in the courtyard, finally to the reception. I'd been seated, as indicated by the glitzy placard, at the end of the connected chain of tables that had been set up specifically for the immediate wedding party. It suited me just fine even though I knew in my heart that as much as Shay had been trying to get along with me during her weekend, the thought of having me sit near her was then too much for her to bear. The wedding planner must have been ordered to switch my placard with whoever the heck it was who was sitting by Bryceson, some middle-aged guy I didn't recognize who had a bad comb-over and wore a dark green tuxedo that was completely out of place. Judging by the looks on Shay and Mom's faces, they hadn't been expecting *that* to sit with the wedding party. He seemed right at home though, joshing with Bryceson and then cheering loudly while holding up his champagne glass high in the air after one of the groomsmen's speech to the bride and groom. I didn't get the jokes and references that had been tossed in, and because everyone else had, and had laughed at each and every one of them, I instantly felt out of place there among them.

I felt completely alone, utterly out of the picture. There'd been this life, these key moments, which I'd obviously missed because I'd been so consumed by my own problems. My heart burned a hole in me, and my temples throbbed. The air around me was suffocating, and I wanted to go. However, I knew that if I left the reception, I'd not hear the end of it from my family, especially Shay, and I couldn't do that to her.

Besides, no matter how anxious I was about being by myself, feeling left out of everything, there was still that lingering sense that something was coming, that something wasn't right. It wasn't just Delia's out-of-character, inappropriate aside, which had alarmed me well enough. It was the feeling one gets—well, the feeling that I often get—before a storm strikes. The air was flat and eerily silent all around, untouched by the white noise of the wedding party. Everything on the outside must have seemed as normal as a wedding ought to appear. The snapshot fragments I remember about the ceremony had been lovely, I suppose, with only a few minor hitches (e.g., Bryceson plopping himself down at the foot of the minister instead of going back to his seat; Shay looking annoyed as Nathan read his vows from a piece of paper he'd kept tucked away in his jacket; someone in the back hiccupping throughout the whole second half of the ceremony). The photography session went well, too, despite the groomsmen acting like assclowns with their flask-sharing and constant quips at the wedding planner, who kept trying to keep them under control while the photographer posed everyone in various shots on the terrace under the fairy lights.

Even the reception itself had been beautifully set up. The dining hall had been decorated in ivory and garnet red, and the hideous moose and elk trophies had been removed from their spots on the walls, replaced with antique mirrors and landscape paintings in gilded frames. Ceiling swags spun from ivory organza had been looped above, meeting at a giant chandelier in the middle of the room.

And the main course. Aside from a little tiff amongst my seatmates, God, it was just…perfection, and it almost made me forget that sense that something was definitely off. Almost. I don't know who'd planned the menu, but I knew it hadn't been anyone from my family. None of us, except for Mom perhaps, had been much of a gourmand. Once the soup bowls had been cleared, we were served either Chateaubriand or spit-roasted Cornish hen. There was even a vegetable Moroccan tagine with couscous to satiate those who'd gone meatless. A couple of the Card cousins—highlighted and svelte twentysomething sisters I'd been sitting in-between—had torn right into the tender slices of meat on their plates, having completely bypassed the soup starter altogether. Not that I blamed them. The broth had been so light on flavor, we may as well have been supping on hot, salted water sprinkled with parsley flakes. If I'd spent more time watching the two of them eat, I probably would've lost my appetite for the Cornish hen and summer vegetables I'd chosen. The meat was moist and tender, and the wine that had been paired with it served to only enhance its fatty-rich flavor.

By the time the three of us had finished, our plates were bare, and one of the girls brought up her plate to her face to lick it clean. Her sister reached across me to swat at the plate-licker's hand.

"Sorry about that," she'd mumbled at me. "If you wanna trade places, I can smack her upside the head."

Plate-Licker let her platter clatter onto the table. Her fingers curled; her hands balled into fists. She then peered around me at her sister, her eyes firing arrows. I sat as far back in my chair as I was able, not wanting to be a part of a fight that was already brewing.

"Cake's coming," she growled at the other, more mannerly one.

"Yeah, so? You don't lick your plate like that in public. You gonna do that with your dessert plate, too?"

"We have to keep it clean for second meal dessert. It'll taste nasty otherwise."

"What the hell are you talking about, 'second meal dessert'? What does that even mean?"

"You know what it means. Don't pretend you don't."

McManners gave her sister a strange look. I couldn't tell if it was meant to direct her to explain herself or to shut up.

"It's like those old Taco Bell ads for 'Fourthmeal.' Remember that?" said Plate-Licker. "Instead of tacos, we're courting dessert."

"That is so fucking retarded."

Plate-Licker shot me an apologetic smirk. "Forgive my 'special' sister for her lack of political correctness." Then she reached over and sharply rapped her sister on the back of her hand with a knuckle, prompting McManners to flinch and attempt to smack her back from across me. I was close to being caught in a twisted knot of hands and arms, being in the middle of their row like that.

"See what I did there? We don't say 'retarded' anymore. That's *rude*," said Plate-Licker. "Instead, we say 'differently abled' or 'special.' I thought you were meant to be a model of good behavior."

"You licked your plate, so evidently, I taught you nothing."

"You know, in some countries, licking the plate clean is a compliment to the chef."

McManners shook her head at her sister. "No, I don't think so."

"Oh, I think so."

"You're wrong."

"It's true."

"You're so wrong, you couldn't be any more wrong."

"Get your cell, and let's look it up then."

"You're thinking of slurping your soup. Like they do in Japan. Not plate licking. It doesn't matter anyway. Our phones are useless in here, remember?"

"Look how clean I made it though. What chef wouldn't take that as a compliment?"

I'd held back my snicker, only for the sake of keeping it together, but I still interjected with a "Why don't I just switch places with one of you" as I pushed my seat back and got up.

Plate-Licker motioned for me to sit back down. "It's fine. It's better if we have a barrier between us," she said, making a face at her sister.

"She's right. We'd probably kill each other. Probably tear each other to shreds," said McManners, shooting her sister a rapid-fire birdie.

"You're *definitely* sisters," I said, my halfassed attempt at cooling them down with polite, normal conversation. "So how many years between the two of you?"

"Two, but it feels like twenty sometimes," said McManners.

Plate-Licker shot her sister a look. "What's that supposed to mean?"

"Never mind."

"You're the oldest anyway, so it'd be like you're in your forties. Almost as old as Aunt Melanie."

"Forty's not that old."

Plate-Licker nodded thoughtfully. "Seriously. She doesn't look a second over thirty. All those collagen injections."

"I heard she's on a liquid diet," said McManners. "But it's just the usual stuff tossed in a smoothie blender with some macha, some kale and pearl powder. Then, presto ala mundo! It's healthy!"

"I can't believe people are stupid enough to ingest pearl powder."

"But think of the benefits in all the crushed gemstones they've not discovered yet. We could make some money testing it out. Topaz, opals, onyx—"

Plate-Licker grimaced at the thought of it. "No thank you. You have fun with your healthy gem powder there—"

"—and for those subscribing to our Platinum offer, there's ruby, emerald, sapphire and diamond powder that'll give you that inner sparkle only celebrities have been able to maintain...until *now*."

"Forget the pearls and rubies. Who was the dipshit who thought kale was tasty and marketed *that*?"

They'd been funny all right, their banter reminding me what brought me here in the first place. I looked over at Shay, who was clapping at the sight of the three-tiered, dark chocolate wedding cake being carted in by a couple of the staff in starched evening uniforms. Mom, who was sitting beside Emma to Shay's right, had on her disapproving scowl when she saw the cake, which surprised me. I would've thought they'd have least agreed on the cake, and since it was an evening wedding reception, why not go for something more decadent? Suited me just fine.

In the middle of chattering with her sister, Plate-Licker gave me a curious once over, and there was something about her stare I didn't care for. It felt heated and crawly all over. There was something about her eyes, something familiar.

"You know the bride's family?" she prodded. "You a relative?"

I don't know why, but I then suddenly had the urge to deflect, deny, deflect. Anything to keep my family safe, protected somehow from whatever it was I knew was there. So I just shrugged in response and pretended to be engrossed in what was going on at the other tables nearby. Noisy family groups. Some sun-crinkled great uncles and eyerolling aunts I barely recognized from wayward family reunions and, still, plenty of people I didn't know.

I suppose I could've taken a good look at the guest roster upon check-in, just to see who all from my family was here, but except for my mom's sister and brother-in-law, Aunt Lil and Uncle Ray, I wasn't close with any of them, especially those on Dad's side, many of whom had, apparently, RSVP'd an "Unfortunately, we're unable to make the wedding due to (fill in the blank with some obviously fabricated situation), but thanks so much for the invite." Figured. The Boones were devout Catholics who frowned upon marrying outside one's religion. Shay had been one of their more recent disappointments, marrying out of the faith, but it must have been expected from us. I mean, Dad was their noted rebel son with his libertarian fantasies and religious skepticism. He loved debating with his family. It actually made him happy to see them squirm in their pews.

I hadn't seen anyone else I recognized from the Boone side though, apart from a total skeeze of a cousin—another bearded, flask-sharing douchenozzle—who'd brought a date who looked like she'd had a rough time of it pouring herself into the sequined dress she'd chosen to wear for the evening's festivities. They were sitting at Aunt Lil and Uncle Ray's table, along with an elderly couple I didn't know, both of whom were paying more attention to poking their forks around their barely-eaten food on their plates than they were the bride and groom.

There were quick flashes as everyone near the main table had out their cell phones and digital cameras, snapping the cutesy image of Shay and Nathan cutting into the chocolate mountain of a cake, both of them laughing with friends and family nearby who cheered them on. Nathan took a huge, crumbling bite and then fed the rest of the piece to Shay, dabbing the frosting on her pert button of a nose. She feigned a look of shock at him and kissed him squarely on the lips so that both of them had frosting on their faces.

Nathan then said something only people in the immediate vicinity could hear, something undoubtedly naughty and entirely inappropriate because the only people who roared and hooted with laughter were Charlie and their other friends. Mom and Dad both grew red-faced under the twinkling lights. Mom's mouth drew in a tight, thin line. Delia tittered into her napkin and then chided Nathan while Rex was—well, he seemed to be off in his own world on his end of the table. His eyes were glassy, unfocused, staring at one of the tables far off in the back somewhere with a half-smile on his face. His hand had its index finger circling his whiskey glass.

Shay shushed Nathan and playfully pushed him back down in his seat. He grabbed her around the waist and pulled her on his lap. She crinkled her nose at him in warning, the look she often gave old boyfriends who'd gone too far with their antics, but Nate didn't notice. I suspect he knew, but he was deliberately choosing to ignore her, instead focusing intently on his best friend. Undoubtedly, it was his first pain-in-the-ass moment as an official husband, and it was all I could do to keep from getting up out of my chair, stomping over to them, taking Shay by the arm and pulling her out of there with me.

After the groomsman's speech, Charlie got up and weaved around his date (Nabhitha was it?) to stand beside Nathan as the wedding planner's harried assistant, who also happened to have taken on the responsibilities of the Emcee, handed him a microphone. He first tested its sound quality by badly beatboxing into it, causing a collective titter to ripple throughout the dining hall. Then he cleared his throat and proceeded to spin a narrative of brotherly nostalgia, one involving a white water rafting trip, far too much weed, and something involving oars, a baggie, and a water moccasin. I could only catch snippets, brief cuts of his story, due to the poor acoustics of the room, but it was evident he was loved by Nathan's friends and family; even my family members, as few as they were there, seemed enrapt by his toast.

For a brief moment, barely quick enough to catch, Charlie glanced over at me all the way down the opposite end of the long chain of tables. The area around his eyes crinkled as he smiled at me, I could see that, but it was so fleeting I had to think back for a moment to gauge whether or not it had been real or just some figment of my imagination. Nabhitha—she of the fluttery lashes, satin skin, and lush locks—must have caught it too because her eyes met mine as well. She then slowly shook her head at me, her expression darkening in recognition. It made me all the more anxious to know if he'd told her about our poorly timed (and my incredibly stupid) late night tryst. Judging by Nabhitha's frown, I think he may have kept it from her, but she'd put everything together right then in that very moment.

By then, everyone was raising their champagne glasses to Charlie's last few words to Shay and Nathan. I quickly overcompensated by standing and lifting my glass. Another foolish move on my part because it suddenly dawned on me that I had the floor and, unfortunately, everyone's attention. The sisters on either side of me rapidly clinked their spoons against their glasses, signaling for the room to listen, both of them grinning up at me.

The planner's assistant/Emcee tottered in her heels towards me, microphone in hand. The effects I normally felt off and on throughout the day were consuming me alive. My throat went arid as I swallowed back the hard stone that had been forming there. My tongue felt like it had just been coated in sandpaper.

"Speech, girl. Speech!" shouted Plate-Licker.

Her sister loudly whooped, the sound of it reverberating back like a boomerang, and one of Nathan's friends howled back.

I gripped the microphone tightly using both hands, one curled over the other, probably out of fear of dropping it. Or perhaps it gave me something tangible to focus on, what I considered to be probably the most embarrassing moment of my entire life. I didn't do public speaking, and everyone who really knew me, like Shay and my parents here, knew that little fact.

Still, I couldn't just set the mic down and run away like a coward. I'd have to say *something*, anything of substance that was true and memorable.

So I took a deep breath and began.

"Okay, so, I'm sure most of you are aware by now that I'm sister of the bride, her one and only sister," I said, "and I'm also fairly certain many of you are aware that I've spent the last couple of weeks in rehab. As for the how's and the why's, well, it's kind of a long story, much of which involves getting off anti-anxiety meds too fast and an ex impregnating and then running off with another woman he barely knew. A story that would be better told crying while sitting in a circle with a bunch of strangers over Styrofoam cups of awful coffee and a few stale donuts."

That got a few uncomfortable chortles, which made me feel a little braver.

"Anyway, over the past year, ever since Shay and Nate got themselves into the whole getting married trend, I confess that I'd not been paying much attention. See, not only was I a little bit...just an eensy bit occupied, I also don't do trends. When tattoos were a thing, I didn't get one. When the Rachel haircut was everywhere back in the nineties, I didn't get one. When yoga pants were worn all over the place, girl, please. No way. Not with these thighs. When Starbucks served those unicorn Frappucinos, I...Well, okay, I tried one, and it was disgusting."

I lobbed that last one in Shay's direction because she was probably the only one in the entire room who'd tried one and actually liked it. Not only that, I had to keep focused, and Shay was the reason why I was even there to begin with. So I hated Nathan and his family, but it was in that moment when I understood why she was going through with it, that trend that's come and gone, come and gone. She was happy.

Shay met my eyes and grinned at me.

"Shay, on the other hand...she loves trends. You never did have any taste, Shay," I said, returning her smirk.

I think that one may have garnered much more laughter than I'd intended, no doubt directed primarily at Nathan's expense, so I tempered it down a bit, if only for my sister. "This time though, this time, I...This time, I think she's got a—"

I just couldn't finish my train of thought there, in that very moment, because right then, I caught sight of something happening off in the distance through the giant windows, just past Shay's shoulder.

If there had been a minute of incredible timing for such an occasion, it was when the sun's glow had long since dipped down into the rolling dusky hills, melting, merging into the violet horizon. The picture windows overlooked the scene from the back zen garden that had been designed to create a pleasant byway one could traverse between one side of the building to the next by capturing the line between land and sky. It also only served to enhance the goings-on inside the dining hall.

It wasn't the beauty of the evening glow over those hills that had initially distracted me though. There was a blur of movement happening outside on the opposite corner of the U-shaped building we were in, on the other side of the garden. One of the catering staff members—a blocky little rock of a guy, sweating in the light of the fairy lights outside— was attempting to get a cart of used plates unstuck from the narrow, winding cobblestoned path, the wheel obviously jammed, and he didn't see the lone, thin figure there, smoking a cigarette, watching, barely noticeable in the shadow of an awning. Smoke curled in front of the figure, cloaking whomever it was in a veil.

The figure stepped into view. It was a man in a fitted pinstriped suit. He had a pale, gaunt face, sunken eyes, and twitchy fingers on one hand. I didn't recognize him, but judging from the suit and boutonniere, I assumed he was a part of the wedding party, the only guests all gussied up around, really, and we all seemed to have taken over the entirety of the resort. The guy flicked his cigarette into the night and slunk his way over to the dining hall employee who was kicking the jammed wheel by that point.

The gaunt man then just stood there, directly behind the catering employee, staring a hole right through the poor guy's back, almost as if he was willing the employee to turn around.

I shook my head, trying to break away from the scene, turning back to the dining hall guests and Shay. "I think I may be wrong about marriage. A friend of mine once said to me that when you found the one, that perfect person who matched you in the best ways you'd never once—"

A swift jerk of movement outside caught my eye again, tearing me away from the audience once more. The gaunt man had just leapt onto the back of the caterer, smacked a hand over his victim's mouth, and was then tearing out the poor guy's throat with his teeth. Blood jettisoned in jet-black spurts, covering the gaunt man's face and the rocks around them in the garden. From a different angle in dusk's violet shadows, the two of them probably looked like a hunchbacked creature in mid-waltz with himself, staggering to the left, to the right, swinging back to the left right before collapsing onto the pebbled ground, a disheveled pile of grubby, stained clothing and heaving beast.

Yeah, I could've chalked it up to the meds.

In fact, at that time, before I knew, I did. After all, of the list of possible withdrawal symptoms, there's…

Blurred vision (I've perfect vision, thanks. No specs—I'm sorry, Mom, *spectacles*, no contacts, no laser eye surgery, none of it).

Delirium (Emotions running high but perfectly normal all things considered. I mean, it's often high during family get-togethers, right? I think I've already established this plenty.).

Derealization (Okay, I was there, right, and things physically felt real. The mic was growing slick with sweat in my hand. My skin felt pinprickly. The air around, chilly due to the fact we were near one of the vents. Don't think I hadn't checked that.).

Hallucinations, auditory and visual.

Stop.

That. Right there. That. I tested that theory, see. Hallucinations, like memories, shift and change, morphing into something else entirely, disappearing altogether, and then becoming something you probably feel that you need and hope to see. Leon had once instructed our therapy group to come back to the present, to the here and now, by looking away for ten seconds, then returning to what we'd seen. I looked away, too rushed to carefully count, then looked back.

Away, then back again.

It was a reflexive lurch forward that snapped me away from the grizzly vision outside, not anything to do with what Leon had instructed. The whole dining hall had gone silent, everyone nervously, uncomfortably, glancing around at each other. A couple of utensils clattering against the china. Throats rattling phlegm, clearing. A few murmurs, the soft hum of it breaking the stillness a little. My heart kept on thumping in my ears.

103

I looked over at Shay, thinking her beautiful, happy face, still rosy warm and candlelit, would provide me some calm and bring me back to my train of thought, something to ease the ice water running throughout my body, spreading to my arms and chest. Like everybody else's around though, Shay's expression had gone hard. Her eyes narrowed at me. Her lips pursed like Mom's. That look, that whole getup was Mom's.

Like mother, like Shay.

Block out everything else around you. They don't matter, girl. They're not important. Breathe, Leon whispered in my thoughts.

I took in a deep breath. Pretended I wasn't standing there like a dolt, the center of attention for once.

And, stupid me, I looked again.

The gaunt man, no longer pale but coated in a film of the sticky stuff, had a couple of friends hunched over and tearing into the body of the catering employee alongside of him, their mouths and chins stained, their eyes glinting in the lantern lights. It was the elderly couple with the visors, the ones who'd been checking in with their odd requests.

Something about plastic sheets, something about clotting.

Not so odd now that I think about it.

The microphone slipped from my hand and clattered to the floor. Its feedback shrieked throughout the dining hall, reverberating off the walls, causing the guests at and nearby my table to wince, a few of them holding hands over their ears at the piercing wail.

"Jesus fucking Christ!" I hadn't meant for anyone to hear that; it just came out.

I felt the bile forming its sour heat in my throat, threatening to force its way out.

It had been loud enough to grab hold of my dad, who'd been seething over at Shay's end of the table the whole damned time. He pushed back from the table, his chair scraping across the wooden floor, and he stood, red-faced and blustery, his hands curling, aiming his anger in my direction.

"No. Not here. Not tonight. That is *unacceptable* behavior, Ansley, and I will not tolerate it happening *here*," he said over the din. I could hear every word. Every, single word he said, even while there were people out there, right outside, eating one of the catering staff.

"Your mother and I have had enough. You do not disrespect your elders. You do not disrespect our guests. Most importantly, you do

104

not disrespect your sister on her wedding day," he continued. "We have tolerated the breakdowns, the theatrics, the *shame* of it long enough. It...*You*...will no longer be an intrusion in our family. I have had *enough*," His words sliced through the silence.

This, all of this happening in front of the gaping dining hall patrons. This, while, just outside, just beyond my Dad from where he stood, a couple more people, two resort staff members in fact, judging from their uniforms, had joined the gore-spattered threesome in the zen garden. The five of them were crouched there, tucking right into dinner. The caterer's arms had been torn almost completely from his corpse, the limbs still barely connected by tendons, red sinewy ribbons of meat. The gaunt man in the pinstripes was even wearing a coil of intestines around his neck like a morbid lei.

Dad shook his head, his heavy brow furrowing his anger. "You're not the slightest bit affected by what I've said, are you? Did you hear me, Ansley, or does my message need repeating? Are you even paying attention? Of course she isn't. My eldest."

Something was either vacuuming all of the oxygen out of the room, or it was just me as it often was. I felt as if I couldn't breathe, standing there. Darting circles of yellow light blinked in and out of existence in front of my eyes, momentarily blinding me, causing me to squint. The dining hall started to spin and blur, the colors whirling, blending together through a watery lens.

And through the bubble, I could still see it happening out there, right there. I tried to speak, but the words wouldn't form. My thoughts, however, were screaming for me to shout, willing me to take action and point out what was occurring outside, right outside that window.

I may have either been frozen in shock or merely under the paralyzing spell of my symptoms, but as it turned out, I wasn't alone. One of the guests at the table that faced ours, a woman I recognized somewhat from Mom's side of the family, shot up out of her chair, her eyes wide with horror, her throat constricting, swallowing. She, too, had been watching what was going on in the garden out there. Her panic forced an ear-piercing scream.

Before anyone could react and see what she was screaming about, what had obviously trapped my attention from the beginning, Delia, her eyes wild and round, wavered up from her seat beside Dad, her sudden movements jerking me back to look directly at her as she yanked Dad by his jacket arm, pulling him towards her.

Delia Card then bit down into the curve of Dad's ear and, using her teeth, ripped it from the side of his head. The skin of his jaw and cheek came right off with his ear, revealing the raw, red muscle and tendons beneath. I had never heard my dad scream until that moment. The sounds coming from him were quaky and shrill, and when Delia tore into his neck, his scream caught in his throat, forming a wet gurgle of a death rattle.

And that— right then, right there—was when everything turned to blood and shit.

TEN

It didn't take long for everyone else to explode from their seats in a chain reaction of noise, carnage, and motion, and I just stood there in the midst of it all, in a daze, unable to budge from my station at my table. I didn't bother attempting to will my legs to get me the fuck out of the place. I didn't even consider hunting for a place to hide it out somewhere, quite possibly the only feasible action I could consider due to the fact it seemed as if every other goddamned person there was a lunatic.

Yeah, I'll chalk it up to shock rather than withdrawals. I think that's reasonable, right? All things considered.

After all, how many people can say they've been stuck there in the middle of Utter Batshit Central, a place where quite a number of people have revealed themselves to be ravenous for human flesh?

Time broke apart.

At the far end of the table, Shay braced Mom behind her as she backed the two towards the French doors behind them, the two of them already spattered in crimson and screaming as Delia had Dad pinned to the table, tearing out his throat. Nathan was at Shay's side as well, moving in, taking his sweet time, his smile showing off those teeth, so *many* teeth. How did we not see that clearly before? How did we miss that? He kept teasing them, circling, laughing, making as if to lunge any moment for her and Mom. Shay held out a hand at him, imploring him to stop, her body stiff and braced with terror.

Amidst the chaos, I didn't see Rex anywhere there with the rest of his awful family. Emma and Bryceson weren't among those at that end of the table either, but a quick glance around the area revealed

Charlie and Nabhitha, the two of them already at the fire exit doors. If it hadn't been for a flash of bright canary yellow there, those shoes Emma wore that were completely mismatched for an evening wedding, I wouldn't have easily spotted her and Bryceson. I'd no idea how they managed to make a break for it in such a short amount of time. Then again, I'd no sense of time at all. Everything around me felt as if it was attempting to push through treacle. While Charlie and another groomsman, one of the burly bearded guys, hurled themselves at the doors, the red-haired hotel clerk from earlier and a couple of other guests had half-circled the little group.

Nabhitha had a hand out at the group readying to pounce, and she kept shouting something at them. I couldn't make out the words, but her tone was firm, so it was probably a warning. It didn't matter though. The crazies, cannibals, rabid freaks of nature—whatever they were—were too far gone to care it seemed. One of the guests among them leapt upon the bearded groomsman, jaws snapping in the guy's face, just as Charlie forced the doors open, stumbling into the night. I looked away just as he pulled Emma and Bryceson with him, and another of the ravenous guests grabbed hold of Nabhitha's hand and yanked her arm so sharply, it came right off in a jettison of blood. I'm not joking. Not at all. Wish I were. But, really though, Her Arm Ripped Right Off.

The screams and shouts grew watery and hollow. My headache had caused the area behind my eyes and across my forehead, all the way to the back of my neck, to tighten as if trapped there. Blood pulsed, thrumming in my ears. There was a faint ringing in one ear that just became louder in time to my breathing, which kept coming at me in sharp, painful puffs of air. I don't know if I was becoming weak with shock, but I felt as if my body had been filled with lead from the top of my head to the soles of my feet.

I could feel something there, something happening to me. It started as a slight twinge in my right arm, just a little one, barely perceptible. Almost like a tiny pinprick, a minute pinch, the kind you might feel whenever you draw blood through one of those ultra-fine baby needles. There was a pulsing pull, and I could feel something ripping from me. The colors, the smells, the noise all around came at me so forcefully, I shuddered, gasping as my lungs filled again.

And the pain, the searing burn of it on my right arm, wrenched me back to what was happening in the dining hall. My arm had been sharply twisted, and one of sisters who'd been sitting at my table, the plate-licker, had grabbed it and was tearing at the flesh of the inside of my forearm with her bloodstained teeth.

So many damned teeth.

She'd managed to chew away a chunk of my forearm, not quite to the bone, but it didn't fucking matter. She was eating the meat of my arm. It was irrational, unbelievable, preposterously obscene. Even worse, she was watching me as she dug in, her bright green eyes glinting at me with a mischievous light, like she was daring me to do something about it.

Listen, I think one's natural inclination, instinctive even, when faced with such a painful dilemma would be to pull the limb away from the lunatic standing there, chowing down on it. You'd be wrong, of course. Consider what would happen if you pulled on it just as I stupidly did: The arm-biter's teeth would snag on the tendons, tearing your arm further all the way to the wrist. I was damned lucky—and I mean SERIOUSLY lucky—said arm-biter's teeth didn't reach an artery. I'll chalk that up to a miracle. Even still, my forearm felt as if it had been scraped raw with a vegetable peeler and then promptly dipped in a bowl of acid. The pain sent a ripple of searing, white-hot agony all the way through my arm up to the shoulder. Tears welled in my eyes, curtaining my line of sight in a watery red glow.

Using my free hand, I felt around behind me and grasped the nearest utensil, a dessert fork, on the dining table and then promptly stabbed it into the back of one of Plate-Licker's hands that gripped my ravaged arm. Her vice-like jaws released my wrist, and she screeched, an eardrum-spitting sound that was instantly swallowed by the mad cacophony all around us. She pried the fork from her hand and threw it aside, her focus, all her fury, on me. Just as she was about to lunge, I had her licked dinner plate in my good hand, and I smacked it down hard on her head. The force of the impact was enough to break the plate in several large pieces and bloodily wound her, knocking her out flat.

"That's my sister, you fucking *bitch*!"

I heard the voice coming from behind me, and something struck my back so hard, I yelped and crumpled to the floor, falling to my hands and knees. I wanted to fold all of my body inwards inside itself, curl its hard edges against the pain, the agony of it. The sharp heel of a shoe ground into my back just between my shoulder blades, pushing me flat on the floor. My arms splayed out to the sides, my cheek firmly smooshed against the polished wood. I tried to wiggle away, but the heel dug right in, swiveling back and forth, back and

109

forth, before it released my upper back and moved down to my lower back. The small of my back felt as if a drill was twisting a hole through all of my meaty layers, searing there, causing me to cry out. I flailed my good arm back behind me, attempting to feel a leg, skin, anything vulnerable. Had I been even just a little bit flexible enough, I might have been able to find something there and strike, but unfortunately, I wasn't.

Naturally, I'd not taken any of the center's free yoga classes. Right then, I hate to say it, I could've used that rubbery flexibility. I stretched my shoulder muscles as much as I could muster, but the burning, the strain of it, was as excruciating as the heel digging into my back.

McManners, no longer particularly mannerly whatsoever, keeping her heel steady and the flat of her shoe smack against me, bent over to spit in my hair and then say over the din, "If she's dead because of you, I will drag your fat ass to the kitchen, find a meat cleaver, and then chop you in small chunks for a stew. How's that sound?"

"Fourth meal. Sounds yummy." I could barely manage a mumble. My left hand fumbled, and then I saw the fork there under the table, just out of reach.

She tipped her heel back, grinding so hard, I felt as if I was going to heave up that Cornish hen I'd eaten a mere hour or so earlier. My eyes went watery-wavery all over again. This time, I let the tears spill, hot and steady.

"With the right seasonings," she said in mid-twist, causing me to gasp. "Maybe some spring greens on the side. Glass of decent Beaujolais. Now that's a nice dinner. None of this Chateaubriand shit and the extra carbs…all the fucking *carbs* they insist on serving."

My fingers skimmed the tines of the fork, so I wiggled them and then stretched them further so they were stroking rather than skimming.

"Like it's a good substitute, Chateaubriand. Keeping us civilized," she said with a snort. "Letting our natural instincts and needs fall by the wayside. Making us forget who we are. As-the-fuck-if."

I finally had the fork in hand. Just needed a good moment, a steady moment, to strike. I couldn't move much at all.

"Chateaubriand. I mean, how pretentious is that anyway?"

"You people and your paleo crap," I muttered.

"What was that?" she said, her voice dripping with venom and ice.

"Or is Atkins still a thing? Fuck if I know. I don't do diets," I said just before I wrenched my body around, forcing her foot—that shoe with that goddamned heel— away, and drove the fork into her calf with as much strength behind it as I could muster.

McManners screamed in pain, gripping her leg, which, in turn, caused her to lose her balance. She went down, crashing against the table, grasping at the table and its tablecloth as she fell. The table tipped on its side as all of the fine china, wine glasses, bottles, silverware clattered to the floor, plummeting, raining over us. She had tangled herself up in the tablecloth and kept clawing at it, trying to get out from underneath it. I crawled over her writhing body, trapping her by planting a knee to either side of her. Then I bent my head over hers, and the blood rattled and whistled in my ears. I could see the outline of her face as she struggled to breathe well, taking large gasping rasps of air, sucking in the material as she did. In and out, and in and out.

I reached over for one of the empty bottles of wine from the floor, its contents having purpled the tablecloth in a Rorschach splotch. Then I turned back to McManners, who was struggling to break free from her food-stained cocoon. She kept twisting this way and that, nearly toppling me over, so I clocked her smack dab in the center of her covered face with the base of the bottle I had in hand. Her head fell back with a clunk. A tiny circle of blood began to spread from her nose, growing into a red blossom.

"Courtesy of my glorious fat ass," I said as I rolled the bottle away.

The pain shooting up my spine from the center of my lower back was strong enough to keep me from standing too quickly. Instead, I barely managed to slide off her body and lean back on my heels. After a minor squabble over shoes and style back when we were all getting measured for our dresses, I'd been lucky that I'd been permitted to wear pumps rather than high heels. Even though Shay spent the rest of that afternoon giving me the Boone silent treatment about it (I still don't understand why high heels are so important in the grand scheme of things), I knew it wouldn't last long. Mom and Dad were the experts at the silent treatment, but Shay and I had long since understood the value of interaction with our family and friends. In other words, we couldn't stay silent for long at all.

The shoes gave me an idea. It wasn't like we all had firearms within easy reach here. Even though it was reasonable enough to assume every local at the wedding was more than likely a gun owner, for this particular event, Mom had mentioned once that everyone had been warned to keep their firearms at home. As for the rebellious ones who were arrogant about their prized possessions and their self-professed expertise in Constitutional rights, there was no doubt in my mind they would've been firing by that point. I hadn't heard any gunshots, so it was probably safe to assume they'd been some of the first on the menu for the crazies, or whatever they were. My dad had apparently been one of them. As much as he and I never got on well, he damned didn't deserve what happened to him. He was my dad. *My* Dad.

It was going to be a gauntlet-like challenge trying to get out of there. I twisted back around to my hands and knees, readying for a bit of a crawl, and I took off one of McManners' high-heeled shoes, the one that had probably been digging holes into my back. Gripping it at the base of the sole, I swung the pointy heel directly down into one of her wrapped thighs. It pierced the tablecloth and her flesh, causing a ring of blood to rim the edges of the hole I'd created. I then loosened, and twisting it a little, freed the heel from the trappings of her skin and the tablecloth. That heel, good enough for me. A broken bottle would've been a much better weapon, sure, but I didn't want to run the risk of accidentally shredding something—or someone— important to me.

In my state as it was, anything could happen, and my withdrawal symptoms weren't necessarily going to be an asset to my overall well-being as I attempted to get the fuck out of there.

#

The dining hall's residents' screams and shouts coupled with the tinkling explosions of glass and china breaking, wood pieces thunking, splintering, had long simmered. However, the wet grunts, the lip smacking, the tearing apart of shreds of whatever physical existence remained, still echoed. The sounds of it brought me back to the situation I was in. Add in a splitting headache that refused to go away and a bad case of the runny sweats, and you'd have my experience there in a nutshell. I cautiously peeked around the makeshift barricade of the dining table on its side, its legs offering some stability.

The lengthy room looked as if bears had ransacked it. I couldn't see where much of the noises were coming from, but from my angle, I could just make out a couple of small groups of wedding guests

112

huddled around corpses, their dresses and suits drenched in gore. Mouths ringed with it. Hands busying themselves prying, tearing, ripping into fabric and flesh.

One group had Aunt Lil splayed out not far from where I hid, her bloodied face directly facing me. She had her eyes squeezed shut, and every so often, she'd emit a puff of air, a tiny sigh or moan. One of the guests who was enjoying his meal of my aunt had his wide back turned to me and was sitting crossed-legged at her side. He adjusted himself a bit, his suit jacket bottom trailing bloody streaks, sliding just enough that I could see what he was doing to her. Her satin emerald sheath dress, probably picked carefully to complement her copper curls, had been torn away from her torso. Her entire ribcage was exposed, the meat dangling from it in ribbons and strings. A cold shudder coursed straight down my spine as she opened her eyes, and her gaze met mine. My heartbeat thrummed a timpani symphony in my ears. She formed the words "Get help" right at me with her crimson lips just before she let out a piercing cry that could've shattered the night. The crossed-legged man had been toying with and tweaking the nipple of a breast dangling there, barely attached by a strand of meaty tendon, and he tore right into it, sliding closer to her as he ate, blocking my view of her face all over again.

A surge of bile burbled in my throat, and I turned away from the sight, ducking back around my makeshift wall and scooting back to the sisters' prone bodies and my own little arts and crafts project. My breath kept coming in tight hitches, so I sat there for a moment, working at the recesses of my mind to form a peaceful image, something calm and soothing. That's when my arm spasmed, the open wound there stinging, startling me back, reminding me I had other things to do as quickly as I could manage, all things considered.

Using the heel and the occasional assistance of a dinner knife, I ripped away several thick strands of tablecloth, taking care to keep my actions quiet and steady. I figured the clusters of crazies out there were too focused on their improvised meals that they wouldn't hear the tearing sounds coming from one corner end of the panel of tables. While I worked at tearing strips, I caught movement out of the corner of my eye coming from the sister who'd bitten my arm. She had come to from the hit I'd given her over the head with the dish and had rolled on her back, her fingers examining her skull, wincing at what she felt there.

113

Using her elbows braced on the floor, she was just about to sit up when I quickly set down the raggedy strip I was working on and slid myself towards her. Before she could react, I grabbed a handful of her hair from the top of her head, sticky with blood, and slammed her head down as hard as I could against the floorboards. The sound of it echoed throughout the dining hall, and I smacked a palm over her mouth just as she was about to yell.

I sat there, so still, feeling the cold edges of panic running its icy fingers through my chest, the back of my neck, up into my brain. I figured the worst that could happen was the obvious: I'd be discovered by one of the crazies who'd promptly rip out my throat, and I'd then be a late dessert, with a side of vanilla ice cream, for the rest of them. Ansley a la mode. Fuck that. Didn't even sound right on a menu. Still, I just sat there, waiting for the worst, hoping for, well, whatever was the second worst possibility. There was one of me versus at least a dozen of them.

Which led me to contemplate the question I ought to have been asking myself all along: What in the holy fuck were these people, and how the hell was I going to get out of there when there was one of me and, quite possibly, a horde of them?

Plate-licker kept squirming around, clawing at my hand, attempting to pry it away from her mouth. She was sprightly and strong. Must have been the extra protein, I don't know. The good news was that I'd weakened her by knocking her skull against the floor. She could've just as easily wiggled away. The bad news was that the wound on that particular arm of mine, its hand over her mouth, was fresh and open, and, of course, she remembered that. Her eyes narrowed; the skin around them crinkled. The bitch was smiling through my fingers. Then she dug her fingernails right into the raw wound, and the wall around me went red.

I bit down on my lip to keep from crying out in pain, and instincts sharply kicked in willing me, begging me to tear my arm away. However, I knew if I did, she'd scream loudly enough to bring those rabid dogs, those crazies, over. Not only that, she had her claws digging in so hard I'd only cause more damage to my arm if I attempted to pull it from her grip. So I did what anyone would have done had they not been thinking straight as I hadn't: I grasped a ball of her hair with my free hand and yanked her head up just before I slammed it back down against the floor. She let out a muffled cough, choking on her spittle beneath my palm, dampening it further. She kicked and squirmed, and kept digging into my arm. Her eyes were red and watery, their capillaries charting mad, fine routes. Nevertheless, I kept my grip firm over her mouth.

And I lifted and then thunked her head back down hard against the wooden floor. This time, her eyes rolled back, and she collapsed with a puff of air in my palm, releasing my arm from her excruciating grip.

My arm felt as if a lit lighter had been teasing its underside over the wound. I wanted to smother it with an ice pack, anything to make the pain stop. There was a large corked bottle of white wine, an Australian Chardonnay, laying on its side nearby, just within reach, one that had merely cracked rather than shattered. It was half-full, one of the bottles we'd started on but never got around to finishing. Didn't matter anyway. For one, it was sour, on the cusp of becoming salad dressing. Secondly, it would have to do, serving an entirely different purpose. I didn't know if it would do what I'd hoped it would, but I figured it certainly couldn't hurt (figuratively, of course) to try it out.

I uncorked the bottle and then poured the wine directly over my wound, drenching it, hopefully cleansing it somewhat. I may as well have been pouring battery acid on it. It took everything I had in me to keep from passing out from the pain.

"Girlie," said a voice, a lazy, masculine drawl. The word itself, enunciated with a slurring, rounded end, said directly behind me at my back, the dining table the only barrier between me and whoever it was.

I quickly wrapped and tied my wounded arm with the strips of tablecloth I'd torn away, creating a sloppy bandage of sorts. I kept my back braced against the tabletop. Sweat beaded my temples. I could feel it dampening my armpits. My pulse went mad. My chest felt like lead. The light danced before my eyes.

Perfect goddamned timing for a panic attack. I would not let it take hold. I would not.

"Come on out from your hidin' place there. Man alive, I tell you what, I smell your meat, puddin' pie," he growled. "Prime cut, girlie girl. Some good eatin'. You bleed fresh and fine. Smellin' so firm n' juicy. I bet you taste wonnnerful."

I didn't recognize his voice whatsoever, but I didn't care either. I wasn't about to indulge him in small talk, no way, no how. Instead, I had my sights honed in on the gauntlet ahead. My choices, as evident, weren't ideal, all things considered:

A) I could have opted for the suicidal route and come out swinging a high-heeled shoe and a bottle, hoping I'd take out a few of them before they pounced.
B) I could have risked running towards the fire exit door, possibly getting caught by a couple of them.
C) The rest of the wedding party's tables were still upright still bearing their dishes, utensils, wine glasses, leftover food and whatnot. A long tablecloth that trailed the floor covered each one. The line of them cut all the way across until it almost reached the area near the kitchen doors, leaving just amount of area around to get by for the servers and their carts and trays.

And each of those tables provided a hiding place, but even still, I'd have to be a sight more than two-steps ahead to keep any of the crazies from reaching me, especially the one directly behind me.

My back groaned at the thought of it. What was probably only forty feet or so away seemed like miles from where I hid, sitting there, braced against the tabletop, with only a slab of wood between me and a sniffing, whuffling crazy.

I could hear the guy sliding around on the floor behind my barrier. So I did what I had to do so as not to be seen. I commando-crawled my way under the long panel of tables, wiggling underneath each tablecloth, one by one, moving as quickly as I could go. I still had the shoe, its spike of a heel would be suitable as a weapon for the moment. Not as noisy as breaking the bottle of wine and using that instead.

It was going to be that kind of bad night for me, silent with bouts of quick movement as best as I could readily manage.

If only I really knew just *how* bad the night could possibly get.

ELEVEN

I'd no clue as to whether or not Mom and Shay had escaped somehow or were there, like Dad had been just after Delia took that bite, spread out au tartare all over one of the wedding party tables. I'd nearly reached the exit having wiggled my way underneath the line, hidden by the tablecloths, one after the other, sliding my body along the waxed floor, when I felt steel fingers close around one of my ankles. Before I could react, I was pulled back underneath the last table of the line, one hand gripping my high- heeled weapon tightly, the other scrabbling for a table leg to hold onto. No such luck. He crawled over me, the weight of his body pinning me beneath him. I couldn't turn my body, couldn't even move it. I was barely able to turn my head to the side. My neck felt as if it had been wrung. Twice in the course of a single evening. How many people could say *that*?

The guy chuckled softly the whole time and gave me a low, appreciative whistle.

He pressed his cheek against my ear. "You're one feisty lil' filly, ain't you?" he said. His breath reeked sharply of garlic and dead things. He licked and then sucked along the shell of my ear, making disgusting slurping sounds as he did. "You taste like sunshine an' honey. I bet you're as tasty on the inside as you are on the outside."

Then he bit down hard on my earlobe, and I swear to Christ I heard the skin pop between his teeth. The awful sting of it, worse than the first bite I'd felt on my arm. I couldn't scream, I could just barely manage to let out a squeak due to the iron weight that had squashed my body, melding it into the floorboards. The hand of my good arm had twisted and was trapped under me, its fingers still closed around the precious shoe.

"Oh, my goodness gracious. I was right. Sticky sweetness on the inside, too," he cooed and made a smacking sound that crackled and snapped in my ear. "It's good to be right n'all. I should crack you wide open like a fruit. Suck that sweet right outta ya."

I think the adrenaline was getting to me, making me loopy, because out of a fucked up nowhere, I'd an image of the guy smashing me over a rock and breaking me apart, like a coconut, and then digging the meat out with his fingers, smacking those bloated lips of his. Somehow, as twisted as it was, I found the thought of it hilarious, even though it would mean my eminent demise, a slow, agonizing one at that.

I did what anyone in a not-quite-right frame of mind would do: I laughed. I mean, just think of the absurdity of it. I laughed so hard, it hurt my sides and back and vibrated against the body of the asshole that had me pinned on the floor and was sucking the juice right out of my mangled earlobe.

I guess it didn't impress him one iota because his lips released my ear with a slurp, and his body went stiff.

"What's the joke, honeypot?"

For some reason, his question was even funnier than the thought of breaking me open like a piece of fruit. Of all the times to stop laughing at the absurd, that was one of them because it only served to anger him. He grabbed a hank of my hair and yanked my head up against his, enveloping me in a noxious cloud of dank breath.

"I'm glad you find this highly amusin', but we ain't here for a comedy show, girl," he growled against my cheek. "None of us 's eaten in the decade gone by, and we are past due for a hearty meal. You an' your kith n' kin serve that purpose, and that one alone, so you'd best keep that in mind before your laughin' and chortlin' gets to me, and I crack apart that pretty skull of yours right here."

I don't know if it was his breath or his response that jerked me alert. I'll chalk it up to both, looking back on it. The revelation itself was enough of a jolt to send that ice water slip-sliding through my veins, as if the horror in front of me, in front of everyone evidently on the menu, wasn't dreadful enough to contemplate. I'd have to keep steady and calm, steady and calm, so steady, so calm, while my ears rang, my eyes watered, and my body burned.

First things first, I'd have to get the son of a bitch off me.

"Can you do me a favor then, before you commence to eating?"

118

He gently let go of my hair, patting it down and smoothing it while breathing in my ear. "What's that, girlie?"

"Do you mind getting off me before you crush my innards? Can't enjoy the sweetbreads if they're pancaked. Am I right or am I right?"

There was a moment of silence, fleeting but there, as he contemplated that. Whoever he was, he wasn't a dummy, but I'd like to think his hunger was strong enough, mean enough, to keep him from making smart decisions. In other words, this sort of hunger was both his best friend and worst enemy as it would keep him less focused and more inclined to make stupid mistakes.

As I predicted, he did what was requested of him, and with his heavy body finally off me, I could suddenly breathe well. He kept a firm, hot hand on my ankle, keeping me trapped, but he didn't see what I'd hidden from him. I snapped around, sliding right into him, and I drove the spiky heel of the dress shoe right into his eye. His pockmarked, ruddy face contorted with rage as he squealed and clawed at the shoe embedded there. Pulling at the makeshift weapon, attempting to remove it, only served to cause him more agony, but I didn't have time to savor the moment.

Before the guy could grab me and pull me back to him, I was already turned around and shoving at the floor, sliding out from underneath the last of the line of tables. I stumbled to my feet. Then I spun around, backing my way towards the kitchen, my eye on the groups that were still engrossed in their feeding, their focus solely on satiating their evident hunger. That inexplicable hunger.

My stomach burbled and churned at the thought of it, that repulsive, inexplicable hunger.

Dad's body was still laying there, splayed out on the middle table, his face partially torn away, his torso a gummy pile of gristle and bone. Delia and one of Nathan's bearded friends, their hair matted with gore, were on all fours on the table, hunched over each side of his body and feasting on his innards. Dad wasn't moving. Wouldn't be anytime soon, if ever. Granted, he and I'd had our obvious difficulties, and I would've never forgiven him for his lack of empathy and compassion. However, no matter our problems, he was still my father, and the sight of him there, lifeless, disgraceful on the table, spread out as a meal—a fucking *meal*—filled me with sorrow. I suppose it was what grief felt like. Actual, heart aching, wrenching grief. What I'd felt after Simon's break-up with me apparently hadn't been grief at all like I'd initially thought. It had just been an empty gut-punch, carving me hollow. Real grief, honest grief, consumed the soul, squeezing and then gnawing at the heart.

It ate my being. And I cried.

My tears momentarily blinded me. I blinked my eyes a couple of times to clear them. I couldn't do what I needed to do if I just stood around nearby, bawling. Grief could come later. As it was, I was right there, prime meat au jus, live and out in the open among the crazies. They were so busy eating though, tearing right into flesh and guts, I don't think they cared if a meal got away one way or another.

Nevertheless, one of them was still on my tail, honing right in on my scent. The guy I'd stabbed in the eye with the shoe heel was worming, wiggling his way out from underneath the table, the shoe still embedded there. He wasn't a big man, nor was he particularly tall, but he was stocky and solid. His suit was creased and splattered with blood. His blood. My blood. Fuck, a mixture of *our* blood. Instinct had me feel around the earlobe he'd bitten. It was sore and sticky, but it didn't feel nearly as awful as I'd pictured. Little indentations on the front and back, like a canine had punctured it. So I'd get a gauge there, big deal. Or it would heal like a piercing. Big fucking deal. It was my arm I was worried about. That possibility of infection.

Didn't human saliva carry the worst sorts of bacteria? I'd cleaned the arm somewhat, as much as wine was able to "clean," but it certainly wasn't going to be enough to prevent infection.

The guy was already up and staggering towards me, reaching out for me with his twitchy fingers. Blood ran from his heel-imbedded, damaged eye down his cheek, dotting a crimson trail down his collar and onto the front of his dirty dress shirt. "I'm gonna eat that tasty arm of yours, girl," he said, panting and leering at me. "First, I'm gonna beat you senseless 'til you're out cold. Then I'm gonna rip that juicy arm right off and have me some good grub."

What was it with the crazies and my arms? I mean, what the hell. Had to give it to him though, he was persistent at least. He'd pinned me down once though; he wouldn't do that again, not if I could help it. I felt behind my back for the kitchen doors, grasping for a handle. I nearly sighed with relief that there were handles there after all. That meant they weren't the kind to swing shut, which would help if I could manage to open them and then close myself in. Then again, I didn't know what the kitchen held in store for me. Knowing the

120

appetites around the place, I wouldn't have doubted a whole cluster of them camped out in the kitchen, making Boone soup on the stovetop.

I tried to step away to the side to dodge his reach, but I banged a shin hard against something. As my (painful) luck would have it, there were two, dainty, upholstered benches on either side of the kitchen doors, and my leg had clanged against one of them. Some cutesy additions from a Pottery Barn or whatever the local home store was in that area. They were undoubtedly placed there as part of the décor because they wouldn't have served anyone practically unless they had been used as last minute seating at a kids' table. Right then, right there, one of them would have to suit me well for something else entirely.

The man must have been tired of having a shoe poking from his eyeball because he stopped within fingers' reach in front of me, gritted his teeth in a grimace, and yanked the shoe, heel and all, right out. The force behind his pull released not only the spiky heel but a gooey strand of gelatinous gunk, the remnants of his damaged eyeball, with it.

Naturally, I threw up everything I'd eaten earlier. Naturally, because that's just how it went. The remnants of a German luncheon and a dinner's worth of roasted hen, doused the man's face, his blood-splattered suit shirt and jacket, his dusty trousers, his scuffed cowboy boots. Now under normal circumstances, the sorts of circumstances that don't involve escaping cannibalistic crazies, I'd have run to the nearest restroom, locked myself in an empty stall, and attempted to heave out the rest of whatever was lingering there in my gut, intent on moving up in the world. Then I probably would've hidden there until everyone had left the building. I'm not the type to show my face after something awful like that. That said, however, there, right there in that particular moment, while the guy immediately forgot he'd gone partially blind and had jumped back away from me in disgust, I ever so politely apologized and wiped the curdled slime from my mouth with the back of my hand. So ladylike. So very wrong.

Yet I couldn't have asked for a timelier, more appropriate diversion. The guy was so distracted by the mess I'd caused all over his Sunday best that he didn't once notice I'd quickly bent and grabbed hold of a leg of one of the little benches, tugging it up, checking its weight. It wasn't as heavy as it could've been with thick slabs of wood, so it would do. Grasping my hands around two of its end legs, I lifted the bench, swung it up and around and struck the guy with it, hitting the side of his jawbone.

He flailed and toppled to the floor, and that's around the time when I fucked it up. Standard rookie mistake, literally looking back at what was happening. It's that sort of thing you yell out at a character in a movie, the heroine who had stupidly stopped and made the mistake of looking back to see the damage. You should never look back because that always gives whomever it is you're running from a bit of extra time to catch up. In other words, it stalls your escape; it makes you, more than likely, easy pickings.

In my case, the commotion I'd caused near the kitchen doors was enough to draw the attention of the little packs of bloodthirsty crazies, sloppily digging into their food. Those crazies included a deranged version of the normally prim and proper Delia Card, not to mention her lumberjack dining partner. My big mistake, and an obvious one that would've had anyone with any common sense screaming at me onscreen, was that I just looked right at her rather than turning tail and running out of there.

She looked right at me, her eyes dark and deep, her bloodstained mouth curling into a half-sneer. She'd been in mid-bite, holding my dad's heart in her hands, cupping it to her lips like a rare treat.

One of the crazies from the group clustered closest to me, a woman in a sparkling, ruby '50's swing dress who'd been tearing into another of the catering staff, let out a mad cackle, spit out the piece of gristle she'd been chewing, pointed right at me and shouted, "Whoooo, y'all, lookie look! Dessert's got legs! Catch it quick before it's gone!"

I backed towards the kitchen doors, bracing the bench against me, a barrier between myself and whoever got closer. Fucking ridiculous weapon. As soon as I felt the door handles digging into my back, I shoved the bench outwards, throwing it at the woman in the ruby dress who, with her crew at her back, was mere steps from me. Then I spun, wrenched open one of the kitchen doors and quickly slid inside the awkwardly narrow corridor in-between the kitchen and dining hall, slamming the door shut behind me, rattling it in its frame. The corridor must have been another cleaning storage area. There were a few shelves bearing cleaning supplies and a couple of mops placed to one side in a bucket against a wall there, so I took both of the mops and shoved each of them through the loops of the door handles to momentarily keep anyone from entering and coming after me.

122

The crazy in the ruby dress hurled herself at the door and then pressed her forehead against the thick frosted windows. She smacked her palms against the glass, and several others joined her, the lot of them creating a thumping beat in time to a rhythm that was frightening in its thunder. Palms turned into fists, and the force of those fists had me turn on my heel and go.

"We're gonna get you, tasty treat!" screeched the one in the ruby dress.

No turning back around though. I had to keep my wits about me from then on. The first thing I had to do before I could look for a way out was find Shay and Mom.

With any luck, they were still alive somewhere. I then remembered though that they'd been cornered against the windows the last time I'd seen them.

When everything went completely bonkers.

Nathan probably had them pinned someplace else. And where *was* our cowboy host, Papa Rex?

Fuck his family. Those freaks.

TWELVE

I rounded a corner of the corridor and found myself in the resort's winding kitchen that had been ransacked. Pots and pans, utensils, smashed crockery, dry goods, all of it scattered about everywhere. The floor was covered in a snowfall trail of flour and grit that crunched underneath my shoes.

There was no sign of anyone there. The place was eerily silent in contrast with the pounding at the door from the dining hall denizens.

"None of us 's eaten in the decade gone by..."

Those words. The ones uttered by the creep under the table.

"...we are well past due for a hearty meal. You an' your kith n' kin serve that purpose, and that one alone..."

The reminder of his words froze me in my tracks as I felt my breath leave my body. My chest felt as if it were coiling and constricting, so I gripped the edge of the sink took in a deep gasp of air, and released it slowly. That little bit of information could be key later. What the hell were they though? If the whole purpose of having a wedding was to eat everyone else on the guest list, especially the bride and her family, why stage it as an all-out wedding? What would be the point of that? They could've just as easily ganged up on everyone during the engagement party, right? Wouldn't have been nearly as pricey.

Rational questions during an irrational time. Make that an absurd time, one soaked in blood and lunacy.

Fucking crazies.

I searched the kitchen for sharp knives, anything sharp at all, but came up short. Not a carving knife in sight, which, considering the situation those of us who didn't eat people were in, wasn't particularly ideal. Looking back on what happened in the dining hall, I didn't recall anyone using utensils, including carving knives, to dig into their actual 'dessert' with all the extra protein.

Dessert. Right. I laughed and then coughed over the bowl of a sink, spitting up threads of mucus that refused to part ways with me.

By then, my headache had split into icy-hot clusters, poking away behind my eyes, at my temples, skewering points into the back of my skull. I turned on the tap and ducked my head down to take in a cold mouthful of water that tasted like chlorine and fresh dirt. I swished it around my mouth, gargled, and spit out the last dregs of bile. Everything, from the air around me to the aftertaste of the water, tasted heavy and metallic.

Stay hydrated, Leon whispered. *Dehydration can settle in without you even being aware of it until it's too late. It'll only exacerbate your symptoms.*

I took another long swig of water, despite the flat taste of it. The cold drilled into my teeth and gums right down to the nerves. Its pain only served to add to the cluster-fucking-hell of a headache I was suffering through.

Don't stay too long in one place, girlie.

(What was that?)

You heard me.

(No. That's not right. Leon would never have called me that.)

You'd better cut and run. Take those tasty arms and legs with you.

If that wasn't enough of a warning that I was losing it, I don't know what was.

Sunshine and honey. Suck the sweet right outta ya. Better get, girlie girl.

Even still, the old, mad subconscious had a point. I had to move. I needed something though, a weapon of any sort. While there weren't any knives around from what I could tell, there were plenty of inventive choices around.

I heard the sound of glass cracking and shattering coming from the doors leading into the corridor from the dining room. Fuck, if I wasn't wasting time clearing my head and figuring out what to use to defend myself. It wouldn't be long before the lot of them came bursting through the doors.

The kitchen curved around a corner and poured into a wide, open space that seemed to be designated for setting up carts and platters. A huge marble-topped kitchen island graced the middle of the room. What was laying there on the center of the island, in a grand display, was enough to cause my legs to turn to jelly and my stomach to go right into somersault mode. I gagged at the sight of it, my body willing my innards to come up, but all I could manage was a wrenching silent heave into my palm.

From what I could tell from the uniform whites that had been neatly folded and placed to the counter nearby—well, that and the name badge that was still pinned to the double-breasted jacket, one that not only included the name but a title—it was the bloated and carved headless body of the resort's chef. The carcass was greasy and shiny with a crisp, golden coating of skin as if it had been buttered and then roasted, and it had even been sliced like a Thanksgiving turkey. Out of all the thoughts that were racing, chasing each other through my brain, what I really wanted to know was when the hell had someone managed to have the time doing that to the poor man without being caught by any of us…normals? Had this been happening during the entire course of the evening? Who had done it? And who had been busy cooking the wedding dinner?

It was as if the gods of awful revelations had been intently listening to my buzzing thoughts. A tall woman in a flowy blue dress with a hem that danced around her ankles stood in the end of the aisle of the kitchen with her back faced to me at a cart where she was bent over and chattering to herself. Her words were manic, her gestures hidden from anyone coming from the dining room like I had. Her arms were busy in their movements, like she was diligently working on something. Still focused on her whatever it was she was doing, she reached over for a sea salt grinder nearby on a countertop and ground its contents over something there on the cart in front of her.

I took off my shoes, one after the other, and brandished both, one in each hand, readying myself. Sure, possibly handy weapons surrounded me, but I figured I'd make too much noise if I attempted to search the cabinets and drawers. There were pots and pans on the floor, but the sound of picking up one from the tiled floor, or possibly dropping it as I often did post-medication, well, it was merely one more risk I didn't want to deal with, not with what was happening. Besides, I had no idea what the crazies were capable of. I mean, their hearing could've easily been akin to bats and their sonar. I crept towards her, keeping my footsteps as silent as I could manage, one shoe in a hand out, ready to strike her with my own shoe's blocky heel. Pumps weren't particularly ideal given the circumstances, as I'd discovered the value of a skinny heel mere minutes before. However, my pumps were practical in that they felt like if I gave a solid swing to the face, they'd break a nose or some teeth. The thought of it had me tighten my grip around them, readying myself.

The tall woman then slammed a fist down on the cart, causing it to rattle with its burden. The sudden sound caused me to jump back, my stockinged feet sliding on the floor. I barely caught myself from falling just by mere luck alone. Maybe it was the adrenalin that kept me focused, maybe it was the fact I was suffering the worst headache and nausea on record, both symptoms virtually demanding me to keep sharp. Even still, bright spots of light bobbed in front of my eyes. I rapidly blinked, willing the spots to vanish, but they remained there, dancing in my line of sight.

"It's not going to match the place settings, *Alice*," growled the tall woman. "It's not going to match the décor. Everything you do is *wrong*. Everything you've done here, *wrong*."

Just the tone of her voice made me halt, wavering there as still and silent as I could be. My breath hurt, caught in my throat like a hard pebble of air.

Her chatter kept coming in a stream. "You'll be fired, you know. Who will want to hire you then? Who would be interested in hiring a middle-aged hag with no taste? Who, Alice? You have nothing worthwhile on your resume. You only work for family, and even your family hates you. You hear that, Alice? They *hate* you. And you know what? You're a failure, Alice. You've always been a big, fat *failure*."

Stupid me with my lousy timing and reflexes, I sucked in my breath a little too sharply, enough that it played in stereo surround sound in my ears.

She'd heard it too. She spun around, revealing herself and all of her madness to me.

I stumbled and slid backwards, dropping the shoes, and my back hit the sharp edge of the kitchen island, causing me to pitch forward onto the floor, painfully to my knees, right at the feet of the tall woman, the wedding planner. As soon as I looked up at her, everything went cold inside. I tilted back into a crab crawl on the floor, moving backwards until my back hit the island.

The wedding planner's once meticulously pinned updo was undone, pieces matted against her sticky face, other pieces snaking out, darting their tongues. A couple of flies flitted about her hair, frantic to find a landing spot, one that would allow them to carry on the bizarre osmosis they'd found with her.

Her leering mouth was rimmed with a thick ring of dried blood. Blood streaked the front of her neck as well and continued down in mottled splatter over the front of her dress that had gone from a bright, cheerful turquoise to a shade of blotchy, dark purple. A man's head—its eyes like runny, poached eggs, mouth open wide in a silent scream— dangled from one hand, the thick grey hair bunched and gathered in her tight grip. She was swinging it like a macabre purse. Judging by the remnants of the neck, the head had been neatly cut away from the body with a surgeon's preciseness.

Or at least a wedding planner's preciseness. A wedding planner who had a touch of obsessive-compulsive disorder.

A wedding planner who had obviously done this sort of thing before.

She casually tossed the head at me, like it was a ball and we were playing catch. The thing landed in between my splayed legs, face-forward into the crotch of my dress. I tried to scream, but my voice caught in my throat, and the scream came out in a tiny squeak of air.

The wedding planner was the only one who found it awfully funny. "Bull's-eye," she said with a giggle. "He can smell you properly now. He can smell your heat. And you know something? You smell so *so* good from where I'm standing."

Gagging, I pulled the head from my lap by the hair and threw it aside. Its bloody imprint marked my gore-streaked dress, another reminder of the monstrous insanity of the evening.

The wedding planner's face darkened, and she stepped towards me so she towered over me with a grim smile stretching her lips. While I'd rid myself of the head, she had apparently reached for a utensil from the cart, the only carving knife I'd seen in the kitchen, unfortunately. And, of course, she'd be the one to have it.

"Who's a naughty girl? We don't play with our food," she purred as she crouched down in front of me. "Well, I suppose it's up to Alice here to teach you how to behave at a formal function. Can't have you running around like a wild thing on the grounds, can we? I suppose it *is* fun to hunt though."

128

Her dress pooled around her as she wiggled around into a cross-legged position, attempting to get comfortable with me. She let out a dramatic sigh, feigning a pout at my expense, her hands and carving knife neatly in her lap in a twisted version of a ladylike pose, prim and wrong. That close, I got a good view of the bits of stringy gristle stuck in between her teeth. Her murky grey eyes were bloodshot. One of them had a burst capillary, mapping the white of the eye in squiggles that intersected with a pool of red. Her nostrils flared as she fumed at me, her hard stare quickening my pulse. She looked like she was contemplating whether I'd be best served hot or cold on a dinner platter, like the poor chef on the island countertop.

A fly had made a landing spot of the center of her greasy widow's peak. It hadn't been as visible until then since I was sitting there across from her. Every few seconds, it skittered and bounced from its resting place, buzzing in front of her eyes, agitated at the slightest movement from its fidgety host.

"What I want to know is, who was the idiot who let you get away?" she said, waving a hand at her persistent friend, trying to shoo it away. "Was it my brother? It was probably my brother. He's always been careless like that. Mama warned us he was gonna be a lot like Daddy. He'd want to appear social at first. Have us get to know our meal before eating it. We can certainly be *polite*, sure, but all in all, it's such a silly exercise in futility, don't you think? Who *socializes* with their food? Who attempts to get to know their food before eating it? Yet it's what Rex wanted of us. And you know how it goes…Whatever Rex wants…"

I guess the expression I wore gave my question away without having to even ask it because Alice, the wedding planner, read my face and nodded. "It took him years to find a mate in Delia. Her family was just as hungry as we were. Hungrier, in fact. They all had the urge for *so* long. They'd not feasted proper since her granddaddy's funeral. A few stragglers there her family knew in passing, some strangers who wouldn't be missed. That was so long ago." She wilted at the thought, her voice dipping into a wistful murmur. "Such a long, long time ago."

I had so many questions for her. Rational, reasonable questions. Questions that would never get rational, reasonable answers from any of these people, the crazies. Certainly nothing from the likes of Alice. Still, I figured it would be best to keep her talking and distracted while I examined the room behind her while we were sitting there on the kitchen floor, a couple of gals just shooting the shit.

I just wanted a weapon within easy reach. Wasn't too much to ask for, was it?

"So you...you people eat like you do because it's...what, it's in the blood?" I asked, somehow managing to keep my voice steady and curious even while I was terrified. Amazing what one can manage with adrenalin pumping, even when one's suffering severe withdrawals. Still, I kept my gaze flitting about from her face to the kitchen space and back again, hoping she'd think it was nerves on my end rather than what I was really doing.

"We 'people'? We 'people' sounds unsure," she said. "You don't need to be so forced around me, around any of us. You can call us whatever you want. It's the least we can offer you, that facade of independence. A little piece of dignity during your final moments."

"You didn't answer my question."

I watched in morbid fascination as the fly landed on her cheek and darted between her lips. Alice cleared her throat and shifted on the floor, moving up onto her knees. She then raised her arms and stretched her back as she reached, letting out a little groan as she did. Then she relaxed with an easy smile on her face. "Excuse me. I've been on my feet all day for the past couple weeks. It's exhausting doing this for a living when families make such extravagant demands of their children's weddings."

"At least this was for family though, right?"

She gave me a funny look. "Doesn't make it easier. It's much harder, in fact, only because when it's not family, we never have to see the clients again. We just hope they're good enough to leave a positive Yelp review," she said with a knowing wink, like I was supposed to empathize with her or something. "When it's family, it's always there, right there, as a reminder of what you did or didn't do. It's in albums, stories, framed photographs, all sorts of reminders. This one...*This* one was especially difficult."

I'd tuned her out a bit, keeping my eyes on her but my focus tight on something I felt behind me on the floor, something that had been making painful indentations against my rear end. My fingers crawled over it, feeling around at its length, its strange, cylindrical shape. Whatever it was, it was solid and a little heavy. If I struck her with it, it would definitely hurt her, perhaps enough to give me enough time to escape.

"But to answer your question, no, we don't 'eat like we do' because of our heritage. Although, that would be an interesting history, one for the local folklore. We love our lore, don't you think? If you have a story, especially one involving mayhaws, steer, and oil, well, honey, you're worth more than your weight in archive."

I smiled in response, unsure of what to say or ask. It was partially because I'd lost interest in anything she had to say. They were monsters. They ate people. End of discussion.

The object I had there in my hand while she prattled on was starting to develop a bit of its own heritage. It was definitely modeled after a gun. It had a thick grip, a muzzle, and a shrunken, slick barrel. There was no hammer and no normal trigger, however. Instead, from what I could feel, the instrument had a dial with raised markings at the top of its grip. It also had a plastic button there in lieu of a trigger, and as if I were delicately treating a firearm, I was so careful not to push it. I mean, I didn't know what the hell it was, but it felt like it could be *something* to use aside from the copper skillet laying near Alice in the midst of all the salt, dried beans and whisper-thin strands of vermicelli that had been scattered all over the floor and countertops.

"There's no history here. Some of us were born with the taste," she said, giving me a curious once over, enough to have me stop what I was doing lest she caught me with my new tool in hand.

It was right then when I realized what it was I had there, so I placed the tool down on the floor behind me on its base, my back acting as a shield. And using that hand, I fidgeted with the tool's dial, turning it slowly counter-clockwise.

"Some of us just grew into it. Believe it or not, there are quite a number of newcomers with us tonight. Got themselves invited to your family's little wedding soiree only because they'd heard the Cards were dealing."

"That's a terrible pun," I said. Anything to keep her interest distracted from what I had hidden and gripped behind me.

Alice leaned in and grinned at me. I nearly gagged from the rank stench of her body odor and breath, a potent combination of raw garlic, sweat, and rotten meat. She'd attempted to mask the smell with a musky perfume, but all it did was make it much worse.

"I think I've chatted with the food long enough," she said. "Daddy'd be so proud."

And with that, Alice pounced, her carving knife swinging at my face. I dodged the blade only just, quickly sliding to the side. I could feel the knife whisper through my hair as it nearly found a decent target. Instead, the blade struck the wood paneling of the island base, splintering it from the impact.

She yanked the knife until it came free in a sprinkle of wood shavings, giving me just enough time to fumble to my feet. My newfound weapon was fast becoming sweaty in my grip at my side. I was worried I'd drop it before I could even use it. However, as pure dumb luck would have it, just as soon as Alice was standing up again, she was already slashing away at the air on front of me like a wild-eyed maniac, and she kept miscalculating my every damned step. After a bit of a bob and weave, I held out the kitchen blowtorch, aiming its burner nozzle right at her mug.

"Dare you, crazy bitch," I said.

She stood there, her glance darting from me to the blowtorch then back to me like she was contemplating the risk. Then she grinned, the stretch of it cracking the dried clots of blood around her mouth and on her cheeks.

"You're using it incorrectly," she said and coughed around a chortle. "Wouldn't know how to set fire to a baked Alaska if you tried, sweetmeat."

"We can find out in a minute if you want."

Her chortle rounded into a laugh, full and hearty. "I don't play with my food."

"Yet you're standing around, wasting time, chatting with it. Thought you didn't do that either. When you think about it, it's kind of funny because you've been doing that for the past ten minutes, boring me to death."

Her grin twisted into a scowl.

"Come to think of it, since you're pretty useless with your knife there, just keep doing what you're doing instead. You can just as easily kill me with small talk about you and your family's tastes. Granted, it might take a bit longer than you intended. It might even delay your cooking time, but at least—"

I got the feeling my running commentary must have ticked her off because she didn't bother with another retort, interrupting my stalling. Instead, she stepped up right towards me, knife out at the ready, her face contorted with hot rage.

And I clicked back the igniter on the blowtorch before she swung. My teeth clenched, grinding down, and I kept my eyes screwed shut during the whole ordeal. I didn't know what was going to happen. I mean, she was right. I didn't know what the hell I was doing with the thing. I felt the windy heat of it and heard a clatter of something dropping to the floor and then her scream, piercing and clear.

I opened my eyes. My finger was still locked on the igniter as a long, lean jet of blue flame shot out from the burner, spurting out at its intended target. Alice's whole head was roasting, a globe of fire enveloping her skull, crisping it. The fire spread over her shoulders, embracing her in a bright, scorching cloak. Her screams had thankfully stopped, but the groaning, choking sounds coming from her during her last few seconds before she fell to the floor in a tower of fire and smoke were enough to grant me the possibility of nightmares for years to come.

There was a blur of movement, creamy fabric and pale arms through the smoke. A blast of white foam over the burning corpse on the floor. I clamped a hand over my nose and mouth to block out the smoke. My eyes burned and watered. The heat alone was enough to make me break out in a itchy sweat all over. My dress must have been utterly ruined by then, its material filthy and damp.

Still, I was somewhat present, somewhat out there in the moment. I'd survived. Again.

I didn't deserve it. Out of all the people at the resort, I didn't understand how it was that I'd managed to get on like I had. Me, of all people. Me, in all places.

When the smoke finally cleared somewhat, the air was still heavy with the stench of smoke, scorched flesh, and burnt hair. Standing there, fire extinguisher sputtering out its last dregs in her hands, was Shay.

(Of all people, in all places)

THIRTEEN

Shay's normally pretty, porcelain face was smudged with streaks of soot, dried blood and sweat. Her dress was in grimy tatters, but amazingly, the bustle and train were still attached to the back. She dropped the extinguisher and then bent at the waist, taking in great gasps of smoky air, causing me to jolt back to the present state we were in. I waved my arms about, attempting to fan the smoke away. There weren't any windows in the kitchen area of the building, but there were vents in the kitchen at least.

I was then there at Shay's side, rubbing her back. I drew her up, pulled her to me, and hugged her tightly. Her arms encircled my neck as she rubbed her face against my hair, breathing in and out in quick hitches.

"I can't believe you're here. You're all right," I said into her hair, patting it down. "I thought they'd—"

"Don't."

"Shay, I swear, I thought Nathan had—"

"Please, please don't say it. If you say the words, they'll be true, and I don't want to live anyplace where that's true. Where something like that happens." She went stiff in my arms. "Oh, my God. What…Who is that?"

I drew back from her, following her line of sight towards the body of the chef, all shiny-roasted there, and headless. I'd almost forgotten about him. His head had been caught in the fire as soon as Alice fell.

I pulled her in to me again, blocking her from the sight of the chef. "Don't look at it. I think he'd been cooking the whole time we were in there during the reception," I said as I held her.

134

She sobbed and coughed against me.

"Not to state the obvious, but we need to hurry out," I whispered. My voice was already scratchy from the smoke that burned my throat and stung my eyes. "And we should keep it nice and quiet. We've probably drawn the attention of some of them out there. First thing we have to do is get some car keys. Maybe Mom's or yours? You drove here, right?"

Shay murmured something soft and unreachable, I didn't quite catch it. We pulled away from each other, and I gently brushed the wet strands of hair away from her face and looked her in the eye, keeping her focus away from that awful countertop centerpiece, urging her to respond clearly.

She must have read my expression searching hers because she nodded and said, "Mom's out there behind her casita, waiting on me. She didn't have the key, so we found a place where she could hide. I told her I'd look for you."

"Where the hell's her key? We all got doubles, right?"

"She didn't bring hers. They were relying on Dad's."

"What, are you kidding? Wasn't she the one who always warned us to take both if we were sharing, just in case? This seems like a great 'just in case' situation."

"Yeah, well, she forgot, Ansley. She was kind of distracted. See, there was this thing going on, this little event she had planned called 'Shay's wedding'."

"Out of all the times to forget her key—"

"Well, it's not like we predicted we were all going to be slaughtered at some point during the evening. That's not what *normally* goes on during a wedding."

"Okay, so what happened to Nathan? The last time I saw you guys at dinner, he looked as if he was—" I stopped before I could finish that thought. Too horrible to consider, too unbelievable to conceive.

Shay visibly shuddered at the sound of his name, the thought of what the rest of my sentence entailed, even unspoken. "He got distracted in the dining room, so we got away. His dad needed him to help with something."

"What, setting up the grill?"

Her face went all slack and grey at that. "So not funny."

"Sorry, bad joke in bad times."

"I told you I didn't want that. I didn't want you to say *that*. Any of it."

135

"I know you did. I'm sorry."

Shay was trembling, so I rubbed her arms to keep her focused and calm. She nodded at the blowtorch I'd set on the kitchen island beside the body once she'd put the fire out. "Is it empty?" she asked.

I picked it up, put it to my ear, and shook the canister grip. A liquid in it swished around. "There's still a little of whatever fuel's left in there."

"Bring it, and see if you can find some lighter fluid to fill it up again. There has to be something else around here we could use," she said, looking around the kitchen. "It's a kitchen, right? So where are all the knives?"

Using my foot, I pointed the knife laying there within mere inches of Alice's scorched corpse. "Besides the one she had? I couldn't find anything."

"Well, then bend down and get hers. She's not using it."

I gave Shay a look, willing her to read my disgust. "Seriously? *You* get it."

She crinkled her nose at the body. "No way. I'm not getting near that."

"I'm not either. Besides the handle is useless. It's all warped. And, need I add, it was *your* idea in the first place."

"You're the one who did it."

"And you're the one who put it out. Besides, I already have this." I wiggled the blowtorch at her. "*You* wanted the knife."

"Are we really doing this while Mom's alone out there in the dark, probably freaking out, wondering where we are?"

"You could've taken her with you, Shay. Why'd you leave her back there?"

Shay shot me a dark grimace in response.

"What, she would've slowed you down? Is that what you were thinking? If it is, you'd best remain ignorant among the ignorant, judging your elders. Judging your betters like that."

She still wasn't interested in answering me. Instead, she started looking around the kitchen, resuming my hunt for a potential weapon. She found a little tin of butane, which she handed to me. While she continued searching, I refilled the built-in canister on the blowtorch.

"Mom can run laps around both of us," I said as I worked. "She's all lean muscle, like a finely oiled machine. I mean, seriously, the woman has worked out five times a week since she was—"

136

"Fifteen years old," snapped Shay as she pulled open a drawer and looked inside. "God. She's said that over and over again since we were little. All the damn time."

"Yep, like we were a couple of lazy slugs who could never compete. That's her all right."

"But you weren't with her when..." Shay stopped, unsure how to finish, and briefly met my eyes. "Mom's not as spry as she used to be."

I wiggled my floury sooty feet back into my pumps, closed up the canister valve with the little lid, and then stared directly at her. There was something off about what she'd brought up, not in the way she said it, but in *what* she said. It something I couldn't quite put my finger on. "With her when what? What are you talking about?"

"Never mind. It's not important right now." Shay went back to shuffling around through the drawers. Then she slammed them shut and scouted the countertops. "How do they not have a knife block? When your kitchen is this big, and there's no knife block...or one of those magnetic holders people have where they just stick them on for easy access. Where is it? Where the hell do they keep their knives?"

She opened a drawer under the kitchen island near me, and I slammed it shut, just missing her fingers, and I stood in front of it, keeping her from searching inside of it.

"What's going on with Mom?" I said. I wasn't about to let her change the subject, even if we were on borrowed time. Besides, I wasn't sure if I'd heard her correctly. Things just never seemed what they were.

"She's had some health issues. Too much strain," answered Shay absently. "Now do you mind? There should be *something* I could use..." Shay gently nudged me aside and opened the drawer. Doing her best to ignore the body there on the countertop, she pulled out a number of odd utensils and tools from the drawer, things best suited for certain, specific occasions, and reached in a bit deeper back and came up with an old-fashioned meat tenderizing mallet, heavy enough that it could certainly do a considerable amount of damage, break a few bones, smash in a skull.

"That should do it," I said right before I felt the burning tickle in the back of my throat and wheezed out a hacking cough. This time, I could presume at the very least, it wasn't a withdrawal symptom making me feel as if I was about to cough out a handful of needles.

Shay swung it a couple of times, testing its heft.

137

"So, tell me, what kind of health issues?" I said as I grabbed her wrist, stopping her swinging, if only to get her attention. I'd foolishly used my right hand of the injured forearm, and I don't know if it was the force behind my actions, but a white streak of pain traveled from my wrist up to my elbow, enough to have me release her wrist, gasping.

She sighed at me. "She had a minor heart attack. She had a decent recovery, but the cardiologist said her heart won't be as strong as it had been," she said, refusing to meet my stare as she did. "It was awhile ago, right around the time Simon split up with you."

I suddenly felt chilled, creepy-crawly, all over.

"Dad said he'd tried to get in touch, but he couldn't reach you, so I tried," she said. "I even emailed you, Ans. You used to respond to emails, even the ones Mom used to send out. You remember? The ones with the links to the cats behaving badly videos?"

"And the jumping baby goats," I said softly.

"I've never seen Dad hurt like that," said Shay. "I caught him—"

Somehow, I knew the rest. Somehow, *some way*. "You once caught him crying on the patio," I whispered.

She froze then, returning my stare with a quizzical frown. "Yeah. How did you know that?"

"We had this conversation earlier, before we went to get our hair done."

"No, we didn't."

"Yeah, we did, Shay. We were outside the ladies room. There was that woman in the orange dress with the little girls…"

"What woman? Little girls? What are you talking about?"

"Come to think of it, where did they go? I haven't seen any of them since all this—"

"We didn't have this conversation before. I'm not lying."

"I'm not either, Shay. We did!"

"I think I'd remember if we did. Kind of an important topic of discussion, don't you think?"

"Okay, then how did I know what you were going to say?"

"Just a weird coincidence. Like when you think someone's gonna call, and they do."

"You *seriously* can't remember?"

"I swear, I don't."

"Well, hell, I guess none of it really matters anyhow."

138

Shay was quiet at that, and then she said, "What happened to your arm?"

"Well, one of your guests wanted more than a slice of your…your weird chocolate wedding cake. Decided my arm would have to do."

"It wasn't weird. It was unique."

"It was weird, Shay."

"Fuck off. It's an evening wedding, and anyone with any taste at all likes chocolate."

"There might've been people who were allergic."

"That's a made up thing, chocolate allergies. That's like being allergic to water or air. It's not real."

"It's real. The Internet says so."

"Now comes the part where you say, 'I know a guy who knows this lady whose brother-in-law is from Canada, and over there, lots of people die every year from chocolate ingestion.'"

"Chocolate-induced hives. Look it up."

"Whatever. It was fabulous, and you know it."

I clumsily round-kicked her, just a tap, from the side, exposing everything underneath my mess of a dress. Shay grinned and grabbed at my foot so I was hopping around, trying not to lose my balance. Bracing myself back against the edge of the island countertop, I pulled my foot away from her grasp swung it at her rear end. She laughed and jumped to the side out of its path, bringing her own foot up to counter it.

No matter how playful we were, no matter how we could easily change the subject in the middle of everything happening while it all went to hell, I still hate myself for being so goddamned self-centered. I should have been there, should have answered. I'd blocked out everyone after my heartbreak, right up until the incident at work. If it hadn't been for Leon, and a few others at the center who'd kept me grounded and aware, I might have done something drastic, like get myself off the grid, estrange myself further from my family. Nothing could've been worse.

Well, that's not entirely true now, is it?

Not that it mattered. We should've been paying attention. We should've been moving by then. Shay suddenly had her foot planted back down on the floor, her eyes round and staring just past my shoulder. You know that feeling you get when your neck goes hot and numb, your back stiffens, the goosebumps spread up your arms because you know—you just *know*—something is there, directly behind you?

"Hi there," said a raspy female voice, one I wish I'd paid more attention to before. "It is *so* nice when late night snacks are already laid out, all peaches n'cream."

I turned around slowly, easing my hand away from the island countertop, the other gripping the canister of the blowtorch. The crazy in the ruby dress had brought some friends with her, including Rex Card himself and a couple of Nathan's bearded hipster-douche friends. They were all gathered in a tight pack at the entrance of the kitchen corridor, and all of them were drenched in a crimson film of gore. A couple of them, much like the pinstriped crazy that had been outside, wore trophy necklaces made from looped intestines around their necks. Most of them, like Rex and Ruby Dress, brandished brass candlesticks and wooden table legs, knives and cleavers.

"So *that*'s where all the knives went," muttered Shay from behind me. "That's not a bit of a bummer at all."

#

Rex stepped forward from the pack, patting Ruby Dress on the shoulder as he passed her. "Now what d'we have goin' on right here, y'all?" he said with a beaming smile, showing off those pearly whites. "It's Missy Prissy and her sissy." He gave Shay a once over, shaking his head appreciatively at her. "You know somethin', darlin', you make such a beautiful bride. I would've been proud to bring you into the fold. But alas, t'wasn't meant to be now, was it? It's a cryin' shame it all was just to appease some appetites. But you know how it is, girl, when folks get all stupid-hungry. They just can't see straight."

He was halfway through the kitchen, almost to where we were standing, when I aimed the torch at him and held up the tin of lighter fluid, tipping it forward ever so slightly in his direction as if I was going to squirt him with it.

"We've already charred your sister there, Rex," I said. "Want me to test this out again?"

His usually disarming smile and cowboy-gracious demeanor had taken a menacing turn. "Did you gals try her?"

"Did we *what*?" Shay's voice was up a couple of octaves, coming out as a squeak. I put my hand out behind me, signaling her to keep her cool.

"Did you try her out? Did y'all take a *bite*?" he pressed, inching closer towards us. "Y'know, she's not always been a wedding planner. She's been on this cooking kick that had her on the local news and some of those fancy national competitions. But she's had this rule she's always stuck to. She always said that it was important…No, it was *essential*, s'how she put it…it was *essential* that a chef test the food himself…or herself, as the case may be. All that testin' though's made her a mite plump n'ripe with all sorts of exotic flavors. I'd break her in myself, but…Well, you know, family n'all. Would be kinda unseemly."

"*Unseemly*," I managed to say around an incredulous half-laugh. Unbelievable. It would be funny if all of it wasn't so *sick*, yet there the Card patriarch was, saying that something amidst all of the insanity, all of the blood and smoke, was *unseemly*. That, itself, was "unseemly."

A lead ball formed in my throat. There was a glint of movement to our side, a shiny bit of red caught twinkling in the light. Ruby had apparently lost patience in the Cards' tradition of talking to their food. She'd come silently around the kitchen island, and she'd just about reached me and Shay, trailing her fingers gracefully along the stone surface of the countertop. She made a clicking sound with her tongue as she moved, her gaze on us steady and unblinking.

"What'd I say? What'd I say, girl? I told you we were gonna get you," she purred.

Rex tightened his lips at her and shook his head, signaling her "no."

She pouted in his direction. "But they're fresh, Rex."

"We're gonna save some of them for later, darlin'," he told her. "You know good and well we're gonna have t'store up 'til winter. They can hold for now. We got us all weekend."

That's precisely when Shay decided it high time to swing the meat tenderizer down hard on Ruby's fingers a couple of times for good measure, mashing them to grit. Ruby let out a ghastly shriek that made my teeth throb and my eardrums ache. I nearly dropped the blowtorch and tin of lighter fluid just from the shock alone, but adrenalin kept me steadfast with my grip just as Rex moved in. I squirted lighter fluid at him, soaking his face and shirtfront with it.

Shay drove the tenderizer hammer against the back of Ruby's skull. There was an audible cracking sound upon impact, and Ruby let out an inhuman groan. She nearly toppled against me, but I sidestepped

141

her tipping body just in time and pulled the igniter as Rex swung his cleaver at me.

The cleaver missed by a couple of inches, but I hadn't. The torch set fire to Rex's shirtfront, coating it in a fiery blaze, and he howled, rushing for the sink tap as—

His pack rushed in for the kill, their sights dead set on me. A couple of others were at Rex's side, helping him put out the flames, and—

Shay knocked the tin out of my hand, grabbed hold of my arm, and yanked me along with her.

The two of us ran.

FOURTEEN

I had no idea what kind of route Shay had us on, but she seemed to know where she was going. Some of Rex's clan were on our tail, but the fire must have spread some because I got the sense there were only a couple of them after us. We rushed out into the night through the back door of the kitchen and found ourselves on an unpaved back alleyway rough on dress shoes, definitely not suited for practical getaway use. We ran in the dark, keeping fast, silent, and focused. I heard the back door of the kitchen slam and a couple of catcalls echoing in the night.

While we ran, I tossed the empty torch. Then I kept trying to rip Shay's train free, attempting to step on the thing as we moved, but once we rounded another corner, weaving around a stucco wall, she stopped us for a second in order to finally detach the stupid thing. She hurriedly gathered it up and shoved it behind a tangle of bushes against the wall.

"Get rid of your shoes, too. You're not gonna get far in those," I whispered, keeping an eye out. It was just dark enough to go slightly unnoticed yet just light enough from the moonlight we could see each other's outlines.

"Are you kidding me? And tear up my feet?" Shay whispered back. "I'm not running in nylons. This place is nothing but dirt and rocks."

"You're gonna trip, and that will be the end of it."

"I'm keeping them on and doing just fine, thank you very much."

She then shushed me before I could retort, and I cupped a hand over my mouth. She motioned for me to stay still and gripped my hand tightly with her free hand, the other still gripping the tenderizer, and she had us creep around and crouch down low against the wall behind the bushes where she'd hidden her train.

A couple in raggedy formal wear ran by, both of them cackling at the night. Several others followed suit, and the last one in the bunch was Rex. He was the only one who stopped close to where we were hidden just take out a pack of cigarettes and a Zippo. When some of the stragglers did an about face, waiting for him, he waved them onwards and lit up a smoke. The flame from the lighter briefly illuminated his face, and I gasped into my palm.

The tattered remnants of Rex's tuxedo shirt and jacket were doing little to cover his charred and blistered chest. He'd been burned all the way up to his chin. His grimacing, worn face was coated in a heavy film of soot. As he took a couple of long drags on his cigarette, Shay shifted a bit, relaxing her posture, her movements causing the brush to rustle. She raised up her hand that was still brandishing the tenderizer, as if readying herself to use it. Alarmed by the possibilities, I braced her, holding her back with a palm out against her.

One of the stragglers Rex had motioned away, a stocky beardo who must have thought plaid jackets were trending, had turned around and headed back in Rex's direction. He was breathless, panting, as soon as he reached Rex.

"Boy, you need to get in shape before you try huntin' in the dark," said Rex around his cigarette. He then took a deep drag and exhaled chalky rings in the air.

The beardo laughed in mid-wheeze. He held up a finger as he got back his breath, bent over. Then he stretched up and said, "Mr. Card, sir, I just wanted to tell you how much I appreciate you letting us take part in all this. It's such an honor."

Rex chuckled, a rattle that came from deep within. My arms broke out in goosebumps at the sound of it. "All of 'this'? What, you can't say what 'this' is, can you now?"

"Well, it's still so new for me. Saying it just kinda makes it sound so…"

"So…what?"

"I don't know. It's wrong, isn't it? It sounds so wrong. Whenever I hear myself say it out loud, it makes me want to take a long shower, wash it off."

"Son, it's been taboo in polite society for a long while now," Rex said softly. "Perfectly understandable."

Beardo looked as if were trying to find the right words. "But I feel like I should... I should talk about this with someone who's been going through the same thing," he said, "someone who's been doing this a long time, longer than any of us. Nate said you'd been...you'd been like this since you were his age."

"An' you thought ol' Papa Card here would be your walkin' words of wisdom. El confidante," Rex scoffed. "Your generation. Hell. All y'all do is 'feel' like talkin' about everything, don't you? On your Youtube channels, your blogs n'vlogs, your Instagrams. You know what? You don't need to say a damned thing if you don't want. All you need to do is to satiate your newfound appetite an' satisfy your nature with God-provided sustenance."

"My girlfriend and I...We've been going through a rough patch. Stress from work. Money problems. Honestly, sir, if it hadn't been for Nathan—if we hadn't met him—we probably would've ended things between us," said Beardo. He kept shifting his weight from one foot to the other, back and forth, like he was anxious. "We didn't know how much we needed this."

Rex nodded and thumped the beardo on the back, squeezed his shoulder. "You're more than welcome to join us durin' feast year. When you're on your own though, you stick to them choice cuts an' no brains, hear? Stay the hell away from whatever pox Dell's trailer park cousins's been tryin' to sell everyone here."

"Nate mentioned something about that. Sounds nasty."

"Yeah, well, it's good what you kids do. Y'all *research.* Because you do, you know goddamned well if you wanna catch the shakes and shimmys, wobblin' around, knee-walkin' like a drunkard, that's what'll happen. And that's your right. You'd best go right ahead and do what they so recommend. Otherwise, steer clear of what they tell you. Choice cuts, and choice cuts only."

"Choice cuts only," repeated the beardo. "I won't forget that, sir."

"Best be movin' on," said Rex motioning for the guy to go on ahead. "Gotta keep up with the rest of 'em before they get it all."

My thighs were hurting by the time Rex took the last couple of puffs and then put out his cigarette, grinding it under his boot. He slowly turned around, the whites of his eyes gleaming, examining the shapes in the darkness. My blood formed slivers of ice that trickled down my back.

Rex halted, frozen in place. Because he'd stepped directly out of our line of sight, I couldn't see what he was doing at first. That is, until he bent over, and suddenly, he was right there, his face probably no more than a couple of feet away from our hiding spot. All he had to do was turn his head, and he'd see us as pale shapes in the shrubbery. Shay suddenly had my hand in her free on and squeezed it so tightly, it went numb and prickly all over. Rex was examining something there on the ground, something he picked up and held in between his fingers. Whatever it was he had, it glinted in the moonlight.

He let out a low, appreciative whistle. "Now what in the world," he muttered. He stood up right beside our hiding spot, pulled out his lighter from his pocket, and flicked the igniter. "Where'd you come from, pretty girl?" he said, chortling, as he examined the finger in the light. The finger with its manicured nail painted a deep shade and its sparkling, diamond ring.

I could swear it was Nabhitha's ring, Nabhitha's finger. As if to confirm my thoughts, Shay cut into my palm with her nails, digging right in.

"Papa, where you hidin'? Come n'get some of this! We got us a wild one here, and hell if she ain't a sight!" Nathan shouted from far off in the dark.

"Yeah, I'm comin'! Y'all just hang on a minute! Give an old man some leeway. I gotta find you kids in the dark, and my eyesight ain't as good as it used t'be!" Rex shouted back, and then he brought the finger up to his nose and took a long whiff. Then he licked and sucked around its crusted, jagged root where it had been severed.

Shay buried her head against my shoulder, averting her eyes. I bit my inner cheek to keep from crying out. When Rex chewed upon the skin and meat around the bone, like he was just enjoying a Buffalo wing at a bar, I silently gagged into my hand.

Rex slid off the ring from the remains of the finger and stuffed it deep in his pants pocket. Then he tossed what was left of the finger into the bushes where we were hidden. It landed, caught in a tangle of bramble directly in front of our faces, its painted nail pointing right at us. I held Shay's head against me, rubbing her neck, keeping her line of sight temporarily blind to what was there. I didn't want her seeing it, a morbid reminder that anyone who was a stranger to the Cards was pretty much at the top of the food chain.

By that time, my thighs and legs felt as if they'd been injected with hot wax, and my injured arm throbbed. I was numb and crackly all over and willed Rex to join his flock, if only so that Shay and I could get up from where we were crouching. It was as if whatever metaphysical entity was in charge had decided to fuck with us because Rex suddenly had second thoughts about throwing away that finger. He reached down into the bramble and dug through, cursing the night as he did, his fingers within easy reach of us.

Shay's breathing went still. I kept an eye on Rex's hand moving in the bushes, inches from our hiding spot. He finally found the finger, and as soon as he had it in his grasp, he pulled his hand away from the bramble. My whole body sagged in relief, but I still clung to Shay because I knew that all it would take was one mishap from either of us, one bit of movement in the bushes, and that would be it.

Whistling a cheerful melody, Rex held up the chewed finger to the moonlight, double checking for whatever it was he wanted to see. Then he slid it into his other pants pocket and walked away into the night, his whistle an eerie afterthought.

I waited until I was absolutely certain there was no one else around, and then I gently let go of Shay. The two of us slid up to our feet, and, holding hands, I let her lead me along the wall behind the chain of bushes. I had no idea where we were headed in, but I trusted that Shay knew exactly where to go.

The real question was, once Mom was in tow with us, how the hell were we going to get out when the crazies had besieged the whole place, and where would we go?

Out in the middle of a dead-land nowhere, our possibilities were awfully slim.

FIFTEEN

I'm sorry, but had I mentioned the evolution of my headache during that timeframe? I know it's not of any significant relevance to what we were going through, and there's nothing quite as boring as hearing about one's ailments, especially when there's a live bloodbath happening. Granted, I hear it gets worse when you get older, and back when the grandparents were still alive and kicking, it was all any of us in my family heard about. For days on end, it was all about the hernias, the arthritis, the back pain, the sinus pressure, the indigestion, the hemorrhoids, and it was always a mixed bag of treats. We never knew which ailment we'd get at what particular place and time.

Rambling. Apologies. But as dull as it may seem, I feel I ought to include something about the raging headache I endured during that point in time, while we were edging our way around the wall to the rear grounds of the resort, where Shay had foolishly left Mom. It wasn't like me to just give in and follow her, and it wasn't like Shay to take the lead. The headache is what kept me behind; it's also what kept me from making taking any risks. My head felt hot and heavy. The night noises had since grown louder. The buzzing drone of the cicadas, punctuated by the occasional faint chorus of mad laughter in the dark, did little to soothe the ache and flashes behind my eyes, the dull pounding in my temples, and the strange, shrill ringing in my ears.

My eyesight was affected by the headache, too. The more I squinted, trying to make out Shay's outline, a misty shape in the moonlight, the worse it felt. I longed to just crawl in a bed, any bed, with a firm pillow and a fluffy blanket and just sleep it away, sleep everything away, hiding from the crazies, burrowing myself down deep in bed as far as I could go.

"We're almost there," whispered Shay. "Should be up ahead somewhere."

The tenderizer gleamed, a sliver in her grip, the head of it still sticky with gore. I was tempted to snatch it from her since I felt a little vulnerable out there in the wide, dark open without a weapon.

"Careful where you step," she said. "There's a little incline, so it'll feel like you're walking on a hill, kind of like you're sideways. But keep to the basin. Step where I step."

I kept on her trail, shadowing her steps, cautious of where I landed. "Where'd you leave her?"

"She should be around here somewhere." But Shay didn't sound as if she was entirely sure of that. "That's her casita up ahead."

I decided to risk it. "Mom!" I whisper-shouted. "We're here. Let's go!"

"Shut the hell up, Ansley," hissed Shay.

"If she's here, she's not gonna be able to see us in the dark like this."

"There's someone on the hill over there, stupid. He'll hear us."

"Call me 'stupid' again, and I swear I will leave you to them. Right here. I don't care if it *is* your day."

"Fine. On *my* day, I call anyone acting stupidly 'stupid.' Thems the rules. Now shut up."

A flickering, yellow light rose and fell, rose and fell, up ahead on a hill behind a row of squat, little buildings. The closer we got, the clearer everything was in the moonlight. The buildings were a few of the resort's casitas, the ones reserved for the parents and families with kids. I only knew that based on their location from the dining hall building. If it hadn't been for the flickering light, I wouldn't have recognized the area where we were at all.

And then there was the smell…

Oh, the delicious scent of it, that salt-crusted, fatty-rich, charred aroma of roasting meat. Even though I'd practically gorged on dinner, and then later, my stomach had felt all acidic and topsy-turvy, my stomach still burbled and moaned, begging me to sit up and take notice. It urged me to consider the possibility that I was actually hungry, even in the worst of times.

149

The flickering light was coming from a campfire that had been set up on the hill. There was a tall figure near the fire, its back to us, roasting a large, crispy carcass on a spit over a blazing fire.

Shay and I hunkered down, keeping as low as we could to the ground without having to crawl on our hands and knees in the dirt and grit. Holding tightly to my hand, Shay led me to a steep outcropping of landscaped stone that formed the base of the hill and kept us blocked from the figure at the top. When the figure at the top of the hill whistled a shrill signal, Shay and I flattened ourselves against the jagged rocks that dug into our backs and tore our dresses. We stayed as perfectly still as we were able, hidden there in the dark shadow of the outcropping.

Someone from just past one of the casitas at the end catcalled in response, the sharp sound of it making Shay jerk. I gave her hand a firm squeeze in acknowledgment, reminding her she still wasn't alone. I turned my head a little so that I could meet her eyes in the dark, but I could barely make her out. If we hadn't been through the insanity of the evening, it would've been easier to see her standing there in her wedding whites. However, we were both covered in blood and grime, almost perfect camouflage in the dark, making it difficult to see us. All things considered, it worked out strangely to our advantage.

"She's near the air conditioner. I told her to hide and wait there," whispered Shay. She kept her voice was barely perceptible. I had to crane towards her to hear her. "See the end of the slope where it's cut off? She should be right there."

From where we were standing, I could see the air conditioner condenser and hear it whirring, but I couldn't see much beyond it. The firelight made the back walls, shrubs and cacti glow, helping the view a little but not enough for me to discern anything that looked remotely Mom-shaped.

"Hey, Patrick?" a masculine voice, rye-crackled and seasoned suddenly said just above our heads, causing both of us to jerk. "I need more of the marinade and a better drip pan. You mind?"

There was a snap-crunch of footsteps cracking twigs, moving towards the voice. "Couldn't find 'em , but I suspect them bitches are close by, lookin' for their mama." And that, *that* was Nathan. I almost didn't recognize his voice. It sounded muffled and odd, like he was talking around a wad of chewing tobacco.

"That any way to talk about your new bride?" said the other.

"I don't give a good goddamn about that girl except how sweet and juicy she's gonna taste," answered Nathan.

150

"Finger lickin' for the pickin'."

"You said it, brother. As for the other one, well...," Nathan said and then hacked and spit.

"She ain't half bad."

"You ain't half wrong."

I felt a shudder worm its way through Shay. Her hand was growing clammy, too. I couldn't see the whites of her eyes anymore as she'd screwed them tightly shut, her face crinkled in horror and disgust. I couldn't even imagine what she was going through.

Her new husband, a monster. An honest to God, human *monster*.

Her wedding, a sham. A nightmare of an excuse for easy access to food.

I still couldn't begin to believe, accept, let alone understand, any of it. Couldn't fathom how they could possibly get away with it. It was all such a long, cruel fever dream.

The other party, the one in charge of the cooking, I didn't recognize his voice, but it wasn't as if it was all that hard to guess if he was a guest of ours or the Cards. I mean, come on.

Not like we had many guests left, I don't think, but who had time to keep score?

"I'll see what we got in the kitchen for you," said Nathan, who was suddenly right there, directly above us at the top of the incline as well. "Speaking of, you hear? We had to cart Auntie Al away."

"Yeah, I heard. Such a shame."

"Cryin' shame. She was a good cook."

"Hey now."

"What's that?"

"Your aunt know how to make a marinade like mine? Let's face it, she never could handle a spit. Couldn't even handle two fires under the meat neither. She just stuck the midsection in an oven and basted it every hour. Sometimes, she'd even forget, and the meat would be all dry an' stringy. This here, my friend, this takes patience and diligence. Your auntie had none of that. She was fidgety. Plumb crazy as a bullbat."

"You shut your trap."

"Man alive, you could hear that woman cluckin' a mile off, but you still wouldn't find her nest."

Nathan spit and then let out a warning whistle, low and sharp. "I mean it, Pat. S'no way to talk of the dead."

151

"What, I hurt her feelings, Nate?" Nathan must have done something next, given some kind of warning gesture like he'd strike because the other one became apologetic. "I'm jokin', friend. No need for that. Heart in humor, that's all. Besides, I can't have you makin' a mess of my beautiful face here."

"A face so ugly your mama takes you everywhere so she don't have to kiss you goodbye."

"And that joke's older than dinosaur pie."

"I have a million more."

"Yeah, I'm sure you do, brother. Keep 'em comin' while I'm on my feet all day, slavin' over a hot roast for y'all. I can't tell you how entertainin' that is for me."

There was a brief moment when they went silent. I heard Shay hyperventilating, so I reached for her and reeled her in close as quietly as I could manage. We clung onto each other there underneath the outcropping, both of us silently willing the two of them to leave. And right then, I had a horrible feeling lurking there, waiting to pounce. I knew exactly what it was, but the part of me that was still in the denial stage refused to grant it any sort of credence.

Nathan hocked another wad just over our hiding place and then said, "Be so good as to remind me once again...? More of that marinade of yours and—What else you want?"

"Bigger drip pan. She needs something wide and sturdy," said the other.

Nathan whooped at that. "Could make a dirty joke out of it, but I'll let your mind play games for once," he said, laughing.

"Now that ain't nice, thinkin' about your mother-in-law in that way."

That was it; that's exactly what was lurking there during their entire awful conversation. Shay's body trembled against mine. She silently sobbed. As for me, I couldn't react. I just couldn't. Aside from the physical pain and difficulty breathing, I felt nothing inside but a cold, wide emptiness, like someone had scraped out the last bits and pieces I had left in me.

I wasn't there; I couldn't be. None of it could've possibly been happening.

"She *was* my mother-in-law," said Nathan, chuckling.

He leapt down from above and landed, feet first, in a crouch, directly beside us. Then he stood up to his full height and, with one arm out, casually leaned against the rocky wall of the outcropping.

"Now she's Sunday dinner," he said, smiling, his teeth gleaming in the dim light. He then grabbed for my sister, but no doubt driven by a sudden surge of adrenalin, Shay was faster. She viciously cracked him across the jaw with the hammer of the tenderizer, and the force behind her swing was enough to send Nathan's head knocking against a stone in the wall.

I pulled her with me before Nathan could regain his composure. The two of us ran off, heading around the little row of casitas towards the back entrance road of the resort. I didn't know where we were going this time since our plan to pick up Mom and get the keys to her car had been cut short.

When Shay had us take an alternate path from the fork in the dirt road, at first, I had no idea what she was up to and had to keep myself from making any noise by asking her. Then I suddenly knew where we were going, and by then, there just wasn't a thing I could do to stop her from leading me back to the casita that doubled as the goddamned honeymoon suite.

And the crazies, well, they knew exactly where to find us.

We were stupidly there on their turf after all.

#

Just as soon as we made it to the wooden door of her casita, a building that was set apart from the rest in its own landscaped area of the resort, Shay had me keep an eye out for trouble. While I played lookout, she first handed me the meat tenderizer, and then she bent and reached up underneath the slip layer of her dress where she'd, apparently, kept a little satin bag snapped to the underside of the waist of her skirt. She quickly unzipped the bag and removed a key.

Sharp whistles coming from all around the resort grounds startled us both. Shay nearly dropped the key, but I steadied her, easing her back to what she was supposed to be doing. She fumbled with the key, rattling it around in the door lock.

"The only resort on the planet that still uses metal keys," she muttered. "And they don't even bother to oil the damn locks."

Right then, someone called her name from far off. She stopped working on the lock just long enough to look around for the source.

I gave her a nudge. "I can do that, and you can watch, if you'd rather."

153

She turned back to the door and twisted at the lock once more. It finally caught, and she swung the door open.

"Shaaaaaaay, my love, my honeypie. In sickness and health. For better, for worse. Hey, where ya goin'? You know I got a key, sweetness," cooed Nathan. He was strolling down the hill from the other end of the road, walking towards us all by himself. The whole side of his face from his cheekbone to the line of his jaw was starting to swell. "I think you broke some of my teeth with that thing, honey. Whole face hurts like a sonofabitch. You might wanna get rid of it before I take it from you and start using it on that pretty mug of yours. Pulverize it to a Picasso."

"I am not giving that boy the satisfaction. Not tonight," she said as she motioned me inside with her. "Not ever. Crazy fucker. Sickness and health my ass."

With that, she slammed the door shut just as Nathan made it to the rocky pathway that led right up to the casita. She locked it from inside, wisely using the heavy deadbolt in lieu of the key lock.

"I just want to say, I'm so proud of you and your newfound rage," I said. "Keep on with your badass self."

Nathan pounded hard on the door and then rattled it, shaking it in its frame. "Shay! Hey, Shay, honey, I'm sorry. I didn't mean it," he said, and I had to hand it to the guy, his tone was almost convincing. "You gotta know I wouldn't really hurt you. You're my wife. Only cowards beat their wives. I wouldn't do that. I was raised right."

"Kinda funny you mention that, buddy, because from here, it looks like you were raised to eat people," I said. Couldn't help myself.

It was enough to get him angrier. "Stay out of this, cunt," he snarled. "This is between the married people. Man and wife. Comprende? Feminazis don't have a say in any of this."

Shay and I exchanged a grimace.

"Did he seriously just call you the c-word?" she said. "He did not."

"He did, *and* he said 'feminazi'. You know, I never thought I'd hear that out of someone's mouth…and in real time."

"Sweet man of mine knows how to charm the ladies."

"For shit's sake, open the door, Shay," he said, punctuating it with another thump. Then his tone softened. "I'm not gonna hurt you, sweetheart. Just wanna talk. That's all. Just talk."

Shay snapped, "Eat a shit sandwich, Nate."

"Not on le menu se soir, ma soeur," I said. That one earned a scowl from my sister.

"Shay, I'm coming back for you, darlin', and I'm bringing some friends," said Nathan, grit in his voice. "You girls can try an' make a run for it, but keep in mind, girl... Better I catch you than my papa. He's none too happy after what you done."

Shay and I exchanged a worried look. We then stood there, quiet and still, waiting for some noise, some sign that Nathan had actually left.

"I think he's gone," said Shay, letting out a big sigh of relief. "I can't believe it. I just can't."

I didn't understand. "You can't believe what?"

She stared at me, a frown lining her face. "I can't believe you were right this time."

Still didn't get it. "Right about...?"

"About Nathan."

"What'd I say about Nathan, aside from the usual?"

"That he wasn't good for me."

I managed a grin. "So the usual."

She laughed, a decent attempt. "The usual, yeah."

"Now that I've seen him in his element," I said, "I don't think he's right for *anybody*."

She snickered and said, "We should find those keys."

Shay rummaged through a handbag that had been left on a sofa near the king-sized four-poster bed. The bridal suite had at least twice the amount of room than my guest casita had on the opposite end of the resort. Someone had set it up nicely with posh candlesticks with white pillar candles placed here and there throughout the room. There was also a champagne bucket that held nuggets of ice and a bottle of Veuve Clicquot on an end table and small bouquets of fresh wildflowers set in delicate crystal vases, none of which were there earlier when we were getting ready. When the hell did that horrid wedding planner manage to squeeze in time to get the place decorated, especially while she was apparently busy roasting the chef?

Of course, Shay's signature travel mess marked the space as her own personal territory. She'd left her customary pile of clothing she'd brought with her dumped on the bed in a jumbled heap. The vanity was still also littered with her stuff, her makeup case having been emptied of all of its sticky and powdery contents.

In contrast, Nathan's post-wedding attire, or what I assumed what he would've worn had the whole experience been authentic, had been left carefully over an armchair. Even his shoes had been buffed and set neatly in front of the chair. If that wasn't a sign that he and Shay would've driven each other bonkers at some point, that they weren't quite right for each other, a touch of cannibalism would have to do the trick.

As mad irony would have it, Nathan's obsessive neat-and-orderly fetish worked to our advantage. While Shay had dumped the contents of her bag all over the sofa and was hunting for her car key in the chaos, I discovered Nathan's cell phone right in plain view, charging on one of the end tables beside the sofa. I picked it up and clicked it on.

"You know the passcode to this thing?" I asked half in Shay's direction, half to the space around me. "I've a feeling it might be something like…oh, I don't know…his mom's birthday…or the day he took his first bite of human flesh…? What do you think?"

Shay held up the car fob for me to see. "Found it!" Then she saw the phone in my hand. "It's not gonna work anyway. Couldn't get a signal."

"I know, but I was just curious if it was different in the honeymoon suite since it came with champagne and flowers," I said as I entered each and every combination of Nathan-numbers I could think of. "Why would anyone come out here if there wasn't a signal anywhere?"

"Yeah, it was one of the reasons why Nate wanted the wedding here," she said, and when I glanced at Shay, a look of realization slowly edged its way over her pretty features. "He said it was ideal for a weekend away from work. Plenty of isolation from everything."

"Doesn't that make you wonder why a place would advertise it has modern necessities like Wifi access if it was an out-and-out lie? Oh, and speaking of, don't you just love how they advertise with the word 'amenities' rather than 'necessities' like it's just something extra and totally frivolous?"

"No Wifi. No reception. And no firearms on the premises," she said, recalling.

"I thought about that," I said, nodding. "Dad must've shit a brick when he found out he couldn't bring his babies."

156

"Delia insisted *no one* bring their guns. I mean, when she said that, and even had it put on the invitations, I was more surprised that Rex agreed to that. But you know something? It makes perfect sense now."

"Wait, hold on. How? How does that make sense at all? They could've just as easily shot us beforehand. Isn't that what hunters do here? I mean, I'm no expert, but isn't it practical for them to keep some distance from their target?" And then it dawned on me. Stupid, stupid me. I knew all along. "Not if they didn't want their prey to be armed, too."

Shay, nodding, slowly made her way over to me. "And not if they wanted the thrill. Isn't hunting all about the challenge of the kill? The excitement?"

We both jumped when the door to the suite started rattling in its hinges once again. "Hey, ladies, time to open up and take your licks!" hollered Nathan. There were a couple of wolf whistles and jeers coming from outside as well, no doubt the "friends" he'd mentioned he'd bring along with him.

"Some challenge," muttered Shay. She jumped again when Nathan, or one of his friends, started thumping hard against the door. It sounded like someone was kicking it rather than rapping on it with a fist.

"How heavy do you think that dresser is?" I asked, nodding in its direction.

Then the room went all fuzzy. My whole body felt covered in pinpricks, and my headache was so bad, I was seeing spots again. The faint, buzzy ringing in my ears and the thumping coming from the door certainly didn't help matters. I felt the room sway and spin, causing me to tightly grip the armchair to keep my balance. Something wasn't right. It wasn't the lunacy we were facing. It was something else, like the moment you have when you're falling from a high point in a deep dream, right on the edge of waking. I felt like my body was wanting me to wake, but my mind was playing obstinate, enjoying the free-fall.

Shay was suddenly there again, right beside me, her grimy face lined with worry. She held my face in her hands, a palm on each cheek, as she met my eyes.

"Hey," she said, nodding at me. "It's okay. You're okay now."

"I'm sorry. I just felt…*funny*. This isn't right. None of this is right."

157

She managed a chuckle, nodding. "Girl, you said it. *None* of it is. Now let's move that dresser and block the door. Give those assholes the challenge they've been wanting."

We made our way over to the dresser and got on either end of it. It was solid and wide enough and looked as if it had been made from some decent heavy wood, like it could last a beating or two.

There was a sudden, massive thunk to the door, and I could swear it was starting to splinter in the frame, even against its deadlock. "We're coming, ladies," Nathan cooed from behind the door. "Better get yourselves all nice an' pretty for the boys here. Put on those smiles, but leave the perfume and hair product. We like you au naturel."

We waited, listening, breathing heavily. There was finally silence on the other end.

"Just when I thought he'd never shut the hell up," I said.

Shay wrinkled her nose. "And did he really just say 'au naturel'? When does it end?"

"Your hubby's disgusting," I braced myself against the dresser. "Okay, let's move this bad boy."

I motioned with my head towards the door, and using all of our combined weight, we slid it carefully from one side of the huge space all the way to the door.

"Don't ever say that again," said Shay as she got her breath back.

"Say what again?"

"'Hubby'. I hate that word."

"Why not? Rhymes with 'tubby' or 'flubby'."

"It's not the rhyming. It's the implication."

"Do you think this will hold?"

Shay made a show of examining the dresser before she said, "It should, but do we have anyplace else to hide?"

"Bathroom seems the only viable option," I said and could hear the panic building in my voice. "Get inside. I'll bring one of those chairs. We can use it to brace the door."

Shay grabbed the mallet, taking it with her into the bathroom, while I picked up one of the dinette chairs and then followed her in.

There was another series of thumps against the door, which was on the verge of cracking, even against the weight of the dresser. The thunks were in time to the whoops and jeers and catcalling happening right outside.

"We're gonna have us some fun with *you*, baby," said Nathan, his voice brittle and mocking. "Sugar'n spice, *everything* nice!"

My heart was doing double time in me. I meant what I said, sure. Let's face reality though. We really didn't know what we were doing. This wasn't one of those emergency situations where plans could've possibly been made in advance, and the escape route was going to be clear. Still, I'll give it to the two of us; by then, it didn't matter. We were letting Sister Adrenalin guide us in all of our madness.

Shay's face had gone red. "Get bent, fuckface!" she hollered before she slammed the bathroom door shut and promptly locked us in.

SIXTEEN
(WHAT IN THE ACTUAL FUCK?)

It's just like them to play. I keep my arm protectively around my sister, all of this during our third or fourth circle of hell of the night.

"Shay! Hey, Shaaaaaay. I really need some painkillers, darlin', so I'm gonna have to break down the door like I did earlier, sweet thing. Hate to do it though. Don't wanna have to foot the bill for it. You know we only put down $500 for incidentals, and I don't want all of it to go to a couple of busted doors just because you wouldn't let me get some teensy pills outta my shave kit." Nathan laughs. It's a cruel cackle, like it wouldn't make a difference in the world. He's been primed to do it anyway.

"Shay, c'mon, sweetheart," he purrs. "You know, we're married now. This kinda thing, lockin' me out. It ain't right. It's hardly befitting a wife. Not in God's eye."

It's quite enough for me, all of it. "Correct me if I'm wrong, Nate, but I don't think God had homegrown cannibals in mind when He created mankind."

"Hush now, bitch," Nathan growls. "Once again, no one asked for your goddamn opinion. Gonna have to stitch that mouth of yours shut just to have some peace n' quiet when we eat you."

Even now, I can't help myself. "Man, I love it when a Christian boy sweet talks me."

"Shay, open the FUCK UP!" roars Nathan, causing us both to flinch. He thumps the door again and there's the sound of something sliding up against it. He must have been leaning against it. There's the thumping of steady footsteps. Low murmuring. Several voices out

160

there, whispering something about us. I don't know how many there could possibly be by now, and I don't even want to know how many of *us* there are left alive. Us. Who would've thought a wedding could turn into an us-versus-them kind of affair, really? Well, all right, maybe since it's a matter of the bride's family versus the groom's family, it makes a little more sense, makes it seem a little more reasonable, but is *this* reasonable?

These thoughts, these tangled thoughts worm and wiggle their way in. My mouth is chalky-dry. It isn't just my arm that burns. Everything hurts, and it's growing harder for me to take deep breaths.

Shay must've seen something in me. A look of concern has spread across her face.

"I'm okay," I whisper. "I just need to get my medication."

"Don't think we should attempt that right now," she says. "Can you manage?"

She'll never understand. No one does, and now, especially now, it's frustrating to even try to convince anyone that I'm not okay, that it's making me sicker every damned day.

"Yeah, I'll be all right." I won't be, but what does it matter. It's either suffer in silence and keep on or...well...get eaten.

Shay and I are back to being quiet, the two of us straining to hear, looking at the other intently. Just as Shay's about to speak, I hold up a finger for her to wait.

It's silent out there in the bedroom.

"Monster," Shay says softly. Her eyes have gone hard and glassy, but the sadness, the regret, the how-did-I-not-know's...evident.

"He said he has pain meds? " I say. Desperate times. Desperate measures. It will relieve the pain in my arm and numb the heat in my head. Before she can answer, I'm already up and rummaging through the Dopp kit that had been left on top of the toilet tank.

"He does, but it has Codeine in it, Ans. You don't want to take that."

"I wish I could transfer the pain I'm experiencing here to you," I say as I search. "You'd be looking for anything you could get. My arm is on fire. It's like someone injected battery acid into it."

"If you have to, take half of one."

Half of one. If only. But she knows that.

In my desperation, I can't find any sort of pill container, but my fingers clasp around something cold, metallic. A key. It feels like one of the casita keys judging from the intricate pattern of its bow. Heavier though, solid, like it would open the gate to a dungeon. I pull it out and hold it up, taking a look at it. It's definitely one of the resort keys, but it's longer and thicker, its casing a dingy wrought iron with a double bit at the end. A heavy skeleton key.

Shay doesn't seem to recognize it either, as she's staring up at it curiously, too. I waggle it at her, and she shakes her head. "Probably for another casita," she said. "It's got the same design as the others."

"It's heavier, like it's for the main gate maybe…?"

She frowns, deep in thought. "What would he be doing with that?"

"It's not like the Cards don't have access since they've pretty much taken up the entire resort."

"Yeah, but why would it be in his shave kit? That means he'd packed it with his stuff when we were getting ready."

"Whatever. I say we keep it. We may need it." Curiouser and curiouser. "Let me ask you something," I say, tucking the key down my dress front. "Who owns this place?"

"Family friend, or so I was told," Shay says.

"Yeah, I remember that part. But who's the friend?"

"I don't know. He has a lot of them. You saw. Pick one. Charlie maybe?"

"No, from what I saw," I say, "he was trying to get away like the rest of us in the madhouse."

"Then my money's on a friend of Rex and Delia's."

"Or Rex and Delia own the place."

She nods. "*That* would make sense. Keeping it insular. Family 'friends,'" she says with a sneer.

"One percenters with their oil money and their fucking barbeques."

Shay shakes her head at the thought of it. "I wonder how long they've been doing this. How many people have gone missing? How is it no one is even asking anything? No one even *knows,* Ansley."

"Rich people. They can do anything to anyone at any time. Must be a dream." I feel something brush lightly against my skin, a slight, cool breeze that soothes the back of my neck, all the way down my arm.

When I'm just about to turn and take a look, the air around us suddenly explodes in sound, thundering hard against the door again and again, rattling the chair rapidly. Shay and I both scream, shaken by the noise. She scrambles to her feet and scoots beside me, brandishing the tenderizer at the ready. There's nothing worthwhile for me to use as a possible weapon except—

"Give us a minute, honeypie," Nathan purrs from beyond the door. "We're comin' in. Be with you in a moment."

—there *is* a way out. How did we not catch it earlier? Distractions, I suppose, but still, how did Shay not remember? I ease the shower curtain back a bit, revealing the little window, probably no larger in size than a kids' cubbyhole, and its ledge with its travel-sized resort bath products along with Shay's favorite grapefruit-scented shower gel lined up in a neat, little row. The window itself is slightly ajar.

"Yeah, I know. I thought of that," she whispers, startling me out of my own thoughts. "There's no way we're going to be able to get out in time through *that*."

There's another cracking thunk against the door, one that grows repetitious, one beat at a time, somewhat synchronous, but the other foot kicking at it occasionally gets out of rhythm.

Even still, the door panels are starting to crack. I don't know if it's the sound of the monsters outside trying to kick their way in or the rattling of the chair frame against it that forces the desperate and dumb idea out of me in the barest nick of time.

#

"They're probably running to the exit road," Nathan says as he holds up the tattered remnants of the skirt slip and torn crinoline from Shay's dress that we'd ditched in the deep bathtub, just leaving that trace of us with the window wide open to the night. A couple of his friends have joined him in the bathroom, one I recognize as the stocky, plaid-jacketed newbie who'd slowed down to talk with Rex.

"Should be easier to trap now," says Plaid Jacket. "We couldn't find Charlie and that hot mom with the kid though. Think we should be worried?"

Shay squeezes my hand tightly. I squeeze back, signaling that I'd heard. The two of us are locked together, face to face, crammed at an awkward angle. We can barely breathe in the tight space of the suite's narrow linen closet, our sides pressed against the wall. We'd barely had any time to detach the few shelves from their hinges and then lean them against the wall on Shay's side. Right now, we can just see what's going on in the bathroom through the narrow slats of the doors.

Nathan drops the dress slip and crinoline remnants back into the tub where we'd left it earlier and closely examines the open window, the toiletries scattered in the tub. He turns back to his friends and smacks P.J. across the cheek, a sharp pop of noise out of nowhere, and Nathan holds up a hand again in a loose threat. P.J. cringes, cowering from the hand, his gaze darting back and forth, from Nathan to Nathan's hand to Nathan.

Nathan softens, smiles, puts on his brotherly charm once more. "Now look. We're kings here, right? This is *our* land, our domain. We got nothin' to worry about. There's nowhere those bitches can possibly go. They don't know the land here." He gives P.J. a friendly shoulder squeeze. "Have faith. It's what gets us through the years we're not able to feed."

"I never knew I needed this until tonight. I told your dad. I just hadn't known."

"How's it feel?"

P.J. cracks a half grin. "Fucking amazing."

"Now why don't you and the rest of the boys get on outta here. Do some huntin'. Impress the rest. Find them before dawn breaks."

"What? What happens at dawn?"

Nathan stares at the guy hard enough, it bores a hole directly through his soul. "Thought you did your research like a good, little college boy. We just shrivel up and fade away," he says coldly.

Then he barks out a laugh, shaking his head. P.J. laughs uncomfortably along with him, looking as if he really wants to get out of there. Can't say I blame him, cannibalistic tendencies or not.

"Lord above, man. You just ate that up, didn't you? Naw. That's when the day staff gets in," Nathan says. "They start rollin' in around six. They're usually supposed to be in at seven, but on account of the grand occasion we got goin' on here, they're scheduled for a special clean up."

Plaid Jacket clucks a nervous chuckle as Nathan playfully socks him hard on the arm, a hit that causes him to wince and recoil when Nathan reaches for him to attempt to give him an apologetic shoulder squeeze.

"You run along now, lil' doggy," says Nathan shooing his friend out the door. "Don't wanna be last at the table again."

As soon as Nathan's friend scoots away, I sense Shay relax, releasing tension, but only just when I give her hand a tap with a finger in warning, pressing firmly down on it. She finally looks at me, reading my expression. Her face is marked in lines from the light filtering in from the slats. Her eyes are round. I shake my head, a slight warning.

When I turn my head to look again, I see Nathan hasn't budged. He just stands there, frozen, listening. He shifts a little, as if he senses something, and icy prickles sprout all the way down my back. His mouth curves ever so slightly, forming a sneer that's only just perceptible. He then swivels around, pulls back, and slams a tightly balled fist against the bathroom mirror over the sink, shattering the glass into webbed cracks. Shay and I twitch at the sudden noise, the shock of it. He thumps the cracked mirror a couple of times with the side of his now-bloody hand, loosening the glass bits, and he pries a large shard from the damaged mirror.

My own hands are growing clammy, cold and sticky with damp. Shay's heavy breathing is so loud in our own cramped space, I worry that Nathan can hear her.

Nathan swivels, facing us dead-on in our hiding spot, grinning, grinding his teeth together. I don't know if he can see us, but I can certainly imagine that he smells us in here. Our blood and sweat, the meaty tang of us. I suck in my breath, set fire to my lungs, my heartbeat undoubtedly loud enough to hear through the slats. Shay tightens her grip on my hand, staring down at the floor as she does. She doesn't want to watch. Her fingernails dig trenches into my palm. We wait, and I keep watching him closely, silently, the two of us frozen there.

Nathan scans the bathroom up and down, all around, like he's looking for something specific. What, I've no idea. He opens the shower stall door, peers inside. Then he shuts the shower door with a bang and scrapes the large shard of mirror glass up and down the closet slats with an idle hand. He's toying with us. The rattling sound of it causes Shay to nearly drop the mallet, so I pry it gently from her shaky hand and grasp it in my own. It's slick with her perspiration, but it doesn't deter me from clasping its handle tightly.

I look Shay in the eye. She's breathing hard and looking right at me as well. "One," I mouth.

Nathan is now facing the door, his sneer curling, his eyes flat. "Heeeeeere, pretty girl of mine," he softly sings.

"Two," we mouth together. Shay nods.

He slides the shard in-and-out through the slats at eye level.

"Three," I finally say, audible enough I hope, and the two of us ram our shoulders into the door.

SEVENTEEN

The force of our shove is enough to smash the rickety door loose from its hinges and have us slam right into Nathan, sending the three of us, colliding into each other, tumbling to the floor.

At first, we're nothing but a messy tangle of bodies, arms and legs and torsos squirming about the bathroom floor in a frenetic game of Twister. I feel a slash of scorching heat across my face, from the corner of my eye to my cheek, and the wound splatters blood over Nathan's cheek and chin. It takes me a fleeting second to realize he'd just used the shard to slice me raw.

Shay screams down at him with a mad rage. I've seen her like this before but can't recall when as everything's a blur of motion, and my head feels numb and strange. Shay attempts to wrangle the shard from Nathan, scratching her own hand in the process. Her face contorted into a spittle-foamy grimace, she closes his hand tightly around the shard, dripping a blend of their blood onto the floor, and he howls.

She and I pin Nathan underneath us. Somehow in the scuffle, I've dropped the mallet, and Nathan tries to twist out from underneath us to grab it with his other hand. Shay shoves at his face, her palm pushing him forcefully back, flattening his cheek and mouth. She grabs a fistful of his hair and then slams the back of his head down hard against the linoleum, unfortunately just not quite hard enough to knock him out. He twists his body, thrashing this way and that, his jaws snapping at me, at Shay. He's laughing like a maniac as the two of us attempt to subdue him. I manage to wrench myself around to the side and stretch my arm out, reaching out for and then snatching up the mallet. I then lock down his flailing arm under my knee. Shay lets go of his damaged hand and then wiggles up to a kneeling position, trapping his other with her shins.

167

"Pretty girl, you shouldn't do this," he hisses at Shay. "We're married, sweetheart. Husband and wife. Better or worse."

The sour stench of urine soaking and heating up the front of his trousers and the metallic tang of blood in the air makes my head feel runny, like I'm losing focus once more in the here and now. All I want to do is rip out his guts and shove them in his open mouth, watch him eat himself alive.

Obviously, I haven't had a lot of time to take my benzo crumb.

These things, hopeless. These things.

Pointless.

(*Remember what I said...*

When you're feeling like everything is sucking all the air from you, you find something solid.)

The mallet feels good in my grip.

"Richer or poorer?" he says and do I detect a pleading tone there? Guilt maybe?

Shay and I exchange a look of disgust.

I hold out the mallet for her.

"In sickness and in health?" he whines.

She takes the tenderizer from me in her clean hand.

"C'mon now, sweetheart," he says, and I swear, are those honest to God tears forming in his eyes? "Sugar'n spice, right?"

He tries wiggling away, but we have him locked down.

Shay has that sort of peculiar, blank expression she used to reserve for all the boyfriends in her life she didn't know what to do with. It's a spacey cross between glazed over with boredom and contemplating something inexplicable, for Shay anyway.

Nathan foolishly takes it upon himself to break the silence on her end. "Til death do us part! That's how it goes, right, darlin'?"

"You talk too much," says Shay before she smashes the mallet down squarely in the center of his handsome mug. The force of her swing is so hard, so vicious, as physically absurd as it sounds, the center of his face pretty much explodes, sending bits of gristle and blood flying, spattering us and everything nearby.

It takes me a moment to remind myself it's okay to breathe. I think I have some Nathan facial matter in my hair, all over the front of my disgusting mess of a dress.

"Goddamn, Shay," I manage to say after swallowing and clearing back the bitter bile forming in my throat and mouth. There's

168

something acrid burbling inside of me, deep and warm, like whatever it is has made a stringy-sticky cocoon and is nesting, waiting for something to happen before it can emerge. It's kind of like that feeling you get when you know you're either going to have a heart attack or vomit at some point, and you're hoping—no, really, you're silently praying, it's the latter. What happens as an end result, though, often catches you by surprise.

Shay doesn't make matters any better to ease that feeling away. She slams down the meat tenderizer again and again, cracking the skull and cartilage, pulverizing whatever was left of Nathan's head that was still possibly in working condition. Whatever is triggering my sister to keep at it, it has her unrecognizable. Pre-wedding Shay would've retched at just the sight of a broken nose; post-wedding Shay, however, isn't even with me right now. This version of Shay has dropped the mask, revealing a gore-cloaked monster with its mouth stretched into a wide, obscene rictus, spittle foaming at the corners, its nostrils flared, its eyes wet and gleaming.

Monster Shay, she's terrifying.

And dare I admit, I may love her all the more, even when we can't stand each other. Sister, slay.

That said, it's now at the point where Shay's just hammering over and over at freshly juiced, red pulp. An onlooker wouldn't have any idea that what remains is even human until he or she saw the lean, angular body in the bloody mess of a tuxedo shirt and black trousers, the grimy dress shoes.

"Shay," I say softly.

She keeps at it, but she's starting to slow down with a splattery thunk, thunk-a, thunk…thunk…

I put a hand to her cheek like she'd done with me, drawing her face up, moving her focus to me. "I think he's pretty much good and gone," I tell her. "I'll take that."

Shay scowls at me. "What?"

"The mallet. Give it."

It doesn't take much from me to pry the thing out of her hand. She's gone all slack and funny, slumping backwards on the floor, a pitiful wretch in what used to be a wedding dress. Couldn't tell by now, that's for sure.

Just before I stagger to my feet and help Shay up, I spot it laying there near Nathan's side, so I swipe it up and stuff yet another thing down my bra while Shay's still in her fugue state. She'd be useless with it now anyway. I don't know if she's about to pass out or what, but she's wavery when standing, so I clasp her arm, steadying her.

"Shay…"

She keeps gaping at the mess she's left on the floor, the mess of what was once a man, I suppose. Some kind of man anyway. Are they even human?

I snap my fingers at her face, trying to get her attention. "Shay. Shay, look at me here."

Shay doesn't, and that's understandable. And, well, she's not passed out at least. That would make things difficult for us both, me especially since I'd be even more responsible for her than I should allowed to be considering the obvious. As my parents would've undoubtedly reminded anyone interested, I'm not cut out to be a caregiver; I'm better at being cared for. Even then, it's complicated.

It's all complicated.

"Shay, we have to go." I turn her head to me, a finger on the side of her chin. "They're gonna come back for Nathan and see all this. We can't be here when they come."

Her eyes flicker back to the here and now, where I want her to be. She meets my gaze and lets out an audible shiver.

"I need you to be with me, hear?"

Shay slowly nods. She's about to look back down at the sight of her husband's body, but I jerk her head up, keeping her eyes trained back on me, my hand firmly cupping her chin as I do.

"*Now*, Shay. You ready to go? I need you to be ready."

She sniffs, nods again, says, "I'm ready."

I then pull her by the hand and guide her out of the bathroom with me.

Fuck this noise. All of it.

#

By the time we're outside and making our way quickly, silently around the guest casitas, the power goes out all over the resort, and we're nothing but hazy shapes in the moonlight. I don't know if it's a deliberate move on the part of the monsters out there, but I wouldn't doubt it in the slightest. They know the terrain. We don't. Game, set, match.

170

My face burns. Arm throbs. Everything's shredded, what's still left of me. No matter. Got to press on.

I've armed Shay with one of the heavier candlesticks from the suite while I brandish the gore-coated meat tenderizer for a change. I figure the candlestick's just fresh enough in that it won't remind Shay of what she left behind in the bridal suite's bathroom. My free hand clasps her own, our fingers interlocking once again as we break into an awkward jog, darting down the narrow dirt path in the dark, only the sliver of moonlight guiding us.

The smoky-sweet scent of basted barbequed meat is fragrant in the humid air, and my stomach rumble-groans its dismay at my thought of running from the smell rather than towards it. The shrill sound of someone screaming pierces the night, halting us. We're both panting, and I didn't realize how fast we'd actually been going until now. The screams are then overpowered by whistling and hollering, then the sound of clapping and cheering. I can't tell where it's coming from. The vast expanse of the dark terrain makes it difficult to pinpoint noise. The last time we'd heard something like this out in the open, our mother was being spit-roasted, and Nathan had chased us.

At least we know now if we're being chased, it won't be Nathan running after us. That's a plus in a way, until, of course, his body's discovered in the bathroom. I shudder to think what the Card elders will do as soon as they find him. Rex and Delia will inevitably make sure Shay and I are both quartered, trussed and served as low country as they'd have us figured.

The morbid bit of me lingering there wonders what "low country" would authentically entail for the two of us.

We've reached the dumpster near the rear parking lot where everyone who isn't a wedding guest had parked their cars earlier. A lone parking lot lamp there seems to be working, and while it's good to be able to see what's in front of us, there are some sights that are best left *unseen*.

There are several packs of eaters in the side parking lot by the murky pool, each pack consisting of anywhere from three to four resort employees in gore-spattered uniforms, each pack crouching around their catch, tearing into their fresh meat. The shrill, wispy song of the cicadas still isn't quite stereo-quality enough to mask the whuffling grunts and noisy chewing punctuated by the occasional blissful groan or sigh signaling their content.

I sneak a peek around our hiding spot behind the dumpster. I've automatically taken on the role of lookout mainly because Shay seems likely to break any minute. She's jittery, fidgety, sensitive of everything around us, and the combination of that with the fact she's ready to pulverize the Card party to mush has me on edge, too, now that I know what she's fully capable of doing.

There's movement coming from beside Delia's SUV not far from Shay's, a dark form, someone there. It's close to the pack, but they're only interested in the meal in front of them. A white, spidery hand reaches around and clamps over a little face that suddenly emerges from the shadow and out in the moonlight. A mouth. A pert little nose. Wide eyes blinking rapidly.

Jesus H. It's Bryceson. Poor kid is gaping at the remnants of what looks like Emma at the back of the car, there on the ground. I can only tell it's Emma because no one else at the wedding had been gutsy enough to wear those canary yellow slingbacks, a slip of color in the dusky light. Members of the pack around the other side of Delia's car are eating her ropy entrails. Someone else has apparently taken charge of the kid, keeping him from crying out for his mother, giving away their hiding place. The hand that's clamped over his mouth is connected to a long, white-sleeved arm. That much I can see from where we are. At least the kid is being protected for the time being.

"See anything?" whispers Shay. Her hand has grown cold and clammy in mine, but it can just as easily be my hand that's sweaty. Even on a summer night, one could go numb all over with shock. This. This is happening. I've been repeating it again and again that This. Is. Happening.

I keep my gaze steady, focusing on the pack on the other side of the SUV underneath the glow of the single light of the lot. They all have their backs to the car, to Bryceson and whomever it is who's keeping him quiet.

How the hell had they got there? What are they thinking?

"It's Bryceson," I whisper back. "He's near Delia's car. He's with someone."

"Who's with him?"

"I don't know."

"Is it Emma?"

"No."

"How do you know? How do you know it's not Emma?"

"I just do."

172

"It could be Emma."

"It's *not* Emma, Shay."

"Who is it then? Who else could it be?"

"I'll let you know when the freaks who are *eating* Emma have left the parking lot."

That shuts her up instantly. And then—

"We need to get him out of there, Ans. We need to do something. They'll see him," she says in my ear. She's starting to hyperventilate. Her breathing comes in light, rapid hitches. "They're gonna see him, or they're gonna smell him. Either way, they're gonna find him."

"Stop it, Shay. We need to keep a clear head," I whisper, keeping my tone soothing and easy. "Listen. Breathe in four seconds, hold for seven, then release for eight. You hear me? Old trick Leon taught me, and I know *you* do this when you meditate. Four. Seven. Eight. Squeeze if you're doing it."

I hear her suck in her breath. She squeezes and then releases my hand. I feel the blood rush back into my joints, flooding my hand with prickly warmth.

"Stay here," I say.

Before I can make a move to leave her, Shay tightly grasps my hand again, pulling at me. "No. No, you can't. They'll see you."

I turn to look at her outline. She had rid herself of the veil, the train and slip, thank God, but I can't believe she still has those goddamned shoes on. She'd been barely able to walk down the cobblestone "aisle" in those clunkers.

I squeeze back. "That's the general idea," I whisper. "I have to get them away from Delia's car. It'll give Bryceson and his friend time to move, but you have to be ready to run, too."

"What? Are you serious? I can't—"

I pull her to me, have her look me in the eye. "Get Bryceson and whoever's with him, and you go as fast as you can to your car. I figure it's anywhere from fifty to sixty feet from Delia's. Don't take the main drive though. Follow the drainage ditch at the lot, and just hide in the shadows where you can. Then get in your car and take the back entrance out."

"But you're just going to—"

I dig down the front of my dress, under one tight corner of a bra cup, and pull out the thing that had been digging into my breast. The other cup still holds the skeleton key we found in the Dopp kit, and

173

I'm more aware now than I had been that it's much more painful in its own resting spot. I hold up the keychain holding the car fob for Shay to see, letting it dangle there in front of her line of sight. Her eyes widen at the sight of it. Then I place it in Shay's palm and close her fingers around it. "You dropped it in the bathroom while you were—Fuck it. Wait for me," I say. "If I don't show soon after you guys are at the rear entrance, no more than ten minutes, you know what to do."

Before she can protest, I'm already off and running.

EIGHTTEEN

How did it come to this? I mean, who could have imagined anything like this was going to happen? By the way, I'm not a runner by any stretch of the imagination, so it didn't take long for the sharp pain to rip through my sides. As much as adrenaline has been my buddy throughout the whole ordeal, it doesn't do shit to keep from reminding me I Don't Run.

Back in the pre-panic days when I hadn't been prescribed anything, I attempted the whole running thing every morning, just before work. Just a mile or two, which turned into five or six or seven, and by then, I'd just reached the point where the pain threshold had turned into that "high" exercise fanatics crow about. That was when Simon stopped talking to me, ignoring my calls, texts, emails, cutting me off completely like the coward he was and probably still is. After that came the surprise of his baby, his marriage, you get the picture.

My shrink later on kept suggesting I get back into exercising, but by then, every time I attempted to run or go to the gym, or even try some incredibly stupid exercise trend like zumba or swinging around stripper poles, it felt as if my lungs were shriveling up to the size and consistency of raisins, like my ability to breathe was rapidly dying, I was dying. Once, while on the elliptical at the gym near my workplace, I even fainted. I'd never fainted before. It's not like in the movies where everything is all in soft-focus, and there's some ridiculous piece of period furniture like a fainting couch where the heroine comes to after the handsome devil wafts some smelling salts under her nose. It's the least glamorous "accident" next to farting, really. I'd just slipped and fallen off the elliptical machine and sprained both ankles somehow in the process.

Anyway, I don't run.

Unless, of course, I've cannibalistic maniacs in hot pursuit of me. I don't know if it's the fear of being caught and eaten or the anger at the thought of being *stupidly* caught and eaten, but whatever it is, adrenaline-fueled or not, I'm finding that running is a heck of a lot easier than it's ever been post-Simon. Granted, I don't know what I'm running on right now, and I'd love to be able to stop and take a few breaths, but I've a feeling our batshit pursuers aren't in the frame of mind or mood or appetite for breaks.

I don't even know where I'm leading them. I'd shouted something that, in hindsight, wasn't particularly bright or inventive—something like "Hey! Steak tartare, everybody! Come and get some, motherfuckers!" If Dad were still around to see all of this, he would've been both terribly impressed that I'd mentioned his favorite dish, ever, next to brisket sandwiches, and horrified I'd done something that, now that I think about it, was so idiotic. Then I remind myself that Dad had been on the impromptu menu earlier *as* his favorite dish, minus the egg yolk, and I get depressed all over again. This isn't what I'd wanted.

This isn't what any of us wanted. This isn't what any of us had rightly and logically anticipated. This is absurd. What the hell am I doing anyway? Where am I going? I don't know where I am right now. Let's see. I'd followed the path around the front of the casitas with some goal in mind, some crazy-stupid end goal. What did I say? What did I tell Shay again? My thoughts, my memory, everything's sort of a jumbled mess in my head. And that noise, that constant keening in my ears won't go away. It could be the withdrawals, tinnitus; it could be the obvious trauma-induced stress. I just can't remember, fuck it all. I think I'm to circle back around at some point from the rear end of the resort, making a wide loop.

Oh, that's right, the back entrance. I have to make it there, reach the car. I just have no idea where I am at the moment. Somehow, I'd taken a turn somewhere along the way in the grey, losing them only just, and now I'm half-jogging, half-stumbling around in patchy beds of brush and weeds, *away* from the parking lot. All of this going on, and I cannot believe my pumps have lasted the entire night. I could've danced well in these babies. It would've been nice, I guess.

My head has gone numb and swimmy again, my mouth bone dry, and my limbs sore. I lean against what I presume to be a wall of some sort, take in a breath, exhale, and I can almost forget about all of what's happening. The night air, while a little sticky and redolent with a smattering of honey-barbequed patrons, has a light breeze to it that cools the sweat and blood on my skin. The rough texture of the wall, the solidity of it beneath my fingers, reminds me where I am and where I need to be.

But that's not quite as important as the sudden, mocking chime of girlish laughter coming from somewhere in the dark, a sound mere steps from where I'm standing. The moon has gone dark, hidden behind a flock of clouds. If it hadn't been for the moonlight, I'd be blindly using the wall as a guide, relying solely on my hearing and my sense of smell and touch. Thankfully, the dim light casts the occasional outlines and shadows, and when I turn around, I see them there, clustered together.

The one who'd been laughing approaches me, and I keep the mallet behind my back, waiting to see just how close she intends to be. She giggles again, and then stifles it back with a pale hand. A flashlight clicks on in her other hand, casting her sunny freckled and blood-smeared face in light and shadow. It's the redhead from the front desk. The others, a couple of panting, snickering teenaged boys with the sort of floppy hairstyle that's deliberate, both in grubby resort uniforms, flank her sides. One of them, who keeps making an awful sucking noise with his lips and teeth, grips a crowbar. He's just about to take a swing, ready to strike at me, when the redhead forcefully shoves him away, causing him to stumble back and fall to the ground.

"She's *not yours*, dipshit!" she snaps at him.

The other one helps his seething friend back up on his feet, and the two of them exchange quick, whispered words back and forth between them, and when the redhead turns to deal with them both, I've turned and am already hightailing it as fast as I can run in these goddamned shoes, tripping along in the dark, my hand trailing the wall as I go. I mean, I could participate, maybe knock a few heads with my weapon of choice, but I'd really rather head back around and try to catch up with my sister.

There's a piercing screech directly behind me, and I can hear catcalls, cackles coming from far off. Undoubtedly, it's the redhead leading the charge, ticked that she wasn't able to chow down in full view of her boy scouts. At least, that's what's going through my overactive imagination as I run. If she catches me, I wonder if she's into the raw bar sort of thing or if she enjoys the barbeque as much as her friendly family/employers here.

The lights of the path leading to the road out of the back gate momentarily dazzle me as I trip along, but I manage to keep running, no matter. I know perfectly well that the dumbest thing a woman in my position can do is stop and turn to see who's following close behind, but I'm tempted nonetheless. I can hear the pound of feet, many feet, behind me, and while I'm sure the image concocted in my feverish brain right now—that of the entire resort staff, a throng of them, joined by stray members of the Card family, after me—is a lot worse than the reality, there's no way in all of hell, even if this is it, I'm about turn around and check. I'm not that kind of twit.

I am, however, the other kind of ninny, the kind who doesn't really watch where she's going since she's so focused on the possibility of an exit.

So, naturally, when I make a turn, I slam right into the driver door of Shay's precious SUV, the impact slamming me back, knocking me to the ground.

"Ansley, get in!" Shay shouts from out the open driver window.

My headache is blinding. I can see only spots of light, the blurry movement of colors shifting; everything else is cast in a watery sheen. The pain rakes its hot talons behind my eyes. I think it's tears. I think I'm crying.

Strong hands gently tug me up from underneath my arm, easing me back to my feet. I wipe at my eyes, and suddenly, it's all there in the moonlight, racing towards the SUV, coming for me. The horde. All of them. I knew it, and I wish, for once, my imagination hadn't been so close to reality. It rarely is. I always imagine the worst, like anyone else, I suppose, hoping for the best outcome. I'm pulled into the back, those strong hands now easing me in just as—

They're upon us. Hands claw for me, grasping only the air there, and—

The passenger door slides shut behind me, nearly taking my leg. I can't breathe. The ball of lead that had been rolling around inside of me is melting into my lungs and hardening there, weighing me down, causing me pain when I attempt to take in air. The last time I remember when I'd felt as if my ribcage was collapsing inward, when the fresh air couldn't enter, I'd slid against my boss' chest, grappling for his suit lapel as I gasped for breath, the firebombs going off behind my eyes. My head had struck the corner of my desk, and everything had just gone dark.

This time, not like it's any different. I feel that tightness, my throat constricting, and the last thing I see before I give myself over to the dark is Charlie's face creasing over with concern. Those brown eyes. Those full lips of his.

My last thought, *I wonder how I really tasted.*

#

The violent impact snaps me alert, ripping me out of the dark. My head whips back and forth like it's on a stalk. Wrenching whiplash. My neck is on fire. We've hit something; the machinery that's been on the move, keeping us relatively safe until now has gone dead. The only sound I hear is a high-pitched whine keening in my ears, masking the noise of everything else happening around me. Charlie is unbuckling his seatbelt from the front passenger seat, twisted around, saying something at me. Then he's up from his seat and ducking back to check on the passenger next to me.

It's Bryceson. He's crying loudly, and the pitch of his voice grows louder when everything comes into focus. The ringing sound is on repeat, warning lights and signals from the vehicle, reminding us of the obvious. I remove my seatbelt slowly, feeling for additional injuries, but aside from my burning arm, my stinging face, my throbbing neck, I'm all right.

Shay is half-buried in the mess of the inflated airbag. She's pulling at it, clawing to release herself from its enveloping cushion.

"Everybody okay?" says Charlie. He's directing it at all of us, even while his focus is on Bryceson. He checks the sobbing boy for injuries, wiping the kid's teary face as he examines him. "Hey, guy. How we doing?" he says calmly to Bryceson while he looks him over. "Anything hurt? You all right there?"

"I think I pooped a little."

Charlie chuckles softly. "Perfectly understandable." He looks at me. "And you. You okay? You poop a little?" He winces when he takes a closer look. Your face. What happened?"

"It's nothing some antiseptic and a few shots of the Jim Beam variety couldn't cure." And yet it hurts just to say that. I unravel myself from the tangle of the seatbelt and scoot in towards my sister.

Shay claws for the side seat control and suddenly slides back, nearly ramming it against me, pushing herself away from the airbag that's starting to sag. She gasps, coughs, expels air. I lean in against the center console, twisting myself around to face her directly. She glances around at everything around us before her gaze settles on me. "You're bleeding again," she says, a croak in her voice. "Did you—Did you break your face?"

It's so hard to smile and even harder *not* to smile. The hot burn rips down the side of my face when I do. "How bad is it now? Does it look broken?"

Shay winces back a grin. "It always does, Tee-tee. The scar's gonna improve things later."

"Best be shutting up now, Ta-ta."

"Hate to interrupt all the tee-tee and ta-ta going on right now," says Charlie, "but if everyone's all right, we're gonna have to move. Right now. Get out there in the dark as quickly as we can and hide out somewhere out there until daylight."

Ignoring the spasms happening in my neck, I shift around from my leaning crouch, taking a look at the darkness outside. That pitch, it's endless. It hides other things, a dark beyond the dark. It hits me, that resultant awareness a few minutes after an accident. I don't even know what happened, never mind where we are. Shay switches off the car, cutting the shrill beep of the alarm as well, and it's like all of the natural noise comes back on at once. I'm suddenly able to hear everything around us.

Charlie slides open the side passenger door, hops outside, and then lifts Bryceson out of the SUV, hefting the kid up against him. He walks around to the front of the vehicle, carrying Bryceson as he does. Shay clicks open the driver door and eases herself out. Before I slide out of the passenger side, I catch a glimpse of Charlie standing in the single bright spotlight of the one working headlight. He and the kid are as bloodied and grimy as Shay and I are. The spiderweb crack of the windshield segments the sight out there in the line of the headlight's beam. It looks as if we'd veered off-road and had slammed into something caught in the middle of clawing at the earth, its protrusions twisted and spiny. The skeleton of a fallen tree.

Out here in the wide-open darkness of the countryside, so vulnerable as we are, I can't see much; it's hard to discern any shapes or shadows. The moon has decided to play a long game of hide-and-seek behind a chain of clouds.

180

My legs are made of rubber, such wobbly, useless things, and I take a tumble. Shay staggers over to me with her hands out, reaching for me, and I grab them, allowing myself to be pulled back up, the two of us wavering.

It takes me a minute to get my air back, to breathe, before I ask the million-dollar question: "What the hell happened?"

Charlie has set Bryceson down and now has him by the hand as they make their way over. "Not like Shay could ease us out of the way. No one could've. I think it was some kind of spike strip or something like it. Someone set it up on the road," says Charlie. "Normally those things are set up by the police, supposed to slow drivers down gradually, forcing them into a stop."

"That wasn't 'gradual,'" says Shay. "We're off road, and we ran into a dead tree. We could've been killed. How was that meant to be 'gradual'?"

Charlie, still holding onto Bryceson's hand, beckons us to follow them both back to the front of the SUV. "That's not normal," he says, pointing at it, urging us to see for ourselves. "But that was definitely intentional. Get us to veer completely off the road like that."

The tires have all been shredded, the front end a crumpled, chaotic crunch of metal and dead tree limbs. On quick glance, for an instance, it looks as if the SUV and the fallen tree had been trying to merge and form into an angry, bizarre mutation.

It's not the time for the how's and why's. It hasn't been for a good while though. "We can't stay out here," I say. "Like Charlie said, we need to go. Right now."

Shay turns in a wide circle, looking all around us. "Where are we going though? Do you see any lights out there? Any houses, farms?"

"Where's the road from here? How far off-road are we?" I aim that at the whole group. I was unconscious, for shit's sake; it's not like I'd have any idea.

Charlie turns in my direction. He looks as tense as the rest of us, clenched and breathing heavily. There's something in his eyes. I can't quite read it, but I'm going with my gut and keeping him at a few feet's distance from me until I know what's going on. "Why? We really shouldn't go back, Ansley," he says.

"No shit. Did I say we should take it back?" I say, and then, remembering the age of the rest of our company, I add a, "Sorry,

181

buddy. Just one of those times," offering Bryceson as friendly a grin as I can offer under the circumstances.

The kid just stares blankly at me in response. He's miles away in his own mind, one grubby hand still entwined with Charlie's, the other with a thumb in his mouth. Comfort where he can get it. What are we going to do with him?

"What I meant was, if we can get back to the road, we can at least travel along, parallel to it, not on it. Doesn't it lead to a gas station not too far from the resort?" I'm not about to add that I'm crazy, sure, but not stupid because there's not really a worse time than now for self-abasement.

"We're not going in that direction, Ansley," Shay mutters, and I barely catch it.

"What do you mean we're not going in that direction? That's the way to that German town. Why *wouldn't* we be going that way? There are *people* that way. There are miles and miles of straight-up *nothing* in the other fucking direction."

Shay gives me a hard look and nods towards Bryceson, as if my goddamned language seriously matters now. I can't believe this. What the hell do they think we're going to do out here? Set up camp under the stars? Toasting marshmallows over a fire? Sharing folksy legends about crazy cannibal families out in the country?

I snort out a chuckle at the thought of it. The mad irony, noted.

Charlie is all smooth and soft rather than blatantly wincing at my laughing like Shay's doing right now. "They're more likely to head towards town while they're after us. It's the logical choice, right?" he says. "I came over from the other direction. There are some houses out there. An RV park, too, if I recall. Can't be more than a few miles at most." He takes a quick glance at his watch. "Yeah," he says, squinting at the thing. "It's going on four thirty." He looks over at me with a weak half-smile. "We might reach the park by dawn if we're on the move now."

I suddenly feel my limbs go prickly. My back straightens, as if lifting by a cord. Something about that sounds familiar. "An RV park? As in trailers?" I turn to Shay who's shaking her head at Charlie. It's familiar to her as well.

"They've got relatives there. Some cousins," she says.

And I remember now, the conversation between Rex and one of the beardos. "From what we heard, they serve the bad meat. Makes them sick."

Shay manages a lopsided grin. "I like the idea of all of them getting sick."

"It's how those horror stories begin, Shay," I say. "Redneck inbred family taking strangers in, cutting them up with chainsaws, and then prepping them for dinner. We've already experienced it with the rich members of the family. But *they*, at least, used fancy, clean utensils to prevent us from getting tetanus. We have sanitary choices here, you know."

"I guess you're right. I mean, if we *had* to be eaten, it's better for us to be treated with care, kind of like those cows in Japan that get massaged before they're turned into steaks."

"Yeah, I'd definitely want five star treatment if I were serving...me. Or someone was serving me to somebody else. You know what I'm trying to say."

Shay nods, her grin widens. It's best to make light, right? "I know what you're trying to say."

"And now I really want a massage," I say. The thought of it warms me, someone's...anyone's touch, as absurd as it seems.

"Now I know what I *don't* want," says Shay. "I don't want steak ever again. That's it, everybody. I'm officially back to vegetarianism. Thanks, Nate, for ruining meat for me *forever*."

"Listen, we go in one direction or the other," Charlie abruptly cuts in, returning us to the subject at hand. "We can't just head into the hills. There's nothing out there."

I'm not entirely convinced in such absolutes. Leon taught me that. Hell, therapy did, that there are more solutions out of the box, that varieties of grey exist in-between, that you can ask for something besides salt or pepper. There are *always* other options besides the ones in front of you.

I turn, facing him. "How can you be so sure there's no one living out there in the hills? You're not familiar with the area, are you? What, have you hiked around here? What do you know, Charlie?"

Now it's Shay's turn to give Charlie a curious once-over, eyebrow raised. Charlie shakes his head; rakes his fingers through his hair, and, with his hands frozen there on his head, he lets out a long, exasperated puff of air, probably meant to be a sigh, at the two, little women staring at him with their flat, suspicious eyes. "I give up," he finally says. "You two can decide what you're gonna do from now on, but I'm gonna take Bryceson here, and we're gonna head up the road in *some* direction that has possibility. I don't care. We're not staying out here by the car where we're live bait."

"Police," Bryceson says, startling us all. He's staring at something, and Shay and I turn to see it, winking in the distance out there in the darkness, the blues and reds going around and around, weaving in and out of the crests and valleys.

Shay lets out a whoop and is just about to make a move up the slope when she steps on something that crunches underneath her bare foot—a detail I'd somehow missed until now—and screams, her voice cutting the still night like a honed blade. I'm at her side in an instant, having her use my shoulder as leverage while she examines her foot. A sharp twig had impaled the sole of her foot. She gently tugs on it, urging it out slowly, carefully, sucking in her breath as she does. I have her sit beside me on the sandy heath and then rip off a strip of her bedraggled dress. It's as if everything about the terrain, from its inhabitants right down to its natural growth, wants to keep us trapped here, in agony and afraid. I help her wrap her injured foot, staunching yet another wound. We're just a mess. I want to laugh it off, but one side of my face is still on fire. It would hurt to laugh. Maybe once we're in our comfy hospital beds, with round the clock care. Maybe then we could share a good, long laugh about surviving hell and everything with it.

Charlie and Bryceson have joined us, Bryceson watches us dress Shay's wound with wide, unblinking eyes. "Why don't you two stay here," says Charlie, a thoughtful frown lining his face. "I'll take Bryceson just over the ridge there, up to the road. We'll be parallel, so we won't miss you when we flag him down."

Shay waves that idea off. "I'm fine. Seriously. Splitting us up isn't an option. Besides, I like the thought of a nice, warm mug of police station coffee." She warbles up on her feet, pushing down on my shoulder as she does, and I'm up as well, having her brace against me before she can fall down all over again.

Still, I'm not entirely ready, not entirely sure, and I can't seriously be the only one who's leery. We'd had our suspicions before. Why do we dive in and trust anyone else now? "I like the thought of being suspicious of everything and everyone in a place that just tried to eat us," I say, my attention directly on Charlie at this very moment. He's oddly hesitant, too. I wonder if he's thinking the same thing I am.

I can feel Shay's tension tightening her body, all the way through her grip on my shoulder. "I know," she says softly. "I'm not so

184

sure either, but it's coming from the direction of the town. Civilization. Cars. Other people. Hiding spots." She looks at me. "Working phones."

"There's also four of us. No one will have to be alone," Charlie adds, offering a tight line of a smile at me. "No, we won't split up."

And there's the sharp whistle of the police siren, making the decision for us all whether we're ready or not.

NINETEEN

One of the nicest people I've ever encountered was a policewoman. No, seriously. She was. Look, I'm not attempting to paint all law enforcement in such broad brush- strokes. I make mistakes. I'm probably making them right now, in fact, placing trust in people I just don't know. That said, that policewoman, she'd been the only one who treated me with care among the three of them who'd pinned me down on the floor of my workplace, while I was kicking and squirming, attempting to get free. I'd gained a few bruises that afternoon, maybe deservedly so, and she'd made sure my injuries were tended to. Maybe it was all about image, keeping the local police from being in another clickbait piece on police brutality. Maybe it had more to do with preventing lawsuits against the city. I'm not convinced though. She spoke to me as if I were just another person rather than a violent offender, a label that sticks to me now with superglue. She'd nodded in sympathy when I was finally permitted to speak for myself (and much to my lawyer's dismay). She'd said she had a brother who'd been overprescribed opiates and couldn't effectively get off them without going into withdrawals. Not quite the same thing, but as close as I'd get in terms of empathy. I won't forget that, ever.

She'd also been the only one who'd offered me an ice pack to reduce the swelling in my own injuries. Everyone else was treating my boss with kid gloves, holding ice packs against his cheek and jawline, giving me angry glances over their shoulders, whispering such awful things they'd really wanted me to overhear. She'd told me to ignore the looks and comments, like it was easy, not a big deal whatsoever. I remember her smile though, natural and knowing, it kept me focused. I didn't forget her; I haven't forgotten her, that kindness of hers, that decency and humanity. When Leon took charge of me at the center, it was as if she'd somehow passed over her empathic persona, imbued him with it. He had the same easy smile when he'd shown me around the facility, introducing me to my temporary new residence.

(*Solidity,* he said, rattling the door to my room in its frame, showing me. *It will remind you what is here. What is now. It will bring you back to where you need to be.*)

The policewoman and her partner who've joined us on the road seem as friendly and concerned over our wrecked and bloodied appearance, reminding me to an extent that not everyone is after us. The two of them are also an interesting study in contrasts. She can't be more than five feet tall with dark, close-cropped hair and a sunny grin, her voice belying her stature, booming and playful. Her partner is a monolith of a man, his face and body carved out of granite. His smile is all business as usual, but he's soft-spoken, easygoing. He'd taken the car a bit of a ways back from where'd we'd driven, looped back around, drove back towards us, and then parked alongside of the hill.

He shakes his head at us as he comes up to us. "Nothing out there. You sure it was a spike strip?"

Shay doesn't hesitate to cut in. "We ran over *something* that shredded the tires. They could've easily pulled it back."

The policewoman stops jotting notes long enough to give her partner a curious look, her eyebrows raised. She turns to Shay. "*Who* could've pulled it back?"

"What?"

"You said 'They could've...' Who are you talking about?"

Shay doesn't answer, and I get it. I get her. She's said too much. I'm inclined to agree because right here, right now, nothing is secure or guaranteed. It's now only about us and our safety. Only our safety is paramount.

The policewoman gives her partner a grim look. He draws his mouth into a tight line, chews on his lower lip. They know something. Neither wants to say a damned thing though, and for four people in danger—four people including a *child*—that's enough cause for the alarm bells to go off. I've been holding Shay steady for too long. My neck and shoulder are aching, going numb. I look over at Charlie who's keeping Bryceson braced against him, both hands on the kid's shoulders. Charlie has his gaze locked steadily on the policeman. I can't read his expression as he's got a mask on. It's almost practiced, like he's dealt with shady shit before. I doubt I'll ever know the full extent of what's going on up there in his head.

I do know he's a shady piece of work himself, keeping his engagement from me, keeping anything at all about himself from me altogether. He idly rumples Bryceson's hair as he stares at the cops.

I guess it's on me then. "Could we get a ride into town at least? We have to get out of this place before—" Nope, I can't. Can't finish this. I'm feeling the same way as everyone else. Uneasy, lost, alone. Damned scared.

The policewoman catches it, holds my look. "Before what?" she says. Then she looks at each and every one of us long and hard. "One of you speak. We obviously can't help you if you don't say anything. What's going on?" She clears her throat, crouches low in front of Bryceson with that friendly smile of hers. "You wanna tell me, big guy? Wanna tell me what's going on?"

Bryceson just stares at her with wide, empty eyes. He's going to have nightmares for years to come. We're all going to have them.

"Hey now," she says in a soft voice, light and smooth, as she examines his dirty, little suit, torn in places, the dried blood spatter on his cheeks and dress shirt. "You been through it, big buddy. Are you hurt?"

He slowly shakes his head at her.

"You got some blood on you though. That's not your blood?"

"It's Mommy's," he primly says. End of.

And just like that, we've become suspects. As soon as Charlie seems about to interject, the monolithic policeman shakes his head at him, holding up a finger to wait, and turns his attention on the kid.

"You wanna tell us what happened to your mommy?" he asks.

Shay and I share an uneasy silence, briefly locking eyes.

Bryceson leans in close to the policewoman. "They ate her," he says.

"Somebody *ate* her?"

Bryceson merely nods his response.

The policewoman's eyes have gone round. It would be almost cartoonish if what he'd said weren't both nuts *and* horrifically true. "Honey, can you tell me who they are?"

A series of piercing shrieks suddenly break open the dark. They're coming from all around us, enclosing us further into our little bubble of relative safety, the beams of light flashing reds and blues around and around. The policewoman jerks up, drawing her pistol in one swift movement. Her partner has done the same.

Shay, Charlie, Bryceson and I draw together in a tight pack, the four of us looking all around for the source of the sounds that cut at our surroundings. The moon is still sunken behind the clouds. Even the stars have hidden away, choosing to stay well out of sight.

When I listen that closely, I hear something else, a familiar, faint drone of insects in the air.

"I'm calling it in," says the policewoman as she backs away towards the car.

It's just at the precise moment when I see the flies. They're circling now, buzzing around the head of the policeman, sensing their human's tension. He then promptly shoots his partner in the head, causing our little group to jump and look on in horror at him when he swivels the pistol right at us. Charlie pulls Bryceson tightly to him, shielding him from the sight. Keeping his gun aimed at us with one steady hand, the policeman swiftly bends, reaches down, unhooks a pair of handcuffs from his partner's belt, and then tosses them to Shay who watches them fall onto the pavement in front of her.

"One for you and one for big sister," the monolith leers, waving the pistol at her, motioning for her to pick up the handcuffs.

"I got them," I say and then glare at the guy as I pick them up.

"Put 'em on now," he says, watching as I lock them in place, binding me to my sister. "There you go. That's a good girl. See how nice and civilized we can all be?"

"If only I'd bet on this," I mutter.

"What's that?" he says, unhooking his own pair of cuffs.

"Nothing."

"Not nothing. What'd you say to me?"

"I didn't say anything to you."

"You said somethin' about placing bets."

"I was talking to my sister."

He's at Shay's side now, grinning down at her, grinning at me. Back and forth. "Your sister a gambler?" he asks Shay.

"Not lately. She's not into risks," she says, shaking her head at me.

The monolith taps me on the shoulder with the butt of his pistol. "Would you risk your sister's life if you had to?"

I turn to look up at him looming over me. Prick. "What would it take to keep that from happening?"

He grins at my question, at me, and walks around us, taking his sweet time. "Feedin' time!" he suddenly calls out into the dark. "Come an' get 'em, y'all!" He follows that with a sharp whistle.

Then he hurriedly snaps his pair of cuffs on Charlie who struggles against the binding as he does. He doesn't want to let go of Bryceson, who has his little arms wrapped around his waist, his face buried in his torso. The monolith then pistol-whips Charlie on the side of his head, knocking him out hard. Charlie crumbles to the ground, and Bryceson is right there at his side, wailing for Charlie to get back up.

The shrieks, barks, catcalls and shouts, whooping and hollering grows louder, closer still, all around us. They're coming.

The policeman skulks back around. He's thinking something over, trying to read me, I don't know. The granite of his face then curves into a sneer full of teeth, so *many* teeth. He stops and says in my ear while unlocking me from Shay, "If you don't want me to kill your sister, all you have to do is make a run for it."

Stupid me for thinking it would be simple, a nice, neat capture. No troubles.

I want to run for her life, for mine, for the others, but I know if I do, I'll be five hundred feet in and out of breath. It'll be much worse with such stakes. I'll be at the point where I'd sooner take a bullet than go through such agony all over again. Lead in my legs. Snakes in my brain. My heart likely to burst. Everything will catch fire, and there'll be nothing left of me but a puddle of human goo.

Hell. It's for Shay.

"Where am I running to?"

He points to nothing out there but darkness, deep and full. "Up over that ridge. Then keep on going."

"What ridge?"

"It's there. You'll reach it when it's right at your feet."

"You spare the kid, too, at least." I'm not doing this until it's set from him. All absolutes, no wiggle room.

If he's agreed, I'll never be sure. He just nods and grins. Shit-eater.

"On the count of three, start running, girl," he says.

"Wait, I'm not ready yet. I just need—"

"One…"

"Fuck! Can I get some kind of guarantee that you won't—"

"Two…"

190

Before he can continue, I'm already sprinting across the road, and then the darkness is upon me.

#

That pain barrier everybody goes on about, I don't think I'll get to the point when it's not an issue for me. Everything hurts. It's bad enough I can't see what's in front of me out here in the actual middle of nowhere. Thus far, I've tripped once, and if it wasn't for the crack of a gunshot, and the image of the entirety of the Card clan and their...*people*... after me, I know I would've just given up, laid myself down on the sandy ground, and promptly passed out. I don't know who shot whom. I'd like to think that Shay somehow managed to wrestle that cop's pistol away. I'd like to think it was Shay who fired it.

It's not my reality though. My reality is the pitch surrounding me every which way I turn, every which way I go. My reality is the panting coming from the dark, the snarling, the low cackling, the hissing. Then the dead silence. The stillness. Where did they all go?

I stop in my tracks, anything for a breath. It feels as if my lungs will burst.

I want to go back. This is pointless. This solves nothing. My sister might have been the one shot. It's just me though, and I have nothing with me. No weapons, no tools, no cell. Sure, there'd likely be no signal out here, but mine had a working flashlight app I could've used as soon as the world went dark. I could've, at least, seen where the hell I was going.

I turn around, despite the warning not to, the one that's burning a hole in my gut. The lights from the police car are tiny specks in the darkness now. Shadows move around the car, their shapes wavery and difficult to discern from here. There's no trace of life out there anymore, even though I know there's life seething at the bit to get at me. They may have gone silent, but I can smell them. The air is pungent with a heady soup of stale cigars and whiskey, aftershave and sweat, blood and musk, basted meat and rot.

Smells like an after-party gone bad.

And I hear something now. At first, I thought it was the faint sound of static crackling in my ears during those awful moments when I was fooled into believing my symptoms had finally subsided. It's not coming from me though. It's coming from all around me. The wet air is alive with the buzzing drone of a swarm of flies.

Then the sky cracks open, revealing a full moon and a crowd of them who've surrounded me. So many of them in filthy, bedraggled suits and evening dresses, some of whom are nearly enveloped in a cloud of flies. Once coiffed and careful hairstyles have since gone mad, greasy strands and straggles, matted knots all askew. Mustaches and beards dangle stray bits of torn flesh. Their faces are sticky and grimy, mouths encircled in crusty rings of blood. Some of them have strings of meat stuck between their teeth.

All those teeth.

The white-hot prickling behind my eyes has started up again with its thrum-thrum-thrumming. Everything else has gone numb from my neck all the way down to my calves. I silently urge my body to move, but it refuses to budge, keeping me rooted there, in the center of the throng. The stench is strong, something awful, tearing at my headache, worsening it in its burning. I want to dip my head in a sink filled with ice.

Just as the moon teases us, disappearing once more behind a cloud, someone steps up from the crowd, edging into the circle, facing me squarely on.

"Sweet girl," says a familiar voice, one laced with honeyed violets and soured milk all at once. I feel her hot, rank breath against my face. "We often enjoy a digestif to mark the end of a wonderful meal. Although as much as we love to hunt, we didn't expect to have to chase the remainder of the menu."

She brushes sticky strands of hair from my face and squeezes my cheeks in a tight grip, her fingernails digging pits in my skin, causing the cut on my cheek to bleed, warm and sticky, all over again. The moon reappears, and she's right there, a horrorshow. Delia Card's once-patrician face, sculpted and refined, resembles runny dough now. Maybe it's her makeup, or lack thereof to be more precise. Maybe the facelift decided not to hold, I don't know. Her usually high and angled cheeks appear as if they're sagging, melting, rippling. The skin around her eyes droops, making her appear heavy-lidded, permanently sleepy. Her lips that had been full, in-bloom, are cruel, thin lines, the skin around them mapped in wrinkles.

And her teeth, those awful, rotting teeth, brown with decay. She must've been wearing dentures before, all these masks, these smokescreens. Delia's something out of a nightmarish fairy tale, the queen of the wastes who eats children and bathes in their blood in order to maintain that high tea-on-silver façade.

"I abhor pretense," she says, like she's reading my mind. "This," she waves around us. "It's in our nature, this. If we weren't conditioned to be otherwise, there'd be no need for us—*any* of us—to hide." She grins, and it cracks and creases the dough of her face. "And why should we? Isn't this the era of 'free-to-be-me,' or whatever it is those repulsive children are calling it?"

Someone grabs my arms from behind me, iron vices, twisting them behind my back as Delia releases my cheeks and runs a fingernail down the cut, digging at it, scooping out the warm, sticky fluid. It burns to high hell, and the salt from my tears makes it sting all the more. She sucks at the fingernail, her eyes glittering in the moonlight. She leans in, our lips almost touching, and I gag at the fetid stench of her breath.

"The things we must do for the good of the family. You'll soon understand, lovely one," she croons just before a hand with a cloth wraps around my mouth, smothering my scream in its noxious fumes, and—

TWENTY

That moment. We know it well. We've seen it many times before.

That one moment where, in a movie, we get the point-of-view of the main character coming to in a dimly lit setting, where the images are blurry, and the little bit of sound is an raspy echo of a voice. It's in that moment when the main character—along with the audience—is then fully awake and alert, and it's revealed that she's in a cell of some kind, an abandoned warehouse, a torture chamber in a secret room of the cute suburban home, a bathtub in a grungy hotel bathroom, a garage that's rigged with lethal booby traps designed by a madman. We know this place.

That moment isn't entirely accurate. For one, the time it takes to come to after blacking out drags on for much longer. I know the runtime for a movie moment is, obviously, much shorter than "real time." I'm not an idiot, despite my apparent current predicament might show. At the very least, however, there could be some realism implied by having the scene black out a few times or something to that effect.

Oh, and the pain. How can a film show a character in the worst possible pain throughout her bones, all the way through to the nerves in her gums, the roots of her teeth? We're given little more onscreen than a wince and a gasp, as if that shows us what enduring pain entails.

In reality, there's a sharp scrape of pain traveling up my arm then down the side of my body, like someone's taken a soldering iron and seared me inside by trailing it up and down, singeing my tendons and nerve-endings. I don't wince and gasp. Instead, I gag and cough up

194

dust and dismay. Dry, sore, wrenching heaves, and it feels like my throat has been smoothed to a slick scar by a piece of sandpaper.

My ears and head feel as if they've been stuffed with cotton. I can't hear anything but what faintly sounds like music playing in water. The song is familiar, but I'm in agony at the moment, just not in the mood to play Name That Tune. It hurts worse behind my eyes, that wretched pulsating pain. This time, I don't know if it can be rightly attributed to withdrawal symptoms, but I seriously doubt anything out of my current predicament helps matters at all for me. I think it has more to do with what's happened, however, since my eyes feel itchy and hot as if they had been doused in something. Maybe it's one of the after-effects of chloroform or whatever agent's keeping me groggy, I don't know, but whatever it was, it's dried out my eyes as much as it has my throat.

It's only now when I get any sense of what's happened with my body. I've been plopped down on a cracked leather sofa like a ragdoll, and I'm lying on my side, one arm twisted underneath me, the other dangling off the sofa. I manage to untangle myself from the invisible knots that bind. My neck and back loudly crackle-pop when I twist and swivel around, pushing myself into a sitting position, and the burn of it tears through me. Tears cast a watery film over my eyes, threatening to spill. I don't care when they finally do. The pain shreds me.

Remember that movie moment I was detailing before? What about the setting of it? The grey, metallic angles of a warehouse space; the moldy, slime-coated bathtub in a filthy institutional bathroom; the dusty, cockroach-littered floor of a nice neighbor's basement torture chamber, and so on…? I'm fully cognizant of my surroundings, and it's nothing like any of that. Not a movie moment I recognize. Instead, I've been planted in the coziest public space of the resort, probably the only space that's even actually comfortable at all. The resort's lounge seems decoratively at odds with everything else in the place. Instead of a Western theme, it looks like something out of a noir, where the paneling is made up of dark wood, and the curtains are made of dusky, velvety material. Instead of vinyl booths and wooden tables and chairs, there are deep, plush armchairs, sofas, and loveseats. The sofa I'd been placed upon, however, is the only bit of furniture I see that's mismatched, like something out of a gentlemen's club. It's a grubby Chesterfield, its lumpy, leathery hide having been professionally cleaned and treated maybe a couple of times in its entire existence.

195

I rub at my sore eyes, scrubbing away fresh tears. They can't blind me now. The music I'd heard is now clearer, something with a twangy, downhome rhythm from a forgotten era. I thought I recognized the song, but I don't. Still, the tune's familiar and weirdly soothing, which ought to unnerve me, but I've since grown numb to all of the horrors of the night. It's kind of nice to hear something calming and warm for a change. Beats all the screaming any day.

When I turn my head a little, my neck smarts, but I catch the murmurs of a conversation coming from somewhere not far behind me. Men's voices, low and controlled. The music then stops, and I sit very still, waiting for the song to change before I move again. Sure enough, my instincts were right. There's an old jukebox against the wall near the double doors leading to the lobby. It whirrs and clicks, switching selections, and it sounds like Lena Horne, her unmistakable trill bringing me focus, clarity, and then I hear the rest as well.

"He suffered." Rex's normally easy drawl is brittle, echoing from the back of the lounge. "My boy *suffered*, and your wayward insistence on keepin' her does not grant me the peace my family so needs. My wife and I. We're not comin' back from this, hear?"

Rex's outburst is answered with silence. Then there's the squeak of tines scraping on a plate, the clink-scrape-scrape-scrape, pause, clink, scrape, pause. Someone's eating, cutting into something and scraping from a dish, and then shoveling the food into a hungry maw.

I freeze where I am. I don't want to move again lest I make a sound, drawing their attention from whatever it is they're doing back there, so I sit there so perfectly still, glancing around the room, looking for a possible weapon within easy reach. If I can't sneak out to look for Shay, at the very least, I can defend myself. The odds aren't great—I'm not dense— but I'd rather have a halfassed fighting chance than none at all. The coffee table in front of me is an old steamer trunk, the edges frayed. There's a half-empty bottle of bourbon, some expensive make my father used to store, and two empty tumblers that look like they'd been carved from blocks of ice.

Rex's voice softens, the sound of it causing me to stiffen. "Look, I recognize the moral import of ceremony and ritual, son. We would be hellbound, if we're not already. These sacraments keep us from becoming savages."

I want to laugh out loud at that. *"...keep us from becoming savages,"* but I keep quiet and controlled. I've my eye on the bourbon bottle. It's the only thing within easy access that may be somewhat useful as a weapon.

The scrape-scrape-scrape of the utensil against china stops and the dish loudly clatters against a hard surface, jolting me from my thoughts of fight-then-flight.

"What *sacraments* are you referring to, Rex?"

His voice sends ice water trickling through my veins, down my spine, and so suddenly, my earlier suspicions are solidified. I need to run.

"What *ritual*?" says Charlie.

I grab for the bottle and am up and off the sofa, whirling around in a spinning tide. My heart in my throat. My grip, clammy and useless. The bottle slips from my hand and shatters on the tiled floor, sending glass shards and bourbon all over the floor beside the sofa.

Charlie stares directly at me from his perch on a barstool at the opposite end of the bar. He wipes his mouth with a linen napkin, his cold gaze focused only on me as he does. Rex stands beside him, primed to move, but Charlie puts a hand on his arm.

"Relax. She's not going anywhere," Charlie says.

I don't know if I find his ability to adeptly turn from tender-heartedness into coldness admirable or frightening. Judging by his flat expression, I'll go with the latter. And I *knew*, somehow, this makes more sense. What doesn't make sense are the why's and the what's. What, for instance—

"What…what about your fiancée?" I say. My voice comes out as a raspy squeak. Can't help it. My throat is dry and scratchy, like I'd swallowed a handful of emery boards.

Charlie offers up a wry grin, his face returning to its boyish softness. That mask, that crafted play, is impressive. Then he turns back to his meal, picking up his steak knife and fork and then back to carving and eating a big hunk of something plump and red on his plate. "What about her?" he says around a piece of meat, chewing, swallowing. A rivulet of blood dribbles down from the corner of his mouth. He pays it no mind. He just eats.

"You were there when she was—I don't understand."

"You don't understand *what*?" he says as he carves into the meat again.

"Oh, that reminds me," says Rex as he rummages around in his pocket. He pulls out the finger with the dark, painted nail, a little

197

ragged around the edges from where he'd been chewing and sucking on it, and plonks it down beside Charlie's plate.

Charlie barely glances at the thing, choosing to focus on his meal instead. "What exactly do you want me to do with that?" he says around another bite.

"Saved it for ya," says Rex. "Thought it'd be a mighty fine souvenir of the evenin'. Some of us need to remind ourselves that we've fed."

"Then some of you need to keep eating. This won't happen again for a while. We won't get anything this fresh for a long time."

Rex picks up the finger and waves it at Charlie, as if taunting him. "You don't want the last bite of her then?"

Charlie answers by sharply smacking Rex's hand away, sending the finger sailing across the other end of the bar. "Fuck your reminders," he growls around a piece of gristle and chews, swallows, his empty, glassy gaze honed in on Rex.

Rex then hunts around in his other leg pocket, finds what he's rummaging around for and slams it down on the counter. "How's about *that* reminder, boy?" he says, nodding at the ring. "I don't need to jog your memory you spent some good goddamned money on that woman and made a heft of empty promises to her."

Charlie stares down at the ring, continuing to carve, shovel, and chew as he appraises it, seemingly deep in thought.

"Wasn't wise on your end to propose," Rex says softly, his tone almost chiding. "One wedding at a time. No getting gluttonous."

"It's not your say, old man."

"It was my boy's first blood. It most assuredly *is* my say."

Charlie swiftly slides off his barstool, clears his throat, once again wipes his mouth and chin with his napkin and faces Rex squarely on, toe-to-toe, head-to-head. "You'd do well if you remembered your place, Rex. This was never about us."

"I am aware."

"Are they ready?"

Rex gives me a quick glance before turning back to Charlie. "They are, but *she* needs to be put in her place for what she did—"

Charlie's hard stare speaks for him and instantly shuts and locks Rex down. Charlie then makes his way around the bar, wiping his hands with the napkin as he moves towards me. A broad, friendly smile crosses his features, one that would've been an invitation before everything.

Before everything.

Before this.

Sorry, Charlie. I'm not fooled.

He sets the napkin onto the bar as he sidles his way over, his smile darkening.

Suddenly, what had been playing in the back of my mind comes on in full Technicolor on a giant screen in front of me. My sister. Jesus Christ. Where was Shay? Another image, a snapshot this time. A little boy, frightened half out of his wits. *Bryceson.* Where was Bryceson? He'd had Bryceson with him earlier, so he must have—

Charlie reads it all over my face. His expression creases into an exaggerated, sad frown, his lower lip sticking out in a full pout. "Oh, no," he says, his voice cracking, on the cusp of laughter. "Where is he? Where oh where could that little lamb be?" He breaks, laughs, shakes his head at me.

I look over at Rex, who just shrugs, nonchalant about it. It wasn't his worry. It wasn't his problem.

The dish on the bar still holds an uneaten slab of meat. Plump. Wholesome. Red.

"Frogs..." Charlie says as he edges closer to me.

His little hands curling around Charlie's waist.

"Snails..."

His face buried in Charlie's torso. Hiding from the horror.

Charlie leans in and says in my ear, "Puppy dogs' tails."

I move backwards, stumbling away from him, striking the back of my leg against the trunk as I do.

He grins, and it's laced with poison. "That's what little boys are made of."

I swallow back the acid forming in my mouth, my throat. I can't speak. My voice refuses me.

Charlie makes a face. "Honestly, it's nothing like that. That's disgusting. I find that little boys taste just as ripe and sweet as little girls, as long as they're scrubbed clean first. Gotta get rid of the mud pies and earthworms 'cause it can all leave such a bad aftertaste. You know how kids are, am I right?" He offers up that smile again, and what had been warm and endearing before now seems entirely off-kilter on him. "He always slices up a kid for me since I'm usually the last one to eat. Freshest stuff around. Kinda nice of him, don't you think?" He nods over my shoulder at Rex. "Papa Rex, your ears burning over there?"

Rex can't contain his rage though. He storms towards me, eyes blazing, fists curling, but Charlie sticks an arm out, blocking him from his target. Charlie shoves Rex away just as he seems about to lunge for me, Charlie's own eyes never leaving mine as he does.

"I won't remind you again that you don't get to make that call," Charlie says over his shoulder to Rex, his voice cold. "Make yourself useful, sir. Just get in there, and see that everything's set up *properly*, everyone's there." He nods primly at me, his smirk twists and curves. "This part is very important. *You* are important for what happens next."

Rex scuttles away, through the swinging doors in the back of the lounge. I hadn't even noticed them there.

The quiet now, it's searing.

"What about Shay? Where is she?" I ask Charlie so softly, for it scrapes my throat, my mouth. That dryness.

He smiles, and it weirdly seems genuine in all of its tenderness, like he really hopes something of me.

Something I can't bear to see, can't bear to know.

Charlie holds out a hand for me, beckoning. *Come. Let me show you.* My own are trembling as I clasp his hand. The air has caught in my chest, stuck there, that ball of lead. He leans in close, taps his forehead against my clammy one. His breath reeks of smoked meat and bourbon, of old world secrets and decay.

"I think they're ready now," he whispers just before he plants a kiss on my forehead. Benediction.

I then let Charlie lead me along, past the bar where he's left the remains of boyflesh on the dish. The flies have congregated nearby, humming a tribute, some of them hovering over the sticky surface.

With one push of the door, he ushers me inside where they're waiting.

#

There's something not quite right about the room, something staged here like it was always meant to be a showcase, theatrical even. The room itself is dark, dimly lit by a chandelier made up of antlers and what looks like old bones. The space itself is wide and lacking in any sort of furniture. The walls are decorated in animal trophies carefully mounted and on closer inspection, as much that's possible in such low lighting, seemingly cared for.

The air is heady with burning sage and the meaty sweat emanating from the bodies of the gathered crowd who step aside as Charlie leads me further into the room. So many faces all becoming a blood-smeared blur. Hands reach out to touch my arms, my face, my hair, a fleeting, airy sensation again and again, causing me to shiver. We're greeted by a barricade of Card family members with Delia at its center. I barely recognize any of them in their filthy dresses and suits, in all their madness, their bloodlust. However, their eyes are bright and alert, their smiles exuding an alien warmth, a strange sense of comfort that had been severely lacking until now. And Delia, she seems almost—

Motherly.

Here, in the haze, she's almost beautiful again. She holds out her arms to me, beckoning me to come to her, to be held, and I do. As soon as she embraces me, I feel her heartbeat deep from within. She smells of warmth and rain, honeyed milk and hay. My heart and mind are becoming quickly undone.

"My dear, my darling one," she says softly, the tinkle-chime of her voice melting me. "No matter how this ends, know that you're welcome and wanted. Know that you're *loved*."

I sense movement from the crowd of them, someone hurriedly shoving others aside and then stepping forward into the circle. Delia releases me and holds out a warning hand in the direction of the interloper. I turn to see that it's Rex, primed to pounce, to rip me apart as I so deserve.

But Delia is having none of it. She shakes her head at her husband. "This was never once about him. You know perfectly well," she says.

"If you can't behave yourself, Rex," Charlie pipes in, "I'll have one of your own muzzle you and then chain you in a corner like an animal."

I don't want to see the look on Rex's face, so I keep my eyes locked with Delia's. She strokes my hair, kisses my cheeks one at a time. Then she takes my face in her warm hands, gazing into my eyes as she does.

"Many of us here now, we've known. We've *always* known," she whispers, and I'm hers, committed now.

It's as if Delia words were meant to signal them, for the crowd splits, revealing the heart of the matter to me against the back wall between two rustic wooden doors. She's been trussed up on a rack and gagged, her smooth, ivory skin completely free of its bridal bondage.

Her hair, once shiny and groomed, is now a damp tangle of knots and nests. Her eyes are panicked, wild, darting this way and that. They rest on me as I approach her from the gathering. She strains against the tight chains and tries to speak around the gag, but it comes out as grunts and bubbles of spittle.

Delia gently urges me forward towards my sister. I step up to wipe her tears from her face and the strands of hair from her face. Shay has never been lovelier as she is in this moment. Her vitality, it's electric. Blood, life, pumping through her. I can hear her heartbeat. I can feel it underneath my fingertips, that energy pulsating.

Maybe it's the anticipation of something great. I've no idea, but I'm more than willing here and now to learn more, and both Delia and Charlie are beside me, hands over mine, stroking warm, bare skin, easing Shay into submission until she's silently weeping. Her body shudders when our hands skim over smooth torso, her nipples, her slender neck, teasing with feather light touches. Charlie's hands then close over mine, cupping them in his. He puts his lips to my ear, the heat of him sending a shiver coursing through me.

"A good bite of her light, Ansley," he says. "That purest morsel will release you. Try it."

My sister, my love, she could do no wrong to anyone. I want that, too.

I lean in close to gently kiss an eye before my teeth clamp down over it, and it pops, its gelatinous, spongy goo flooding my mouth with its brine. Spots of light dance in front of my own line of sight as I tear into her face, from the base of her eye socket, to her jawline, ripping away the tender flesh and eating it whole, gorging on it. There's white noise, scratchy static in the room, but I can't hear well at any rate for the wretched, grating sound of her screaming around the gag. Half of her beautiful face is in red, weeping ribbons, her eye socket now filled with blood.

The pain I'd felt for so long, my old friend, my worst enemy, it's gone. In its place, absolute clarity and what I think may be the apex of nirvana.

How did I not know of this? How was I not aware?

When I turn to Charlie, he's still there beside me, smiling at me. But everyone else…

When did they all leave? Delia and Rex, too, they're gone. I must have been so consumed by my hunger, by my need, I didn't even notice them go. Not like I could hear anything in the moment.

There are only a few of us in the room, a room that has since grown foggy with a smoky haze, remnants of a fire that had never been lit to begin with. While its scent is redolent with that burning sage and the tang of blood, my lungs have never been clearer. My headache is finally gone.

I've never felt better. Who would've thought?

Shay has passed out from the pain. When she comes to, perhaps I'll eat the rest.

Charlie sucks the blood and goo from Shay's eye socket like it's a seashell. The sound of it is lewd and raw. I should be nauseated by it. Instead though, I feel nothing. Not a sense of emptiness, or even a sense of hollow sadness. I just feel nothing. Sheer apathy, perhaps.

The shadowy shape to the other side of Shay, a wavery figure in the haze, grows into a recognizable form. He offers me a little wave in recognition. Warm, friendly, open face. Pride brimming in his eyes. He's wearing that stupid arcade tee shirt, that ugly corded jacket with the patched elbows, the worn jeans, and Nikes.

I can't move; my feet are failing me. My mind is playing games. How is this even happening?

"Leon? What are you—?"

"Remember what I said the other day?" Leon suddenly says, abruptly cutting me off. He's not even paying the slightest bit of attention to the meal we've made of my sister. His focus is entirely on me, and he's choosing his words carefully.

Charlie laps and chews at the raw layers of meat exposed on my sister's face.

And my breath, it's suddenly ripped from me. I'm gasping for air.

Leon turns my head so that I'm looking at him instead, and I'm trying to reach deep within me, to get myself to breathe. His smile curls into a thoughtful frown.

"When you're feeling like everything is sucking all the air from you, you find something solid," he says.

Something solid. I don't know if I even have—

Wait a minute. There *is* something. I don't even know if it's still there. I feel along the side of my breast, and it's still trapped there

203

in my bra. Ridiculous. I reach down inside and pull it out. The key has probably left an angry indentation, but right now, if it's my way out—

I look up at Leon, knowing the rest of the words by heart, but even still, I want to hear it from him, the source of it.

He beams at me and says, "Look at it. Hold it. Use its solidity."

The key feels heavy and just right in the palm of my hand.

"It'll remind you what is here. What is now. It will bring you back to where you need to be." He nods in the direction of wooden door number two, to the right of my ruined sister, my first ever homegrown meal.

I make my way slowly around Charlie, keeping a wary eye on him as I walk past. He doesn't even look up from his grazing, doesn't even seem to care. As soon as I'm at the door, I glance back at Leon. He motions for me to keep going.

"You will be released from the lie that's keeping you bound, little sister," Leon says right as I use the key to unlock the door.

TWENTY-ONE

At first, there's only the light, and it's blinding.

It's not what you think, that cliché of the end of the tunnel.

Right when everything starts to come into focus, all the grating colors and cacophony forming into something tangible, something *comprehensible*, the light is just a powerful beam aimed directly at my face, and I can't seem to move. A deer caught in headlights. Now that's the right cliché.

I've been caught, but I can't seem to grasp what's here, what I've been caught doing. I'm sitting crossed-legged on a carpeted floor. Its texture is strangely sticky, pliant, under my hands.

My hands. They're gloved in blood. This is not what gives me pause. This is not what makes me question everything until now.

The sound that had been a high-pitched drone in my head strikes me hard first. The shrill screams come from several women and men all at once, and I hear the first whole series of words, a solid line of inquiry, straight to the point.

It's the voice of my mother, screaming, "What did you do to her, Ansley? What did you *do*?"

How is my mother here? It's a logical question, considering she'd been last seen roasting on a spit not too long ago. The smell of her cooking made me hungry. I remember that.

Memories can be tricky devils though. Sometimes, they're simply what you *think* you remember, but in fact, somebody else has recalled it for you. What you recall is, in fact, completely fabricated, fooled by your mind, crafted by your own suffering. You know that sort of suffering very well.

Someone pulls me up on my feet from underneath my arms, and I don't want to go. I can't go. I need answers. Here in the bridal suite (the *bridal suite?*), it's crowded with people in dresses and suits, people in blue and white uniforms.

One of the blue uniforms, I instantly recognize her with her short hair and tiny features. *But she's dead.* She offers a comforting hand on my shoulder as her partner (*eater*) has my hands behind my back and locks the handcuffs on. The policewoman is having me focus on her and nothing else, her line of sight drawing me to her. *But she's dead.*

When I shake loose my thoughts looping circles, around and around, I realize she's been speaking to me. For how long though, I've no idea. Her actual voice is soothing, like a soft, welcoming blanket. It's certainly practiced. "Miss Boone, are you here with us? Do you need me to repeat your rights?"

She'd recited my Miranda rights. I know what this entails now. The handcuffs are tight. My arms are strained and aching. I've no idea what I've done, even still. My mother is kneeling there on the floor, rocking and weeping, my father behind her, attempting to pull her away from the sight of Shay lying there, sprawled out, still in her wedding gown. Its bodice and sleeves, while perfectly intact, are splattered in blood.

There's a flash-pop of a lightbulb as a photo's been snapped. The brief burst of light reveals Shay's ravaged face. Her remaining eye stares up at the ceiling, as if the answer to everything about what has happened to her exists somewhere in the void.

My headache lingers, a buzz of an afterthought, a reminder.

How could this be possible? I mean, everyone is alive and whole. Nathan has crouched beside Mom and is holding her now, his wet, red glare directed up at me. Dad is screaming something, but I can't understand him, can't comprehend or make any sense of what he's saying. Rex and a groomsman pull him away from the gathering around Shay's body. He's pointing and flailing, trying to grab for me. It takes another police officer to keep him barricaded from reaching me.

There's something else in his eyes, underneath the hot rage. Bafflement? Sadness? Horror? Shock? Pity? I won't be able to find out anytime soon what any of this means, what exactly happened, but then again, as my thoughts come together in a jumbled collection of images and I'm led out of the room, out into the courtyard of the resort, heading for that police motorcade and ambulance, nothing about this makes any sense in the end. You must realize this, right? Even by now?

That *Delirium.*

That *Derealization.*

Hallucinations, auditory and visual.

Stop.

That. Right there.

Play it back.

Leon had warned me about it again and again and had softly passed on that information on to my mother. I had been there. She knew, so I can't be solely to blame.

And hallucinations, like memories, they shift and change, morphing into something else entirely, disappearing altogether, and then becoming something I will definitely *need* to see for myself because none of this was ever meant to be.

Still, perhaps a nice, long stint in a cell will be a much more effective detox program. And, well, hey, my insurance won't be affected either. Have to look on the bright side of things.

Right after I wash the bitter taste of my sister out of my mouth.

THE END

ACKNOWLEDGEMENTS

Many heartfelt thanks to the following people:

My family and friends, who always encouraged me to persist, persist, persist, even when it all went sour.

Jeff Strand, for his ever-patient mentorship and friendship. I only hope, one day, to be able to pass it on to someone else.

Johanna Kopp, Cori Endicott Large, Renee Laurent, and Rebecka Ramos, who were there when I first put this insanity to paper and whose feedback was invaluable.

Jarod Barbee and Patrick Harrison III, for giving a new girl a chance to make some waves in a genre we love.

Lynne Hansen, for the amazing cover to this baby, and Tiffany Messerschmidt, for the encouragement *and* the inspiration behind the cover concept.

William Tucker, for bringing me back to the writing life.

Finally, J. Frank James, wherever he may be, who took a chance long ago on a kid who wanted to write *something*.

KENZIE JENNINGS is an English professor currently residing and sweltering in the humid tourist hub of central Florida. She has written pieces for a handful of news and entertainment publications and literary magazines throughout the years. Back when she was young and impetuous, she had two screenplays optioned by a couple of production companies, but her screenwriting career ended there, and she hasn't looked back since. *Reception* is her debut novel.

DEATH'S HEAD PRESS

WATCH FOR THESE OTHER DHP TITLES!

AND HELL FOLLOWED an anthology

The Hard Goodbye by Chris Miller

Catfish in the Cradle by Wile E. Young

Notches by M. Ennenbach

Dig Two Graves an anthology

Rope Burns an anthology

Breaking Bizarro an anthology

Dawn of the Living-Impaired and Other Messed Up Zombie Stories
by Christine Morgan

Stronger Than Hate by Robert Essig

Master of Pain by Wrath James White and Kristopher Rufty

Made in the USA
Middletown, DE
10 January 2020